The Monster Was Right Behind Her

When Robin Lefler had first fallen through the soil of Risa, the prospect of trying to climb back to the top never occurred to her. It was far too high, and there was no way she was going to be able to find enough foot- or handholds. Now, however, she had no choice.

She grabbed hold of the wall and started to climb, as fast and hard as she could. Her fingers dug, almost on their own, into nooks and crannies that she never would have seen before.

She didn't look down, but she could sense the thing bubbling around down there. It was not, thank God, climbing the walls. But it was waiting for her to lose her grip, to plunge back down into it.

And she had the nauseating feeling that if she fell into it again, she was not going to be getting out anytime soon—if ever.

STAR TREK®
NEW FRONTIER

EXCALIBUR

RENAISSANCE

PETER DAVID

POCKET BOOKS

New York   London   Toronto   Sydney   Singapore

An *Original* Publication of POCKET BOOKS

POCKET BOOKS, a division of Simon & Schuster, Inc.
1230 Avenue of the Americas, New York, NY 10020

A VIACOM COMPANY

STAR TREK is a Registered Trademark of
Paramount Pictures.

This book is published by Pocket Books, a division of
Simon & Schuster, Inc., under exclusive license from
Paramount Pictures.

ISBN: 0-671-04239-4

First Pocket Books printing September 2000

10 9 8 7 6 5 4 3 2

POCKET and colophon are registered trademarks of
Simon & Schuster, Inc.

Printed in the U.S.A.

Dear 'Xana:

It's been simply ages since you've gotten a communiqué from your favorite "aunt," and I felt it was time that I attended to that oversight.

You've heard, of course, about the *Excalibur* blowing up. I don't need to bore you with all the details surrounding the ship's destruction: the unexpected emergency in engineering, the incredibly noble sacrifice of Captain Mackenzie Calhoun . . . These are all things that have been covered *ad nauseum* in so many other venues. So there's really no need for me to go over events that have been so thoroughly examined elsewhere. Besides, why dwell on it? Look to the future, that's what I've always said.

There was a postmortem of sorts involving the command crew. As I'm sure you know, there's a

Starfleet "cooling-off" mandate that follows any experience as traumatic as the loss of an entire ship. Particularly when the loss involves something as catastrophic as the death of the ship's captain.

Calhoun. I never knew what to make of him. He was utterly unorthodox, and not like any of the captains it's been my pleasure and honor to serve with and alongside. His cowboy sensibilities, not to mention his underlying streak of warrior brashness, informed and shaped much of the crew as well. He was their center and, without that center, they could not hold. I don't know if that's a strength or not. I've been around long enough to know that no crew, no ship, should be that dependent upon one person. The vacuum of space is unforgiving, and if the leader is lost in a crisis situation, the crew cannot afford to find itself at loose ends, or even disconcerted, for a moment. That moment, after all, can wind up costing the rest of the crew its life. The chain of command should be above all. The new captain should be able to step in without missing a beat. I don't know that the crew of the *Excalibur* would necessarily have been able to do that. Oh, there was a time when they thought their captain dead, but they carried on well enough. On that occasion, however, they were certain that somehow Calhoun had survived, and the determination to prove him still alive guided their subsequent actions.

Then again, I may be underestimating them. I have, after all, served in the company of some truly great crews. So—to be fair—it could be that I'm holding them to an impossibly high standard.

The sad thing is, I'll never have the opportunity to know for sure. The ship is gone. The captain is gone. The crew is dispersing even as we speak. Some of the general crew and noncoms are forgoing the "cooling-off" period, and are being allowed to do so on a case-by-case basis.

The command crew is another story.

Commander Shelby, well . . . she has proven to be the most resilient of the lot. Who would have thought? Considering that she was closest to Calhoun—they were even engaged to be married at one point—you would think that she would be the *least* likely to bounce back as fast as she did. It may very well be that she simply did not want to pass up the opportunity for command that had finally been handed to her. Obviously, she was cleared by the Starfleet Surgeon General's office for mental fitness, or she wouldn't have taken a run at getting command of the *Exeter* when the position of captain came open. Impressively enough, my contacts in Starfleet have informed me that she is, in fact, getting the rank and command that she has sought for so long.

Ah, my contacts in Starfleet. Far more than even Robin would suspect. Then again, considering how long I've been around, I'd be remiss if I *didn't* have my ways of obtaining information.

Thanks to those ways, I can keep you up-to-date on the other rather colorful members of our little command crew.

Zak Kebron and Mark McHenry . . . now there are two names I never expected to mention together. But apparently our former security chief and conn officer, respectively, undertook an expedition at the behest of certain Starfleet intelligence types to a world that was being plagued by—how best to put it? Pranksters. Pranksters from a local interplanetary university, who thought it would be amusing to visit the uneducated residents of an underdeveloped world and terrorize them. So Kebron and McHenry agreed to do a bit of "undercover" work and attend to it.

Science Officer Soleta decided to take time to visit Vulcan, spend time with her father. For some odd reason, however, she became involved with a Romulan who had been a prisoner of the Federation, but had been released. Even my sources can give me only the sketchiest information about this. I'm sure she knows what she's doing. Perhaps she has found him a potentially interesting subject for scientific study.

Soleta has always been a bit of a puzzle to me. Goodness knows, I've known enough Vulcans. I know how they think, how they behave. But there's always been something about Soleta that was a bit . . . off. Not *entirely* off, mind you. I remember another Vulcan . . . a half-breed. When he was young, he was actually known to crack a wide smile every now and then. Soleta, to the best of my knowledge, is pureblood Vulcan, so I wouldn't know to what I should attribute any unusual behavior on her part. Perhaps spending time with a Romulan will help to refocus her, help her to understand what it is that Vulcans evolved into in leaving behind the mind-set of the offshoot race that eventually became the Romulans. After all, it's not as if she's part Romulan herself. I mean . . . that would explain a good deal, I suppose. But it's too far-fetched. Then again, you know me, 'Xana. Always coming up with half-baked, wild speculations that have no relationship whatsoever to reality.

I have no idea what Si Cwan and Kalinda are out and about doing. They're not part of Starfleet, what with the two of them being former members of the Thallonian royal family. So I haven't been able to keep track of their subsequent activities. Something of a pity, really. Robin clearly has feelings for Cwan, perhaps even feelings of love. But she has never really had the opportunity to tell him just how she feels. This bothers me a great deal, because Robin should never feel daunted by anything . . . most especially making her feelings clear to someone. In any event, it's a moot subject. Si Cwan is off attending to his business, Robin to hers, and the chances are that they will never see each other again. As for love . . .

Love. Ah, what a transient emotion, 'Xana. You and I, we've had this discussion before, I know. You believe it to be some great, overwhelming, all-powerful emotion, but I know better. You have to trust me on this. It's fun, for what it is, and it certainly has its entertainment value. It resulted in the birth of Robin, as well as others. But it's no different from any other human sentiment, and less reliable than many. At this point in my very long life—aside from maternal love—I doubt I can feel anything along the lines of romantic affection anymore. I'm a bit . . . worn-out on that score. Loved too many, lost too many.

Speaking of love and its rather odd permutations, there's nothing stranger than the current relationship between chief engineer Burgoyne and chief medical officer Selar. In the throes of the Vulcan mating drive, they wound up conceiving a child, recently born, whom they named Xyon, after the late son of the equally late captain. But Selar appears a bit . . . testy about the situation. A testy Vulcan is a rather startling concept, in and of itself. As for the child . . . it certainly appears Vulcan enough. Then again, Hermats such as Burgoyne are possessed of both male and female attributes, and so who knows what little Xyon's biological makeup might be.

As for Burgoyne hirself, I'm not sure how s/he regards Selar at this point. S/he not only conceived the child with Selar, but also delivered it under circumstances that could only be described as adverse. Hir affection for Selar seems genuine and unswerving, but Selar doesn't quite seem to know how to return those sentiments. I hope, for both their sakes, that they are able to come to some sort of accord. After all, they have a child to be concerned about now, and that has got to make all the difference in the world.

I should know. I have my own child to consider, certainly. Robin and I are even now making plans as to how we're going to be spending time together. Granted, we'd been together on the *Excalibur,* but there was always ship's business to contend with. For the first time in a long time, we actually have an opportunity to be together as mother and daughter, and I have no intention of letting that opportunity slip away. Perhaps, underneath it all, I really am an old sentimentalist. Never let daughters get too far away from you,

'Xana. They might start to think they don't need their mothers, and then where would we all be? Out of work, that's where.

That was intended to be amusing. I don't know that I've succeeded, but humor is something that I've never really gotten the hang of.

So, that brings you up-to-date with me. I know your life has been full and active. After I spend time with Robin, I'll try to swing by and say hello, and we can catch up on old times. Please let your own lovely daughter know that I send her warmest regards. And to you as well, I remain . . .

Your favorite "Aunt,"
Morgan

BURGOYNE & SELAR

SELAR STARED AT THE DESERT in the middle of Burgoyne's living room, then looked in astonishment at the Hermat. She held their child close to her, looked as if she wanted to say something, said nothing, and instead looked back at the desert.

"Too much?" inquired Burgoyne solicitously.

Cautiously Selar walked the perimeter of the red desert sands. She felt heat radiating from the sands. A heat lamp above gave a fair approximation of a desert sun. "This," she said slowly, "is insane."

Burgoyne looked rather surprised. "I don't know why you would say that."

"Why I would say that?" The Vulcan doctor had walked around the desert and wound up back next to Burgoyne. The infant, Xyon, cooed blissfully. "Burgoyne . . . there is a desert . . . in the living room. Why is there a desert in the living room?"

"Not enough space in the den."

"That is not the point," Selar said with forced patience.

"Yes, I suspected it wasn't," Burgoyne admitted. "You don't like it?"

"That is also not the point. It has nothing to do with like or dislike. The question is why you felt a need to construct a replica of a desert in a room normally reserved for matters of socialization."

"For you."

"I do not recall asking you to construct such a thing."

"Yes, I know you didn't ask. I was doing it to try to make you feel at home."

Selar let out a long, patient, and—ultimately—emotionless sigh. "Burgoyne," she said finally, "we need to talk."

"All right," Burgoyne said reasonably. S/he went to a chest of drawers and pulled out a couple of large blankets. This action puzzled Selar somewhat, but things were quickly made clear when Burgoyne spread the blankets out on the sand and dropped down onto one of them. S/he patted the other one, indicating that Selar should take a seat next to hir. Selar was sorely tempted to remain standing, but decided that matters would be simpler if she just humored the Hermat for a while. So she sat on the blanket that was a few inches away from Burgoyne.

Burgoyne looked quite ready to listen to anything that Selar was prepared to say. "Go ahead," s/he prompted.

"Burgoyne," she said slowly, "first, I should acknowledge the efforts to which you have gone. Obviously, you are aware that my native Vulcan is somewhat arid and desert-like in many places. Unlike the other Starfleet personnel who are taking advantage of the cooling-off period, you have chosen not to reside in

San Francisco, in proximity to the Academy. Instead, you have obtained this lovely residence here in Nevada, on a stretch of territory that is not unlike Vulcan."

"I wanted to make you comfortable."

"I know. Your attention to my comfort and to any desires that I either might have, or that you *think* I might have, has been very . . ." She cast about in her mind for the right word. "Flattering," she finally settled on. "And I have been willing to accommodate your endeavors because . . . frankly, I had not developed a workable strategy to the contrary. However—"

"However what?" s/he prompted. "You can tell me anything, Selar. You know that."

"No. I do not know that," Selar replied. "There are many things that I cannot tell you because it is a waste of time. There are things that you do not wish to hear, and, therefore, you tend not to hear them."

"What sort of things? I'm listening now."

"Burgoyne . . ." She drew a deep breath. "I do not love you."

"Yes, you do," Burgoyne said cheerily.

Selar let the breath out, shaking her head. "You see?"

"Yes, I do see. I see that you're afraid—"

"No. I am not afraid." She rose and walked around the interior desert, shaking her head in a combination of frustration and amusement. "I am Vulcan. I am logical. I am able to put the reasonable aspects of a relationship ahead of any foolish emotional entanglements. And, logically, it is utterly unreasonable to think that any long-term relationship between us could work."

"Excuse me, Selar," Burgoyne said, indicating the child who was happily burbling on the blanket, "but we already have a long term commitment, and that's him. He's as much my child as he is yours."

Selar was silent.

"I said, 'He's as much—' "

"I heard you, Burgoyne," she said softly. "My hearing is quite acute, as I am sure you are aware."

Burgoyne leaned back against the nearest wall, watching Selar with open confusion. "Are you disagreeing?" s/he asked. There was something in hir tone that seemed vaguely warning.

"The child has Vulcan ears, and the face is of a generally Vulcan cast. As for his reproductive system . . ."

"He is singularly male. Yes, I know."

She raised an eyebrow. "You say that with a hint of regret."

Burgoyne's lips thinned. "You keep talking about how you know nothing about emotions, Selar. About how above them you are. So, if it's all the same to you, don't start attributing emotions to *how* I say things, considering you claim to be unfamiliar with them."

"Very well," she said. "The point is . . . your genetic contribution seems minimal to nonexistent."

"I'm still his father."

"And for that, you will always have my gratitude. But—"

"Gratitude," Burgoyne interrupted her, snorting disdainfully. "You know, Selar, I'm starting to wonder if you know the meaning of the word."

"Gratitude. Noun. An appreciative awareness or—"

"That's not what I mean and you know it!" It seemed as if Burgoyne's meticulously crafted control was starting to erode. Selar couldn't help but think that if Burgoyne was in some sort of "competition" to see who could keep themselves reserved longer, s/he didn't have a prayer. S/he was pacing furiously.

Still sitting on the floor, Xyon's attention was now

caught by hir, and he watched hir as s/he moved back and forth.

"How much more do I have to be there for you? I was there for you when you were in the grip of *pon farr.* I was there for you, for emotional support, during your pregnancy. I saved your life—"

"Burgoyne, I know that—"

"Saved your life!" s/he shouted over her. "I was so linked into your mind that I fought monsters and kept you alive so that you could give birth to our son in a hostile environment—"

"Technically, it was a single monster, not plural."

"Who cares?"

"I care. We might as well be precise."

Burgoyne covered hir face with hir hands. "Selar . . . does it matter whether it was one monster, two, or twenty? The point is, you owe me your life, and the life of Xyon."

"I am very well aware of that," Selar said reasonably. "But what did you expect of me, Burgoyne? Did you believe that I would come to love you because of those things?"

"I believed that, at the very least, you wouldn't reject me out of hand."

"It is not out of hand. It is . . ."

"What? What is it?"

Selar looked away. "Burgoyne . . . you want me to give something of which I am not capable."

"I don't believe that," Burgoyne said firmly. "I don't believe that you're incapable of love. Incapable of acknowledging that you are capable, perhaps, but that's as far as I'll take it." S/he shook hir head in exasperation. "You know what? I'm starting to wonder why I even bother."

"As am I," Selar said reasonably. "What did you think was going to happen here, Burgoyne?" She steadied herself. "It is my fault. You see, Burgoyne . . . I was operating out of gratitude. Believe it or not," she added dryly.

"Let's just say I'm skeptical," Burgoyne said, but s/he sounded uncertain.

"I agreed to come out here, to reside with you in this domicile, because I believed that you were . . . entitled in some way. That, after everything you had been through in connection with me and this child—"

"Xyon."

"Yes. Xyon." She frowned. "I know his name."

"That may be, but you never say it. You just say, 'this child.' You should refer to him by his name. It's as if you're trying to distance yourself even now."

"I am trying to do nothing of the kind. The point is, Burgoyne, that you had gone to a great deal of effort to create a safe and nurturing environment for both my child—"

"Our child," Burgoyne immediately corrected.

"Our child . . . and me," Selar continued. "And I have resided here for eleven days, thirteen hours and fifty-seven minutes. I have given you time to get to know your child—"

"Our child."

This time Selar took longer to make the correction. An observer might have concluded that the unflappable Vulcan was becoming just the least bit annoyed. "Our child," she said slowly. "But I believe that I have falsely given you the impression that this could possibly attain some sort of long-term status, when such is not the case."

"Would you like to know," Burgoyne said, "what I consider not to be the case?"

"I suspect you will tell me whether I desire to know or not."

"Absolutely true." Burgoyne took a steadying breath. "I thought I could walk away, Selar. I thought I could accommodate your biological need, provide you with a child, and then turn away and leave him or her in your hands. And I suppose I also thought that we would have time to sort things out. After all, we were going to be continuing to serve on the same ship. Neither of us was going anywhere. So you could say that a false sense of security set in. Well, we're not on a ship together, and if we're going to raise this child as a couple—"

"Burgoyne." Even Selar's endless patience was waning "We are *not* a couple. We are not going to raise this child together. I am his mother."

"And I am his father."

"But according to Vulcan law, my interests in the child hold sway."

"Ah," said Burgoyne. S/he had stopped pacing, and was now facing Selar in a rather challenging pose. "So now we get down to it."

"Get down to what?"

"You feel that you're more important to Xyon's future than I am. You're intending to cut me out of all interest in his development and growth."

"For you to be 'cut out,'" Selar said, with what she felt to be fairly reasonable consideration, "you would have had to be 'cut in' in the first place. You have not been. It has always been my intention to be this child's primary parent."

"Why?"

"Why?" Selar blinked at the question.

"Yes. Why?" S/he gestured toward Xyon, who—it

seemed to Selar—was actually beginning to look a little concerned, as if aware that his parents were having a disagreement. "You keep telling me how incapable you are of love. What kind of a mother are you going to be if you can't even love your child?"

"A Vulcan mother. One who will teach Xyon about his heritage and raise him in the Vulcan way, as per Vulcan law."

"Well, you know what?" Burgoyne said defiantly. "We Hermats have a few laws of our own. That child right there is as much Hermat as he is Vulcan, no matter what the biological tests might say right now."

"I think," she told him, "that if you do some serious study into the matter, instead of confining your awareness on the topic to emotional outbursts, you will find that not to be the case. Vulcan genes tend to dominate. This is true in Vulcan/Human pairings, and is true as well in this union. Burgoyne, I think it would be best if you were reasonable."

"I *am* being reasonable. Xyon's entitled to know of his Hermat heritage."

"But he needs to be raised as a Vulcan."

Burgoyne actually looked concerned. "What are you saying?"

"I am saying that it is my intention to return with Xyon to Vulcan, to reside there, and to raise him as a Vulcan. He will be taught the orderly discipline of logic, he will be—"

"He will be my son, with no opportunity to truly grasp his heritage."

"His heritage?" She shook her head and actually looked amused, or as close to that as she came. "Burgoyne, this is foolishness. The fact that he is *your* son flatly contradicts that he could even have a heritage.

Hermats do not have sons, or daughters. All of you are mixed genders."

"We prefer the term 'blend.' "

"Blend. If that is your phrase of choice, fine. The point is, your calling him your son precludes the very claim to Hermat upbringing that you bandy about. If he has one heritage, then he is not Hermat."

"You don't understand his potential."

"Potential? To what are you referring?"

Burgoyne looked left and right, as if s/he were about to impart some great, secret knowledge. In a lowered voice, s/he said, "There is a prophecy . . . a Hermat prophecy, going back centuries. A prophecy that says there will come a child . . . a child who is Hermat, but not *of* Hermat . . . a child with pointed ears and alien head, but of Hermat heart. One who will unite the fractious Hermat population and guide us forward into a golden age. And that prophesied child . . . could very well be our son."

Selar was stunned. She looked from the baby back to Burgoyne. "Is any of that true?" she inquired.

Burgoyne opened hir mouth to continue the boasts, then sighed and sagged, like a deflated balloon. "No. It's all lies," s/he admitted. "But it sounded good, didn't it?"

Selar's lips twitched ever so slightly. "Sometimes, Burgoyne, I have no idea what to think of you."

"Then think of this," Burgoyne told her. "You said these past eleven days were so that I could get to know the child. Eleven days? *Eleven days,* Selar? The truth is that people spend a lifetime getting to know their children, and even at the end of that, they can still be as much of a mystery as they were at the beginning. The sad thing is that you don't understand that. The fortunate thing is that I do. The child needs both of us, Selar. Both of us. It is only . . . logical."

"But I do not love you, Burgoyne," she said firmly. "I feel as close to you as . . ."

"You'll allow yourself to be?"

She frowned slightly at that. "This is accomplishing nothing, Burgoyne."

Burgoyne seemed about to argue further, but then s/he sighed, looking fatigued. "You know . . . you're probably right. I admit that. But I will do so only if you admit that perhaps we've hit a stalemate simply because we're going back and forth over the same ground. That perhaps tomorrow might bring fresher views and new insights."

"I do not know that I agree," said Selar, "but I concur that it is possible. You are suggesting that we 'sleep on it,' as they say."

"As they say," agreed Burgoyne readily.

"Very well, Burgoyne. I owe you much, I admit that. So I certainly owe you a night's consideration. Let us consider matters tomorrow."

Burgoyne bobbed hir head . . . and then reached toward Selar with hir right hand, the first two fingers extended. Selar was a bit surprised, but hid it with practiced ease. She hesitated a moment, and then extended the first two fingers of her own right hand. Their fingers touched, caressed each other gently in the Vulcan custom that served as an open display of affection.

"There," smiled Burgoyne, hir pointed teeth slightly exposed. "That wasn't so horrible now, was it? The world didn't come to an end. Maybe there is hope for us, Selar. What do you think?"

"There are always . . . possibilities," Selar said diplomatically.

Dreams tumbled about in Burgoyne's head, images that s/he could not determine, nor did s/he wish to.

They were too upsetting in nature, and were best left for another time.

S/he awoke and sat up in hir bed, then glanced at the chronometer. But that simply verified what s/he knew instinctively: it was the middle of the night. S/he had no idea why . . . but suddenly s/he wanted Selar. There was no rhyme, no "logic" to it. It wasn't as if Selar would be interested. And even if she was, it was insane to think that an act of passion in the middle of the night could settle the differences between them.

"Then again, at least it would be a start," Burgoyne murmured to hirself. With that thought in mind, s/he padded out of hir bedroom and down the hall to where Selar slept. The door, s/he was pleased to see, was unlocked. That might be considered a very good sign.

S/he stepped quietly into the room, allowing hir cat-like eyes to adjust to the dimness, and padded over to the bed. S/he knelt down upon it . . . and, instantly, the absence of warmth indicated to hir that the bed was empty.

This did not immediately concern hir. S/he reasoned that the baby must have stirred, cried for his mother. Hermat parents tended to keep their children in the room with them during the early days. Selar had not felt it necessary: with those impressive ears of hers, there was no way Selar would not hear him should he stir in the night. So Selar was undoubtedly in the adjoining room, tending to little Xyon's needs.

That was what Burgoyne kept telling hirself, right up to the point where s/he entered the baby's room and found that empty as well.

They're in another room. They're outside for a walk. These and other explanations tumbled about in Burgoyne's head as s/he went from one room to the next, and to the next, still fighting down a combination of anger and panic. But as s/he moved through the house, s/he went faster and faster until—by the time s/he was inspecting the exterior in the last, flagging hope that Selar and Xyon would be out there—s/he was practically sprinting.

S/he bolted to the outside. The desert air was surprisingly sharp in hir lungs as s/he bounded around the perimeter of the house. By now s/he was moving on all fours, balancing the spring in hir powerful legs with hir knuckles. S/he moved away from the house, hir nostrils flaring, trying to catch a scent in the air. And s/he picked one up. No . . . there were three. There was Selar, and Xyon . . . and there was the faint, burning whiff of ozone that told hir a small ship had come.

Come and gone.

Gone . . . with Selar and hir son.

Burgoyne crouched, looking at the blood-red full moon that hung in the sky, and then s/he threw back hir head and let out a scream that sent small animals scurrying. A scream that carried across the desolation of the peaceful night desert, and seemed to go on until morning.

ROBIN & MORGAN

ROBIN LEFLER GAPED at her mother and shook her head. "No. Absolutely not."

There was no sunlight coming through the window of the San Francisco apartment that Robin shared with her mother, Morgan Primus. A cloudy day had been scheduled, with some light rain mandated for later in the afternoon. At that moment, however, weather was the last thing Robin was thinking about.

"You'll change your mind, Robin," Morgan said with confidence. She was busy moving about the apartment, packing a case.

Robin's eyes widened as she realized just what it was her mother was packing. "Mother! Those are *my* things!"

"Yes, I know," Morgan said matter-of-factly. "I didn't think you were going to pack them."

"I wasn't!"

"See? Mother knows best." She held up several

blouses and shook her head. "You inherited your father's clothing sense. I loved him dearly but, good God, the man couldn't dress himself worth a damn. Thank heavens for Starfleet uniforms. You never have to figure out what you're going to wear to work."

Robin took several quick steps forward and snatched the shirts from her mother's hands. Morgan looked a bit surprised as Robin threw them back into the drawer. She then turned to face her mother, arms straight down and fists balled—not as if she were going to try to hit her, but rather out of an obvious desire to try to contain her annoyance.

"Risa, Mother? *Risa?*"

"Yes," said Morgan. "Risa."

"I cannot believe you booked us for a stay at Risa!"

"Why ever not?"

"It's so . . . so . . ." She gestured helplessly. "I mean . . . it used to be okay. There used to be a variety of resorts, and they certainly had some free-spirited beliefs about . . . romance. But now it's just so . . . so . . ."

"So what?"

"So prepackaged!" Robin finally managed to say. "Everything is so manufactured!"

"That's an odd thing to say, coming from someone who spent the last several years of her life inside a starship. How manufactured a life is that?"

"We use starships to go places, Mother. *Real* places."

"You're acting as if Risa isn't a real place. As if it's a . . . a holodeck simulation or something."

"It's only a few steps above one!" Robin dropped down onto the edge of her bed. "Have you seen their advertising, Mother? Have you?"

"Yes, of course I have. Anyone who's spent more than twenty minutes surveying the ether-web has."

" *'Come to Risa, there's no place nice-uh?'* " Robin looked as if she was going to be sick. "What kind of an awful slogan is that?"

"It seems rather effective to me."

"Effective? How effective? It doesn't make *me* want to go there!"

"Yes, but it makes you remember the name of the place. That's the important thing."

"It's plush! Luxurious!"

Morgan cocked an eyebrow. "You say that as if it's a bad thing."

"It's not a bad thing, but . . . there's no sense of adventure there!"

"Spending time together with nothing requiring our attention will certainly be adventure enough, don't you think?"

"Mom . . . there's nothing on Risa but gigantic resort hotels. All the beaches, the natural splendor of the place, has been co-opted."

" 'Natural splendor'?" Morgan sounded as if she wanted to laugh. "Robin, you seem to be forgetting something. When Risa was in its 'natural' state, there was hardly splendor. It rained ninety percent of the time and the planet was geologically unstable. Only because of the weather-control system was the planetary climate made over into what it currently is. The people of Risa embraced the changes, and the subsequent tourist trade."

"Some of them did," Robin said sourly. "Others felt that if the Risan gods had intended their planet to be a 'paradise,' they would have made it one in the first place. Instead, everything that was unique about the Risan culture—with the exception of their eager attitudes about . . . romance—has been subsumed by a tourist mentality."

"I don't believe it," said Morgan.

"It's true! That's exactly what's happened!"

"No, I mean I can't believe you used 'subsumed' in a sentence."

Robin blew air through her lips impatiently, not even bothering to address that comment. "And the worst is that new place, the one you want to book us at . . . what's it called? Oh, right—'El Dorado.' What sort of incredibly stupid name is that?"

"Well, aside from the literary reference, I tend to suspect that the hotel's founder, Laurence Dorado . . . L. Dorado . . . didn't think it such a foolish name at all."

Robin decided to try a different tack. She rose from the bed, draped an arm around her mother's shoulder, and said wheedlingly, "Mother . . . how about mountain climbing? Now *that* would be an adventure! There's a mountain range on Qontosia that has the most magnificent vistas on—"

"What, and wreck my nails?" said Morgan dryly. "Where's the relaxation in that? The stimulation . . ."

"Stimulation?" Robin looked at her blankly. "What do you mean . . . ?" And then, suddenly, she understood. "Of course! I get it!"

"You get it?"

"Yes! You're looking for romance!"

Morgan winced. "Robin . . ."

"Oh, have I got the planet for you! Argelius II. So hedonistic it makes Risa look like kindergarten. As a matter of fact—and I can't believe I'm telling you this, me, talking to my mother this way—" She lowered her voice, sounding conspiratorial. "On Argelius II, I know a place where the men are soooo—"

"I know the place."

Robin blinked. "You do?"

"Robin, I've gotten around quite a bit in my extended life, as you know. You'd be amazed at how few things I *haven't* seen. And, believe it or not, Risa happens to be one of them. Besides, you're judging it purely from the advertisements. There's other things there."

"Like what?"

"Archaeological digs, for one thing. I understand that some people go there for a vacation and spend the entire time rooting about in old ruins."

"Really?" Robin felt some stirring of interest.

"Really."

"Huh . . . you know . . . it could be kind of interesting at that." Robin stroked her chin thoughtfully. "We could camp out."

"We could, absolutely."

"Rough it."

"Roughing it would be very exciting," Morgan agreed.

"The two of us, spending our days by ourselves, digging around in ruins, scrounging about, seeing what we can find, maybe uncovering some great secret of an ancient civilization." Robin's enthusiasm was beginning to build. Not only did she start walking back and forth across the room, at one point she actually walked right across the bed. "And at night, the two of us in a tent, talking about all kinds of things, with nothing to distract us. No crowds, no loud noise, no red alert signals. No running around like our lives depended on it."

"We could do all that," Morgan told her.

"Mother, you've got yourself a deal," Robin told her. She started rummaging around in her drawers. "I'll have to bring stuff that's durable, since we'll be excavating. I've still got some dig tools in the other room, so that will help."

"And bring a nice dress or two."

That stopped Robin cold. "A nice dress? For excavating?"

"There's never an excuse for not looking our best."

Slowly, Robin fixed a level and not-particularly-inviting stare on Morgan. "Mother . . . you already booked us a room at El Dorado, didn't you?"

"Have you seen the things they have there?" Morgan asked by way of defending herself. "Swimming pools. Beaches—"

"Mother!"

"Nine restaurants featuring cuisine from all over the galaxy—real cuisine, prepared from scratch. Not things manufactured by replicators."

Robin noticed that her mother had started putting her clothes into the suitcase again. She promptly began yanking them out once more. "Mother, what about camping? About the dig? You said we would—"

"Ah-ah," Morgan corrected her. "I said we 'could.' That's not the same thing as saying we would. We 'could' flap our arms and fly to Venus, but I wouldn't hold my breath if I were you."

"Mother!" she fairly howled in exasperation. "Be reasonable!"

"You be reasonable! They also have an art museum on Risa, not to mention rides and attractions . . ."

"Oh, yes, rides." Robin rolled her eyes. "Climb on a shuttle and experience a simulation that puts you right in the middle of a black hole, or plunges you into the heart of a sun. As if anyone could survive experiences like that."

"Well, no one could, Robin. That's somewhat the point."

"Mother . . . I was onboard a starship when we dove straight toward a sun while trying to shake a Redeemer ship that was trying to blow us out of space. How is some 'ride' supposed to approximate that?"

"Because it's fun, Robin! Fighting for your life isn't fun. Experiencing danger firsthand when it's not really dangerous at all, that can be fun." She saw the disapproving look on her daughter's face and sighed heavily. "Robin . . . think about it. Does it really matter where we go, as long as we're going to be spending time together? Really? In the final analysis?"

"I suppose not," Robin admitted.

"Then why not have it be someplace that's lavish? Someplace I'm really going to enjoy?"

"What about me? Doesn't it matter if *I'm* going to enjoy it or not?"

"You will enjoy it, if you'll just relax long enough to get that stick out of your—"

"But—!"

"Exactly."

"No, I was starting to say, 'But you're not hearing me! You're not listening to what I'm saying!' "

"Actually, I think it's more a case of I'm not listening to what you aren't saying."

Robin totally lost track of the conversation. "I'm not following," she admitted.

"This is about Si Cwan."

"*What?*"

"You're concerned because Risa also has a reputation for being very romantic, and you're resistant to the notion that you might become involved with someone."

"Hey, *I* was the one who suggested Argelius II!"

"Hedonism and romance are two entirely different things."

Robin clapped her hands to her ears. "Mother, we are not having this conversation."

27

"One of us is. The other just isn't listening to it."

"I'm not resisting the Risa suggestion because I'm afraid of having a romantic fling! And there's nothing to 'get over' as far as Si Cwan is concerned, because nothing ever happened! What is it that I'm afraid of, exactly? That I might run into another man and have nothing happen all over again?"

"I don't know what you're afraid of, Robin."

"I'm not afraid of anything!"

"Then let's go to Risa!"

"Fine!" Robin practically exploded. "We'll go to Risa, all right? We'll go to damned Risa!" She started hauling clothes back out of the drawers and stuffing them into the suitcase. She made no effort to fold them or arrange them in any sort of neat or reusable fashion. She just shoved them in pell-mell. "We'll go, and we'll stay at the damned resort, and eat at the damned restaurants, and I'll fall in love with half the damned men in the place. Are you happy?"

"Well, I'd be happier with less use of the word 'damn,' if it's all the same to you."

Robin stabbed a finger at her. "You are driving me insane."

"That's what mothers are for," Morgan reminded her sweetly. Then she scowled as Robin grabbed up another blouse. "Not that one. It makes you look fat."

"I'll wear it over my head. That way I'll look like the fathead that I am."

"Wonderful idea, Robin. You'll be keeping the men away with a stick if you do that."

Robin moaned as she continued to pack, and wondered whether it was too late to call the weather bureau and ask for a lightning strike directed squarely at her skull. Or her mother's. She couldn't quite decide.

BURGOYNE

TANZI 419 LOOKED UP from hir desk and was most surprised to see Burgoyne 172 standing in the doorway. S/he rose, putting aside the material s/he'd been working on, and gestured toward the chair opposite hir desk. "Burgoyne! It is good to see you! I was not expecting it—"

"You are an accomplished liar, as always, Tanzi," Burgoyne said with surprising affability, considering the sentiment. "You must have known I would show up. I've been trying to get in touch with you for days." Just to show off, s/he covered the distance between the door and the chair with a single bound, landing squarely in the chair and crouching on it. "Amazing how you always have something else to do. Things here in the Hermat Embassy that busy?"

"Oh, you can't even begin to believe it," Tanzi said. S/he flashed that ready smile that had seen hir through so many difficult situations. Hir hair was long and silver, and s/he carried hirself with a dignity that existed mostly within hir own head. "First, we had an incident with—"

"I'll come straight to the point," Burgoyne interrupted, displaying absolutely no interest in Tanzi's incident or anything else having to do with life around the Hermat Embassy. Outside the window the classic spires of the New York skyline glistened in the day's scheduled sunlight. "There's been a bit of an incident involving . . . well . . ."

"Your son."

Burgoyne blinked in amazement. Tanzi's expression had changed, going from pleasant to all business. "I assume that's what you're here to discuss."

"Well . . . yes," said Burgoyne, making no effort to keep the surprise from hir face. "I didn't know you knew about him."

" 'Him.' " Tanzi shook hir head and laughed softly. "Who would have thought I'd ever hear that word coming from your mouth, Burgoyne, in regards to your own flesh and blood. Then again, you always were something of a rebel, weren't you? An upstart."

"You engaged in enough acts of rebellion at my side, Tanzi, and don't you pretend you didn't," Burgoyne said, pointing at hir. There was still a cordial pleasantness in hir voice, but something else as well. A warning: vague, but there nevertheless. "We've known each other too long, go back too far, to start playing games with one another."

"True. So true," admitted Tanzi.

"She told you, didn't she? Selar. She was in contact with you," Burgoyne guessed.

Tanzi nodded. "Not . . . her, precisely. Her brother. He's in the Vulcan dipcorps . . ."

"The what?"

"Diplomatic corps," Tanzi said by way of clarification. S/he leaned back in hir chair and, looking so at ease that it served to make Burgoyne feel a lack of ease, s/he put hir feet on hir desk. "Told me all the details . . . at least, as much as he felt was appropriate to share. The child was conceived during some sort of . . . mating ritual?"

"Something like that," Burgoyne admitted.

"Would *you* care to tell me about it?"

"Actually . . . I think not. I don't feel it's my place to tell. Vulcans tend to be somewhat reticent in discussing such things."

"How interesting," said Tanzi with clear amusement. "You're all worried about people's feelings all of a sudden."

"It's hardly 'all of a sudden,' Tanzi, and I can't say I'm enthusiastic about your attitude."

Tanzi did not appear to be particularly concerned about whether Burgoyne was enthused or not. Instead, s/he was consulting files that s/he was calling up on hir computer screen. "From my reading of this," s/he continued, "Selar was not exactly in her right mind when this mating urge seized her. In some respects, you took advantage of her to satisfy your own interests and curiosities."

"I did no such thing!" Burgoyne said, hir face becoming flushed with anger. Then s/he quickly reined hirself in, all too aware that losing hir temper at this point would not do hir the slightest bit of good. "Tanzi, it wasn't like that, I swear," s/he said. "We developed a sort of bond between us. Not only that, but the 'mating ritual,' as you call it, strengthened that bond. It caused us to . . . well . . . commune with each other, in a way—"

"Ahhh." Tanzi seemed thoughtful. "So you're saying that the Vulcan mental capacities might very well have robbed you of *your* judgment."

"No! That's not what I'm saying at all!" Burgoyne was feeling more frustrated by the moment.

"Let's just say that, however it happened, a child was conceived and born. Correct?"

"Correct." Burgoyne was simply relieved to be past the questionable circumstances under which s/he and Selar had joined with one another.

"And now Doctor Selar has taken the child—or at least is en route—to Vulcan, where it is her intention to raise the child in the Vulcan way."

Burgoyne bobbed hir head. "That is my belief. And, since that was conveyed to you by her brother, it would appear that's exactly right."

Tanzi sat back, interlacing hir fingers. "And what, precisely, do you expect the Hermat Directorate to do about it? Or me, as I am attached to the embassy?"

"I want you to go back to the Directorate and present my case to whomever it should be presented to," Burgoyne said eagerly. "She should not be allowed to get away with this. I want my rights as the father enforced."

"And why, precisely, would the Directorate help you in such an endeavor?"

At first Burgoyne wasn't entirely certain s/he had heard the question correctly. "I'm sorry, did you say . . . why?" When Tanzi nodded, a dumbfounded Burgoyne finally managed to say, "Because this is a Hermat child! A Hermat national! What Selar has done is the equivalent of kidnapping!"

"It is kidnapping only if someone is being transported against their will," Tanzi said patiently. "Furthermore, since she is the child's mother, naturally she is within her rights to take the child anywhere she chooses. Besides, Burgoyne, you are proceeding from a false assumption."

"And what would that be?" Burgoyne demanded.

Tanzi actually looked sympathetic, although whether s/he genuinely was or was simply putting on a good act Burgoyne could not determine. "That the child in question is even remotely under Hermat jurisdiction. All the evidence I've managed to garner points out that he is not, starting with the very fact that we can refer to him as 'he.' "

"Tanzi—"

Tanzi spoke right over hir. "The simple truth, as you should already know, is that the Directorate does not recognize half-breeds as Hermat citizens, deserving of protection under Hermat law. One is either Hermat or one is not. The essence of who we are is that we are both male and female. We contain the physical and spiritual essence of both. To possess only half those attributes is to be something other than what we are."

"There is precedent," Burgoyne said. "I checked. Some years ago, one of the Elders spawned a child out of the race, with a human. He was given status as a Hermat citizen—"

"You speak of Lebroq, and yes, that occurred. But the circumstances were different, starting with the fact that Lebroq was, in that instance, the human equivalent of the mother, not the father. Furthermore, Lebroq was indeed an Elder, and highly placed in our society . . ."

"And I'm not? Is that it? A parent is a parent, irrespective of which half of the biological contribution s/he falls on . . ."

"Perhaps in theory, Burgoyne. But the fact is that some parents are more equal than others. And let us be candid with one another, Burgoyne. You have not earned yourself any friends with your behavior."

"Behavior." Burgoyne felt an anger building behind hir eyes. "What is that supposed to mean?"

"You know precisely what it means," replied Tanzi. S/he was looking less sympathetic with each passing moment. "How many times have you spoken out against the Directorate, Burgoyne? How many times have you held up our ways, our philosophies, as something to be lampooned? What words did you use to describe the Hermat teachings? Let me think . . . oh, yes. 'Stodgy.' 'Boring.' How did you describe the Directorate? 'An assemblage of dreary drones, leeching the gods-given sense of joy and tactile sensation from our very being.' "

"That's completely out of context."

"Oh, really? And what was the context, Burgoyne?"

"Well . . . I was . . ." Burgoyne cleared hir throat. "I was speaking of . . . of dreary drones in general, not just the Directorate."

"Mm-hmm." Despite hirself, Tanzi smiled ruefully. "Burgoyne, we were playmates together. Students together. I can't find it in me to judge you too har̶̶̶, even to really judge you at all. But there are others who feel quite differently, and even if you had some sort of position that was truly tenable under Hermat law, they wouldn't be inclined to go any effort for you. As it is, they're not going to extend themselves at all. You've simply made too many enemies, offended too many people with your outspoken criticisms of the status quo."

"And because of that my child is to be punished?"

In spite of the seriousness of the situation, Tanzi laughed curtly. "Your child is hardly being punished. Your child is going to be raised among one of the most intelligent, most sophisticated races in the entire Federation. There is nothing that you have told me that even begins to indicate the child will be abused or mistreated in any way. The only thing that's being upset here, Burgoyne, is your vanity."

"Vanity!"

"Yes, vanity. You want the opportunity to raise a child in a culture that he is clearly not a part of."

"He's not Vulcan. Despite his outward appearance, he never will be, and he'll never fit in there. My every instinct tells me that."

"Unfortunately, Burgoyne, I'm afraid that simply doesn't carry very much weight. Slon has already spoken with me, I have spoken with representatives of the Directorate, and the decisions have already been made. The course is clear. If you want to go to the Directorate and fervently express what your instincts are telling you, then naturally you are entitled to do so. I can tell you right now, though, that not only will you be wasting your time, but you're also just going to embarrass yourself. Is that what you want?"

"What I want is the support of my own people as try to retain some sort of relevance to my son's life."

"Burgoyne." Tanzi reached over and took hir hand. "For your own sake . . . for your sanity . . . let it go."

"I can't."

"It will destroy you if you let it."

"I can't, I said."

Tanzi let out a heavy sigh. "Then you proceed on your own. I'm sorry, Burgoyne. But that's simply the way it's going to be."

Burgoyne rose from the chair. Tanzi remained seated. "I don't believe you're sorry. I don't believe you're sorry at all."

"What you believe, in this instance, really doesn't matter."

"Yes, that's becoming increasingly clear. Well, you know what, Tanzi? This isn't over. It isn't even close to over." Burgoyne turned on hir heel and headed for the door.

"When it is over," Tanzi suggested, "call me. Maybe we can get together for dinner or . . . something."

Burgoyne turned and looked at hir incredulously, trying to determine whether the suggestiveness in Tanzi's voice was hir imagination.

Obviously it wasn't, because Tanzi shrugged hir slim shoulders. "It has been a while, Burgoyne. Perhaps some 'quality time' spent with one of your own race would help realign you along the proper course."

"I don't want realignment," Burgoyne said tightly. "I want my son."

"Then good luck to you, Burgoyne. Believe it or not, I mean that sincerely."

"It'd be easier to believe if you were offering me help instead of a social engagement."

"Sometimes, Burgoyne, you have to believe in things despite evidence to the contrary."

"You know, Tanzi," Burgoyne said sadly, "I could swear that's exactly what I was trying to put across to you just now." And s/he departed, leaving Tanzi in thoughtful silence.

THE GREETER

ROBIN LAY BACK ON HER BED and slowly sank into it, then thudded the mattress gently as she repeated over and over to herself, like a mantra, "I won't like this place . . . I won't like this place . . . I won't like this place . . ."

The door to Robin's bedroom opened and Morgan was standing there. She had booked them a suite with a common sitting area and bedrooms on either side, ensuring privacy. "Well?" she queried.

Taking a deep breath, Robin prepared to lie to her mother. Instead, the words, "I love it," popped out of her mouth of their own accord. Upon hearing that sentence, which sounded as if a stranger had spoken it, Robin moaned and flopped her head back onto the pillow. The pillow conformed perfectly to the shape of her head with a slight hiss of air. *I'm in hell. I'm in hell, and I can get gourmet meals delivered twenty-six hours a day.*

Morgan beamed at her. "That's wonderful. Thank you for admitting it."

Robin grunted.

The truth was, she had been dazzled the moment their commercial shuttle had gotten within range of El Dorado. The advertisements she had seen for it did not even begin to do it justice. She had been to cities that were smaller . . . maybe even planets. It was like nothing she had expected. Much of the exterior of the resort was done up in elaborate gold mosaics. As a result, El Dorado seemed to shimmer with a life of its own during the day, particularly at certain hours, when the sun's rays caused the place to turn into a miniature version of the sun itself, glowing in all directions and visible for miles.

The El Dorado had been designed with a motif similar to what one would expect to see in Central American ruins, where Aztecs had once lived. No ancient tribes had ever resided in El Dorado, of course. It was of far too recent vintage, having been constructed and opened only a few years ago . . . and had promptly sucked up almost all vacation business.

Risa had been a popular getaway spot for ages, mostly because of its unique and perpetually temperate weather, its convenient location, and the open and friendly nature of its citizens. Assorted places had sprung up over the years to accommodate travelers who came to visit beautiful Risa for those reasons. Then developers had come in, built up El Dorado, and opened it, all within a fairly brief period. It became the tourist sensation of the area. It didn't matter that the glorious beaches had been manufactured specifically for the resort, the waters produced via wave generators. It didn't matter that filters had been erected that hovered over the sky and specially conditioned the sun's rays to provide maximum tanning. It didn't matter that none of the restaurants were family-owned and operated (like most of the other "quaint" Risa eateries), but instead were created for, and run by, the resort. In short, it was of no consequence to anyone that Risa's unique and relaxed character had been usurped and replaced by a resort hotel that could easily have been dropped on any world and been exactly the same.

The place did phenomenal business anyway.

Robin Lefler was a purist who respected and valued traditions that were native to various worlds. She was not someone who embraced commerce over everything. She was . . . she was . . .

Good lord, what a comfortable bed.

She was angry with herself for liking the place.

She had to admit it: She had gasped in appreciative amazement when she'd first beheld the sprawling complex. It was an architectural masterpiece. The interior had been just as impressive, with a massive waterfall smack in the middle of the main lobby . . . a fake sun, hanging high at the top of the lobby's great dome, bathing the people below in a gentle, caressing light . . . long, carpeted hallways . . . an efficient, helpful, and courteous staff. It was nothing short of astounding.

I want to live here forever . . .

"Shut up!" she said angrily to herself.

Morgan Primus looked startled. "What? What did I say?"

"Nothing, Mother, it's not you. It's me. Don't listen to me. Even I don't listen to me." She let out a sigh. "I hate being so immature that I have trouble liking a place just because it's someplace that you wanted to come."

"That's all right, dear," Morgan said reasonably. "I

get immature myself sometimes. And considering how long I've been around, I've really got no excuse for it. So don't worry about it. Come, get dressed."

"For what?"

"Well," she placed her hands on her hips, "you're not planning just to lie around on the bed all day."

"Actually, that doesn't sound like such a bad notion from where I sit. Why? What did you have in mind?"

"It's cocktail hour. I figured we could go to the main bar, just off the lobby. You must have seen it. From what I understand, they just redid it with a new theme."

"A new theme." Robin sighed loudly. "What have I gotten myself into? So what's the theme?"

Morgan frowned a moment, trying to recall, and then her face brightened. "Oh, right. 'The Engineering Room.' That's what they call it now."

"Why?"

"I don't know. Perhaps after one drink you'll do things on impulse. Either that or you'll become totally warped."

"I couldn't be any more warped by the situation than I already am." Robin eyed her mother thoughtfully. "Would you please explain to me how all this is supposed to bring us closer as mother and daughter?"

"You just have to give this place a chance, Robin. Get into the spirit of things here. Promise me you'll do that?"

"All right, all right. As long as you promise me," she replied, "that you'll stop talking about pushing me into a romance or something. I'm not looking for a man."

Morgan raised a questioning eyebrow.

"*Or* a woman, Mother."

"Just curious."

"Mother, at the moment, I'm really not interested in starting up any new relationships, considering that I haven't managed to sort out the ones I've already had. All right?"

"That's fine, honey. I can understand that. To be honest, I feel the exact same way. If there's one thing I'm not looking for, it's romance."

"That's a relief." Then Robin frowned. "On the other hand, maybe it's not. After all, isn't that when it usually happens?"

"That," Morgan informed her, "is a popular myth. And believe me, I know all the myths, all the nonsense, all the come-ons. The fact is, Robin, that whether you like it or not, men will probably be approaching you. They'll probably haul out every old line in existence."

Robin couldn't help but be amused. Getting tips from her mother as to how to handle advances from men . . .

"What's the oldest line, Mother?"

"They'll say, 'I could swear I know you from somewhere.' That's the oldest, most fake line of them all. It seeks to establish some preexisting relationship in order to save time. Promise me you won't fall for it."

"I won't, Mother," Robin promised solemnly, even raising one hand as if swearing to some higher power. "Now let's go down to the Engineering Room. And let's hope our warp cores don't get breached."

Morgan stared at her. "What's that supposed to mean?" she asked after a moment.

"You know . . . I'm not sure. But it sounded good, didn't it?"

Her mother considered it a moment. "No," she finally said.

Robin was starting to decide that maybe this entire thing hadn't been such a good idea after all.

* * *

They could hear the activity from the Engineering Room all the way across the lobby. There was laughter, music playing, and lights flickering at a slow, steady throb. "Oh, it's just like every engineering room *I've* ever been to," Robin noted with a touch of wry amusement.

"Robin . . . ," her mother said warningly.

"All right, all right, I know. I'm supposed to get into it. Give it a chance, get into the spirit of it. Fine, Mother, whatever you say. But I'll tell you right now, if the decibel level inside is anything like what it appears to be outside, I'm going to be able to take maybe five minutes of it before my head explodes."

They walked in through the main door. The interior was exactly what Robin had been expecting—flashing lights, loud music. She stifled a laugh as she saw that the center of the Engineering Room had a tall column, stretching to the ceiling, that was a rough approximation of a matter-antimatter mix chamber. But instead of matter and antimatter (obviously), the "chamber" had different types of alcohol brewing together and combining in taps that were being briskly operated by several bartenders.

It was quite an experience for Robin. The drink of preference on starships was synthehol, since its inebriating effects were simulated and could be shaken off at a moment's notice. After all, on a starship the concept of "off-hours" was really just that: a concept. The truth was that the call for all hands to battle stations could come at any time, and if that occurred, no one needed inebriated crew members rushing to their posts. So it was only recently that Robin had availed herself of a newfound liberty to explore alcoholic beverages.

Someone was walking toward them briskly, and Robin did a double take as she saw that he was sporting an old-style Starfleet uniform. She couldn't quite believe it; the only time she'd ever seen a uniform like it was in a museum, carefully preserved. It had to be seventy years old if it was a day. She wondered why in the world anyone would be wearing such an out-of-date ensemble, and then it hit her: It was simply a costume. For some reason, to add an air of "reality," they had a costumed actor sporting the outfit of an old-style Starfleet officer.

He approached them with such confidence that she immediately twigged to the fact that he worked there. He was a portly old gentleman, with gray hair and a bristling gray/black mustache. As he walked past others, they appeared to be greeting him by name or clapping him on the shoulder, as if they derived some sort of remarkable pleasure simply by being in his presence. Merriment twinkled in his eyes.

"That old fellow seems glad to be here," she murmured to her mother. "Then again, at his age, he's probably glad to be anywhere."

But she was astounded to see that her mother was staring at him, wide-eyed, as if she couldn't quite believe it. "Oh, my God," she muttered.

"What is it?"

He approached them, a hand outstretched in greeting, and said, "Welcome to the Engineering Room, on behalf of the management of the El Dorado. Ah'm . . ." Then he stopped dead in his tracks, his hand simply dangling there. His gaze was fixed upon Morgan with such intensity that Robin felt as if something physical was being transmitted from his eyes directly to Morgan's face.

"You are . . . ?" Robin prompted him.

"Scott. Montgomery Scott." He was still staring at

Morgan. And then, in an incredulous whisper, he said, "Christine?"

Robin looked from Scott to her mother and back. "Who?"

"You have me confused with someone else, I'm afraid," Morgan said, sounding rather apologetic. "My name is Morgan, Morgan Primus. This is my daughter, Robin. She's with Starfleet," she added, almost as an afterthought.

"So was I." Scott sounded as if he was in a fog. Then, abruptly remembering his job, he took Morgan's hand suavely in his own and kissed her knuckles. But his gaze never left her face. "It's uncanny," he said. "The hair is different, but . . . ye could be 'er twin."

"I'm afraid I don't know what you're talking about."

"Ah'm . . . sorry." He seemed to be having trouble finding words. "It's just that . . . ah could swear ah know ye from somewhere."

It was all Robin could do to stifle a laugh. They had barely been at the resort an hour, and already this Scott fellow had come forward with her mother's favorite bad pick-up line. . . .

But then something clicked in Robin's head. "Wait a minute . . . Montgomery Scott. Not . . . *the* Montgomery Scott."

"Aye, lassie."

She still couldn't quite believe it. "Montgomery Scott . . . from Captain Kirk's *Enterprise?*"

"Well, lassie." He smiled at her, as if pleased to be momentarily relieved of the utter befuddlement he was obviously feeling in regards to her mother. "Ah prefer t'think of it as Montgomery Scott's *Enterprise,* upon which Captain Kirk and all those other great people had the honor of serving. But then, most engineers tend to feel a wee bit possessive of their bairns."

" 'Bairns'?" inquired Robin.

"Children," Morgan promptly said.

"Aye, that's right." He stared openly at Morgan once more. There was no subtlety or artifice about him. If you were the focus of his attention, you knew it immediately. Robin had to listen carefully as he spoke, since his brogue was at times so thick she practically needed a machete to cut through it. "It's absolutely uncanny. The resemblance, ah mean. To Christine."

"Well, I'm not this 'Christine' person," Morgan said cheerfully. "Sorry to disappoint you."

"Oh, ah knew ye couldn't be. She's long gone, bless 'er, along with the rest of 'em . . . well . . . almost the rest of 'em. . . ."

"How can you be the original Montgomery Scott?" Robin demanded. "You would have to be . . . I don't know . . . over a hundred years old . . . which isn't impossible, of course, but you look much better than any hundred-year-old I know . . ."

"Actually, lassie—"

"Could you stop calling me that? Please?" Robin sounded slightly pained.

Scott didn't pretend to understand, but he shrugged and said, "Actually, lass . . . ah just celebrated muh one hundred fiftieth birthday."

"You seem wonderfully well-preserved for a man of your 'advanced' years, Mr. Scott," Morgan commented.

He beamed. "Call me 'Scotty,' why don't ye? Everyone else does. As for muh 'well-preserved' status, well . . . ah have a confession to make."

"You're a clone?" Robin guessed.

"No, no . . . the original item," and he bowed slightly

as he said it. "Perhaps ye ladies would allow me t'buy ye a drink."

"I wouldn't have it any other way," Morgan said lightly. She noticed the confused look in Robin's eye and gestured for her to be quiet, even as Scotty walked her over to the bar and ordered her a screwdriver.

" 'Christine'? Who the hell is 'Christine'?" Robin wondered out loud, but no one quite heard her.

The three of them had been sitting at a table for quite some time. The man known as Scotty regaled them—quite colorfully—with the tale of how a bizarre transporter mishap and a desperate bid for survival had stranded him more than half a century after the time he had once called his own.

"Now I wish I'd stayed with the *Enterprise*," said Robin. "Such interesting things happened after I left. Not that it was exactly dull before that. . . ."

"So, what happened?" asked Morgan eagerly. She leaned forward on the table, swirling the contents of her glass idly. "After you left with the shuttle, I mean?"

Robin looked at her mother carefully, and with some degree of amusement. She couldn't recall a time when she had seen her mom quite as worked up or interested in something. After all, her "immortal" mother was able to lay claim to having seen and heard just about everything. As a result, Morgan wore a permanent blasé attitude with pride, as if it were a mantle. But there was something about Scotty that was connecting with her.

Robin could see some basis for the interest. The Scotsman was certainly something of a raconteur, with a wonderful way of telling a story. And the accent was to die for.

"Ach, well, I'd love t'tell ye that I had all manner of

incredible adventures. But the fact is that it was, well . . . a bit dull. Out of curiosity, the first place I went was to the Norpin V retirement colony, where I was supposed to be spendin' muh golden years."

"Norpin V? Wasn't that the place that—"

He nodded to Robin. "Wiped out by the worst series of planetary hurricanes anyone ever saw, more'n fifty years ago. If ah had been there, ah wouldn't be talkin' to ye now."

"Well, if you'd been there back then, I doubt you'd be alive today in any event," Morgan pointed out.

He raised his eyebrows, and looked positively impish doing so. "Don't underestimate muh longevity, Morgan. There's any number of reasons ah'm known as a miracle worker."

"Really?" said Morgan with obvious interest. "Would you like to enumerate some of them?"

"Well," Scotty cast a glance Robin's way, "not in front of the wee one."

"Oh, my God," muttered Robin, her face flushing. Morgan, for her part, simply laughed. Desperately trying to angle the conversation back toward something less potentially humiliating, Robin said, "So how did you wind up here, Scotty? I mean, you obviously work here. Why? You're an engineering genius; you should be getting your hands dirty in an engineering bay somewhere. Not working as a . . . what do you do here again?"

"I'm a greeter, darlin'. I shake the hands of folks who come in, welcome 'em to the Engineering Room." That drew a chuckle from him as he glanced around the place. "And ye know what? One out of maybe ten gets that sort of wide-eyed look of wonder, and they say, 'Are ye really him? The legend?' Those one in ten make it a bit fun."

"But how—?"

"Ach, but ye are a single-minded thing, aren't ye? Well, the simple truth is that the good people here on Risa were having trouble with their newly installed computer systems. Serious problems. And ye know what they found out? They found out that computer installation is too bloody easy."

"I'm not following," admitted Robin.

But Morgan said immediately, "He's saying that the quality of those installing them is dropping off."

He touched his finger to his nose. "Ye have it exactly right," he agreed. "Everything is so foolproof, the systems so efficient, that a lot of people nowadays billin' themselves as computer installers . . . why, they don't know the least thing about what's truly makin' the bloody things function. They think if they insert tab 'a' into slot 'b,' why, that's all there is to it. And, unfortunately for the folks here on Risa who were counting on their installers to do the job, they found out differently. Computer systems analysis is becomin' a lost art, outside of Starfleet. Even in Starfleet, it's so standardized. Same mnemonic circuits, same database, even the same computer voice . . ." He stopped talking, staring once again at Morgan.

Morgan looked at him with curiosity. "Is something wrong?"

"It's just that . . . yer voice. Even yer voice sounds like . . ." And then he waved dismissively. "Ach, forget it. Ah'm losing muh mind and that's all there is to it. So, in any event . . . the Risa management needed someone who understood the systems from the ground up. And how many people are there around who fill that bill, I ask ye?"

"Not many," said Robin.

He thumped the table. "Not many indeed. There's exactly two people still suckin' oxygen who could get the job done the way it ought to be done."

"Going on the assumption that you're one," said Robin, "who's the other?"

It was Morgan who answered. "Spock," she said immediately.

"Right again. Morgan, ye are quite the knowledgeable lady."

"Well, I've been around a while. Picked up a few things," Morgan told him modestly.

"Ahhh, but ah'll bet ye haven't been around quite as long as ah have," Scotty replied.

"Oh, you'd probably lose that—*owwww!*" Robin suddenly yelped.

Scotty looked at her with concern. "Are ye okay, lass?" he inquired solicitously.

Robin was firing a dirty look at her mother, whose face had gone resolutely deadpan. She flexed her foot, the instep of which had been thoroughly crunched by the heel of Morgan's boot under the table. "Sorry. Pulled a muscle. Nothing to be alarmed about."

"You're absolutely right, Scotty," continued Morgan with a quick, satisfied smile in Robin's direction.

"And what's this?"

Robin looked up to see a short, avuncular fellow with thinning hair and a too-eager-to-please manner. His hands were in constant movement, his fingertips tapping against each other. "My, my, my," he said, in a voice that sounded like an odd combination of friendly and nervous, "are we seeing a hint of romance here?"

"Romance, Mr. Quincy?" Scotty sounded somewhat surprised. "Ah'm just doin' muh job."

"Ah, but I've never seen you spending quite so much

time with any one guest . . . I'm sorry, guests," he amended, turning to Robin. "I didn't see you there, Miss."

"Yes, I'm just that memorable." Robin said.

"These are special guests, Mr. Quincy," Scott informed him. "The lassie—lass—here is from Starfleet."

"Starfleet!" This time Quincy rubbed his palms together. "We do quite a nice business with Starfleet. Always appreciate the business. And you, ma'am? Are you also—?" He looked questioningly at Morgan.

"I've . . . dabbled," said Morgan. "But it's no longer my number-one priority."

"Ah. Well, I'm Theodore Quincy. I'm the manager here at El Dorado. I didn't mean to intrude . . ."

"Ah was just regaling the ladies with the explanation of how ah came to be here," said Scott.

"Oh, well . . . !" Unbidden, Quincy snagged a chair and pulled it over. "As it turned out, we had a few initial problems with our computer systems, and we brought in Mr. Scott here to smooth out the rough edges."

"So we heard," Robin said.

"We were so pleased with the job he did that we invited him to spend a week or so, on the house," continued Quincy. "And it was amazing. When people found out who he was, they were flocking to him. He became his own media event. Well, I'll tell you, there are no flies on Theodore Quincy."

Robin looked him up and down and saw that there were not, in fact, any insects swarming on him. So it was certainly true, although the significance of the absence of flies eluded her.

"I spoke to the owners, and before you could say, 'Milk it for all it's worth,' we'd offered Scott here a full-time position."

"It's a lot more interestin' than retirement, ah have to admit that," Scotty told them. "And yet, it's not that entirely different."

"We immediately redid this lounge area," Quincy said, gesturing to the bar surrounding them. "Everything from basic concept to final execution, inside of forty-eight hours. Then we installed Scotty here and the rest is history."

Scotty winced visibly, but forced a game smile. "Ah prefer not t'think of muhself as history."

"Oh, of course not, Scott," Quincy immediately clarified. "You have a tremendous amount still to contribute."

"And you find this interesting?" Morgan appeared a bit puzzled. "Standing around in a facsimile engineering bay, appealing to people's nostalgia and encouraging people to have a good time—which they were likely going to do already—when you're clearly capable of so much more."

"What would ye suggest, Morgan?" Scotty asked reasonably. 'Ah'm not exactly a spring chicken, ye know. It's not like ah'm going to—ah dinna know— take command of a ship, or perhaps start a family."

"I suppose. It's just . . ." She shook her head. "It seems like a waste of material to me."

"Ah, ye are sweet to say so, Morgan," he smiled. "And ah admit . . . every so often, ah find muhself thinkin' about how it would be t'be pressed back into service. I got muhself into some pretty fixes through the years, ah did. There's somethin' about tryin' to string together operating systems, or jury-rigging engines while under split-second pressure with lives at stake . . ." He let out a sigh. "Makes a man feel alive."

"Sounds dangerous," Quincy commented.

"That's the point, isn't it?" Scotty sighed.

"So you see, Mr. Quincy," Morgan told him, "there's

no 'romance' here. Just Mr. Scott doing his job and making our first hours here at El Dorado as pleasant as possible."

"And I trust the rest of your stay will be equally as pleasant," Quincy said. He smiled wanly. "Hopefully you'll be able to feel sufficiently alive without putting your lives at stake." They all laughed at that.

They wouldn't be laughing later.

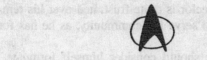

SELAR

SELAR INSPECTED THE OFFICE with approval. Her brother, Slon, stood nearby with arms folded, watching her with his customary detached disinterest. Although Slon was her younger brother, he was a head taller than she, with a very triangular face and exceedingly curved eyebrows that gave his face a look of perpetual disdain. This could not have been more at odds with his personality, for he had a far more wry outlook to life than just about any other Vulcan Selar could think of.

"This seems quite adequate," she said after a sufficient time of looking over the facilities.

"High praise from you," Slon replied.

He had a tone that was slightly baiting, one that he adopted with no one else. As always, she let it pass without comment. "And Dr. Seclor was quite certain that the arrangement was satisfactory with him?"

"More than certain," said Slon. "The timing of it was

53

quite good, actually. He needed to take time off to recover from his bout with xenopolycythemia, but he had no wish to leave his patients and clientele in the lurch. Your expressed interest in setting up a practice here on Vulcan for a period of several months was, as I said, well-timed. Dr. Seclor is quite frustrated over his temporary inability to serve his community, as he has for so long."

"Doctor Seclor should consider himself fortunate," Selar said primly. "Less than a century ago, his ailment would have been terminal. The strain that affects Vulcans is particularly vicious. Better to be out of commission for a relatively brief time than deceased for substantially longer."

"As always, Selar, your way with words remains uniquely your own." He walked around the office, his hands draped behind his back. "So I can inform Dr. Seclor that you will attend to his patient list."

"Yes. This arrangement will suit everyone's needs. And, who knows . . ."

Her voice trailed off, but Slon was not about to let it stop there. "Who knows what?" he asked.

She did not answer immediately, but he did not push it. He knew Selar well enough to know that she would say what was on her mind sooner or later . . . and if he pushed the subject, it would be later rather than sooner.

"Perhaps," she said thoughtfully, "it will be permanent."

"You would leave Starfleet?" he asked. Naturally, he covered his surprise, but Selar could tell that he was caught off guard. "I had thought it was the only place where you were happy. Or, at least, what passes for happiness in you."

"I have . . . been considering it. I do not know that a

Starfleet vessel is the best place for a child to be brought up."

"Nor do you know that it is the worst. There have been extensive studies done upon children raised in such an environment. There have been no indications that any psychological harm was done to them."

"My child is not a study or a statistic," Selar informed him, in that annoyingly superior tone she was so capable of adopting. "I am concerned purely about Xyon's well-being and overall health. On that basis, I believe he would be better off being raised on Vulcan, in a Vulcan environment."

"He is your child . . ."

Slon didn't complete the sentence, but instead let it hang there. The lengthy pause naturally caught Selar's attention. "You think I am wrong to desire this thing."

"I did not say that."

"You did not have to."

Slon appeared less than amused. "In addition to your capabilities as a doctor, are you adding 'mind reader' to your list of accomplishments, Selar?"

"No. Having the status of being your sister is sufficient." She tilted her head slightly as she regarded him. "Do you think I will be an inadequate mother?"

He took a deep breath. "I will be honest, Selar—"

"Can you be any other way?"

"No. To be honest, I have difficulty picturing you as *any* sort of mother. You have never struck me as the motherly type. Your possessiveness of the child seems . . . odd."

"That," replied Selar, "is because you have no children, Slon. You have never experienced *pon farr* . . . nor will you."

"Yes," sighed Slon, "as you and our parents never cease bringing to my attention."

"That reminds me . . . how is your 'friend,' Sotok? Are you and he still together?"

"On and off . . . at the moment, off, but eventually, on, I would suspect. He is well . . . much to the annoyance of Father. He still believes that, were it not for my involvement with Sotok, my 'true' nature would have presented itself, and the *pon farr* urges would have swept me up in their inevitable tide of reproductive drive."

Despite her Vulcan discipline, she actually felt slightly sorry for him, and allowed that to slip into her tone. "You should not concern yourself, Slon. Father may argue against the 'logic' of the situation, but ultimately his, and Mother's, feelings for you are undiminished."

"They have no feelings for me. Or for you."

"True. That is why they remain undiminished."

He raised an eyebrow. "You, Selar, have acquired a somewhat mordant wit."

"I prefer to think of it as 'bedside manner.' "

"And patients appreciate it?"

"No," she admitted. "However, they place far greater concern upon the likelihood that I will enable them to remain alive. Since I am skilled at that, they overlook any other concerns regarding my conduct."

"That is very fortunate for you. Let us hope that your patients' general survival rate remains high. It would not be beneficial to your career if they should turn on you."

"You," Selar told him, "are avoiding the question."

"Am I?"

"Yes. Answer me straight, Slon. Do you think I will be a good mother for Xyon?"

"I try to make a habit, Selar, of only presenting my opinion in those instances where I believe the questioner might act upon that opinion. I do not consider that to be likely here. You will do what you will do, as you always have."

"But you think I am wrong to do so."

"Not wrong for you. You will do what you feel is right."

"You are fencing with me, Slon. That is unworthy of you. Say precisely what you mean, or cease saying anything at all."

His eyes narrowed at that. "Very well. I think it unwise that you have elected to exclude the father from the process of raising the child."

"You cannot be serious."

"I am Vulcan, Selar. I do not know how *not* to be serious."

"Your syntax is mangled, but the sentiment is clear enough." She took a deep breath. "Burgoyne and I . . . are not a possibility, Slon."

"Why? Do you find hir that repugnant?"

"No. No, s/he is not repugnant at all. S/he is . . ." Selar paused, calling an image of Burgoyne to her mind, and was inwardly surprised to discover that image was not altogether displeasing. "S/he is loving and caring. Protective and brave. Fiercely loyal. Very concerned about the welfare of our child. Dedicated and hardworking."

"Ah. Very well. I can see why you have no possible future together," Slon said with a waspish, cutting edge to his voice.

"Slon . . ."

"Is the problem Burgoyne . . . or is it you?"

"I do not have a problem," Selar told him.

"That may very well be your problem," said Slon. He shook his head. "I do not mean to lecture you, Selar, or to seem as if I doubt your judgment."

"In that case, the happenstance by which you are accomplishing both of those ends is truly impressive."

"I simply think that you are cutting off options that might be of benefit to you, and to Xyon, and that you are doing them for reasons you do not fully appreciate or understand."

"And you do?"

"Not entirely," he admitted. "I have known you for as far back as I can remember, my dear older sister. Our people are not compassionate, even under the best of circumstances, and you have followed that spirit to the letter. That is to be expected. But for all that . . . you have changed. You are colder, more ruthless, more uncaring than the Selar I recall. You went about your profession with efficiency because that was what the job entailed. You dealt with your drives as a Vulcan because you felt it your duty. But lately . . . I am not sure . . . you seem to use your detachment as a shield, a cloak that will protect you from harm."

"What sort of harm?"

"I would think that you would know."

"I do not know how I *would* know, Slon," she said reasonably. "This is, after all, your own scenario that you are spinning here. If you do not know the origin of this mythical 'harm' from which I am protecting myself, then I do not consider myself bound by it."

"You are not bound by it in any event," he said. "I am simply . . . thinking out loud. That is all."

"You would be well-advised, then, to think more softly. Quieter thoughts usually result in more accurate thoughts."

"I shall try to keep that in mind in the future, Selar."

ROBIN & MORGAN

ROBIN SAT UP IN BED, blinking against the darkness. She checked the chronometer and couldn't believe what it was telling her. Oh-three hundred hours? *Oh-three-hundred?*

She slid her legs out from under the covers. The rug was fuzzy against her feet as she rose from the bed and padded to the common area, then peered through the still-open door to her mother's empty bedroom. "Where the hell is she?" Robin said to no one with utter incredulity. Even as she voiced the question, though, she already knew the answer: She was out with him. With "Scotty," as she had been every night since they'd arrived.

"Half light," she said, and the lights in the room obediently came on halfway. Just then the door to the room slid open and Morgan entered, her face a little flushed. She'd obviously been running . . . or, perhaps, engaged in some other physical activity. She froze just inside the door when she saw the look from her daughter.

"Oh. Hello," she said.

"Hello," said Robin. If her voice had been any more icy, mist would have floated from her mouth. "Another late night?"

There was a silence. "If you were about to use the bathroom, don't hesitate on my account."

"Thank you for your permission, Mother. I'm ever so gratified." She went in and used it. By the time she came out, minutes later, Morgan was in nightclothes and sliding under the covers of her own bed. "All tuckered out?" she asked.

Morgan didn't notice—or at least appeared not to notice—the dripping sarcasm in her tone. "A bit, yes."

"And what, exactly, tired you out so?"

"Well, it was a busy evening," Morgan said. "First, we got stinking drunk. And then, to work off the alcohol, we went at each other in a manner similar to crazed weasels."

"Mother!" Robin couldn't believe it. She wanted to slam her hands over her ears. She very nearly did. "I don't want to hear this! I do *not* want to hear this!"

"Good lord, Robin, you have your father's sense of humor."

"Dad didn't have a sense of humor."

"Ah. My point was sufficiently obvious, then." She smiled. "Nothing like that happened, Robin. More's the pity, actually . . . I wouldn't mind. . . ."

"I'm not listening to this."

"We talked, Robin. We talked. And later . . . well, there are three different dance clubs here. You should try one."

"Really." Robin flopped down on the edge of the bed. "And who, exactly, do you suggest that I go dancing with, Mother?"

"I don't know. Find someone."

"That's not what this was supposed to be about, Mother. This was supposed to be about you and me, finding each other. Not you finding someone and me finding someone."

"But don't you see?" said Morgan. "If you found someone, then we would have something to talk about together. It would be like . . . like being teenagers together. All right, granted, I'd be working from very distant memory in my case."

"Oh, I don't know about that," Robin said tartly. "Considering the way you've been behaving, I'd say you've got the hang of it well enough."

For a moment Morgan's dark eyes flashed in anger, but then comprehension and compassion superseded. "I've disappointed you, haven't I?" she said.

"Oh, how could you tell?" Robin still sounded annoyed, but felt a little bit less so since it appeared that her mother was actually starting to understand.

Morgan sighed heavily. "I'm sorry, Robin," she said. She sat up and ran her fingers through her daughter's hair. "Look, believe it or not, it's just . . . been quite a while since any man paid attention to me the way Scotty does. And here's the really funny thing: I thought I didn't care. I thought I was beyond that. I thought that if another man never gave me the time of day, it would be perfectly fine with me. I didn't want it, I didn't need it. . . ." She laughed softly to herself, clearly amused by it. "It just goes to prove that, no matter how long you live, you always have things to learn. You know what, Robin? I won't spend any more time with him."

"Mother, no . . ."

"It's okay. It'll be fine. I'll explain to him that—"

"That what?" Robin asked. "That your grown daughter was acting like a spoiled child? 'Mommy, Mommy, pay attention to me!' How foolish would that sound? How foolish would that actually *be?* Because that's really the truth of it, and we both know it."

"Well, yes, it is, but I want to be respectful of your feelings."

"And I should be respectful of yours, Mom. I mean . . . oh, hell, the whole thing with you and Scotty is only part of the problem."

"Really? And what's the rest of the problem?"

Robin smiled wryly, as if she were confessing a major sin. "I like this place."

"No!" Morgan gasped in mock-horror and put her hand to her breast as if to calm the rapid beating of her shocked heart. "Oh, my dear lord, we have to get you out of here immediately before you start having fun!"

"Okay, okay," laughed Robin. "I guess I deserved that. It's just that . . . well, Risa, as you know, wasn't exactly my idea of a fun place. It wasn't what I wanted to do. But I've been walking around, and, you know . . . everyone here is having a good time except me. The beaches are crowded, and the surf created by the water generators moves in and out steadily. The restaurants are superb. There's a zoo, did you know that?"

"No, I didn't."

"Animals from worlds even *I've* never been to, living in exact replications of their own habitats. And I . . ." She looked chagrined. "I went on the fly-into-the-sun ride."

"Oh, Robin, you didn't!" The words sounded severe, but there was nothing except amusement in her voice.

"I did. God help me, I did. And I screamed in 'terror.' It was incredible. I really felt like I was right in the middle of a solar core, and for one moment . . ." She dropped her voice conspiratorially. "For one moment, I actually felt as if it was the end. That there was some sort of malfunction, and we really were going to be incinerated. I thought we were all dead, and suddenly we 'came out the other side,' and . . . well, it was just remarkable. At some point, I'll probably try out the black-hole ride."

"So what are you saying, Robin?"

"I'm saying that you're obviously enjoying things your way, and rather than complain about that, I'm just going to start enjoying them my way. You said yourself there were archaeological dig sites. I think I'll check out a few of them. See what's there, experience them for myself. I'll camp out a night or two. That way you won't have to be out and feeling guilty about me sitting here by myself."

"Oh, Robin, you're wrong—"

"Now, Mother, I'm certain that my getting off by myself for a day or two wouldn't be such a bad thing."

"Oh, I'm not disputing that," Morgan said flatly. "I was just saying you're wrong if you thought I was feeling guilty. I was off having too much of a good time to feel guilty for so much as a microsecond."

"Oh." Robin smiled wanly. "Well . . . thank you for clearing that up, Mother."

SELAR

SHE WAS NOT EXPECTING to see Burgoyne sitting there in her outer office. And yet, somehow, she was not the least bit shocked. Selar had known that, sooner or later, s/he would be there. In fact, all the times she had envisioned exactly this moment, it had occurred precisely like this. Odd how some things in life were truly as predictable as all that.

Burgoyne was standing, but did not approach her. S/he looked surprisingly at ease. "You don't seem surprised to see me, Selar."

"I am not," Selar replied. "I had hoped that you would be wise enough not to pursue me. To honor my wishes in this instance."

"I honor your wishes as precisely as you honor mine. No more, no less." S/he cocked hir head. "You look well. Very much as I remember you."

"It has only been a few weeks, Burgoyne."

"Really. It seems much longer."

No patients had yet arrived; Selar's first appointment was not for an hour. She had been looking forward to taking the time to settle herself, go over records of her patients, perhaps even catch up on news. That, obviously, was not going to be the case now.

Burgoyne was looking more carefully at her. "On closer observation," s/he said, "you do not look quite as well as I thought. In fact, you look exhausted."

"I had a long night with Xyon," she admitted. "He has been unconscionably fussy."

"Unconscionably?" Despite the seriousness of the moment, Burgoyne couldn't help but smile slightly. "He is an infant. I doubt he has much truck with, or even concept of, such esoteric matters as conscience."

"It is inconvenient, nevertheless. As unreasonable as it may sound, I had—on some level—been expecting Xyon to be the equivalent of a miniature adult Vulcan, rather than an infant not in control of any aspect of his being."

"As a doctor, I would think you would be quite familiar with the developmental patterns of infants." Burgoyne was trying to look relaxed, but came across as merely ill at ease.

"I am. But the familiarity of it is somewhat different from the experiencing of it." She took a deep breath. "Would you care to sit?"

"Unnecessary. I have been sitting for quite some time. Most of it was spent in the offices of various Hermat officials, seeking aid in my cause. And then, of course, there was the time I spent in the transports that brought me out here. Once here, I have spent a good deal of time doing further research in Vulcan law and tradition, in continued pursuit of—"

"Your cause, yes, as you've said." Now it was Selar

who sat. She did so very stiffly, her hands resting lightly on her thighs. "Then I suppose we should get to the heart of why you are here."

"I suppose we might as well," Burgoyne said dourly, "considering that you don't seem inclined to say so much as 'hello.' "

"Would that make a difference?"

"It might."

"Very well: Hello, Burgoyne."

"Hello."

There was silence for a moment. "Did it make a difference?" asked Selar.

Burgoyne appeared to consider it. "No. No, not really."

"Ah."

"You should not have left, Selar. I deserved better than that."

To her own surprise, Selar looked down, suddenly having developed a tremendous interest in the floor. "You . . . are right," she admitted. "You are right, Burgoyne. You deserved better than that. In fact . . . you deserve better than what I can offer you. Your fixation on me surpasses all logical understanding."

"Love isn't about logic."

"Yes, it is," countered Selar. "Love is the romantic gloss put upon fundamental biological drives for the purpose of making them appear more than they already are. No one wishes to think of themselves as slaves to their desire to reproduce. Humans are particularly noted for such absurd behavior. I had hoped that Hermats were above such nonsense. Certainly we Vulcans are."

"That," Burgoyne said, "is not something I would take a great deal of pride in, if I were you."

"But you are not me, Burgoyne."

"Yes. Yes, you've made that abundantly clear." S/he

took a deep breath. "You have made it clear that you do not reciprocate my feelings, Selar—"

"Cannot."

"And doesn't that bother you?" s/he asked. "Doesn't it bother you that you find yourself incapable of even feeling such a fundamental and important emotion? Yes, yes, I know," s/he waved hir hands around dismissively, "I know how you and your people go on about emotions. But my understanding has always been that you *feel* them; you just don't *display* them. After all, where is the discipline in controlling something that you have no experience of? It would be like a eunuch taking a vow of celibacy."

"A very vivid comparison. No, Burgoyne, it does not bother me. It is something without which I have been able to function quite well, thank you."

"Have you? If that's what you believe, Selar, then you're deluding yourself."

Selar sighed. "This is getting us nowhere, Burgoyne. You have come a long way and obviously spent a good deal of time in your 'cause.' What do you wish? I will hear you out, of course. It is certainly the least that I can do."

"My concerns involve a bit more than the least that one can do. Xyon is mine, Selar, as much as he is yours."

"Vulcan law says differently. So, I suspect, does Hermat law, for if it was aligned with you, you wouldn't be here alone."

"Nevertheless . . . if we are not to reside together, Selar, then I want Xyon to be with me at least half the time."

"That," she said stiffly, "is not going to happen."

"I shall make it happen."

"How? Through sheer force of will?"

Burgoyne smiled thinly. "What about the Time of Awakening?"

Selar blinked in confusion. "You speak . . . of Surak?"

"Surak, yes. Interesting fellow. Father of your civilization, as I understand it."

She nodded. "Yes. But how is that applicable?"

"You spoke of sheer force of will. As near as I can determine, Surak forged Vulcan society into its current state almost entirely through force of will. He preached logic, stoicism—these and other aspects that were not part of your warlike culture up to that point." Burgoyne was speaking with ease and confidence; one would have thought s/he was a full Vulcan scholar. "From my reading, there were certainly some bumps and bruises along the way. Some odd traditions arose from those days. The transition from a society of barbarian, warlike attitudes to a society based on logic was certainly not a smooth one."

"No, it was not," agreed Selar. "But I do not see the parallel."

"The parallel is that, at some point, Surak had to look out upon the world the way it was, and he had to say to *somebody,* 'I can make it better.' Except that to look upon this barbaric world of savage, warrior Vulcans and say that it could be transformed into a society of dispassionate logic was, in fact, a totally illogical thing to do. It made no sense. No reasonable being could look at black and say, 'I'll think I'll make it white.' Surak must have, could only have, made the decision and embarked on his course of action based solely on an act not of logic, but of utter faith. Your meticulously crafted world of logic hinges on a decision that was, on the face of it, completely illogical."

"Burgoyne . . . allowing you for a moment your rather unique interpretation of our history, which you, as an outsider, are naturally far more qualified to make than any of us who are native to this planet—"

"Blinding sarcasm. You're learning."

"I am a quick study. Allowing you that, Burgoyne . . . are you saying, in essence, that you intend to convince me, or whatever authorities you choose to approach, that you should be accorded these rights you seek based not upon logic, but upon sheer will power?"

"Something like that. I'll use force of will . . . force of arms if necessary."

"Force of arms?" She cocked an eyebrow, more amused than anything. "Are you threatening me with violence, Burgoyne?"

"No," s/he replied. "But at times this can be a violent universe, Selar. We're just living in it." S/he paused, clearly trying to think of something else to say, but then s/he shrugged. "I suppose I'm done here." S/he turned to leave.

"Would you like to see him? To see Xyon?" Selar asked quietly.

S/he turned back to her, clear surprise on hir face. "I . . . didn't even think to ask. I just figured you'd say no."

"Perhaps, in the final analysis, that is why we are not compatible, Burgoyne. You see . . . you think you know me. But you do not. I am not without . . ."

"Compassion?"

"No, I am without compassion. Compassion can be a serious impediment to the practice of medicine. If one feels compassion for one's patients, it can interfere with clear and correct judgment. But I am not without consideration for the feelings of others. Come." Without another word, she turned and walked out of the office, carefully calculating that the conversation had consumed eleven minutes and nineteen seconds. Spending five more minutes with Burgoyne and Xyon would not act as an impediment to the timely and speedy processing of her patients.

Her home was only a short distance from her office. When she arrived with Burgoyne in tow, the nurse she had hired to attend to Xyon rose with a mildly quizzical expression. "I was not expecting you to return for seven hours and forty-three minutes," she said.

"There was an . . . unexpected circumstance," Selar said judiciously, casting a sidelong glance at Burgoyne. Burgoyne, for hir part, had gone over to the side of Xyon's bed and was smiling down at him. "If you would excuse us . . ."

The nurse, whose name was T'Fil, inclined her head slightly in acknowledgment and walked into another room. Selar turned back to Burgoyne and started, unable even with all her training to cover her surprise. "What are you doing?" she demanded with a bit more edge in her voice than she would have liked.

Burgoyne had extended two fingers, and Xyon had grabbed one in each of his chubby little hands. With the child gripping hir firmly, Burgoyne had lifted the infant into the air, his tiny feet hovering an inch or so above the mattress and pumping the air joyously.

"What are you doing?" she said again.

"Just playing. Quite a grip, huh?"

"You will hurt him," Selar told hir. "Put him down."

"I'm not hurting him. Look at the grip on him." To demonstrate, Burgoyne raised and lowered the child slightly. Xyon cooed. "See?"

"Put him down! Now!"

Her tone was so emphatic, so strident, that Burgoyne automatically settled Xyon back down on the infant bed. But s/he was looking at Selar with clear surprise. "An emotional outburst. Who would have thought?"

"It was not an emotional outburst, Burgoyne. I simply deemed it necessary to increase the volume of my voice in order to get your attention."

"Mm-hmm," said Burgoyne noncommittally. S/he was looking down at Xyon and smiling. "He's coming along nicely. He has my eyes, don't you think?"

"He has his own eyes. Have you seen him for a sufficient period of time?"

"I could look at him for a lifetime and it would be insufficient. He's looking back at me, you know. He's focusing right on me. I think he knows who I am."

"Very unlikely. Vulcan children are slow developers . . . not unusual, considering the length of time we live. Children of that age simply do not focus or pay sustained attention in the manner that you are describing."

"It's impressive, Selar, how you can know so much about everything . . . and at the same time, know so very little."

Xyon, starting to look a bit concerned—as if he could sense the tension in the air—began to cry. Burgoyne reflexively reached down for him, but Selar quickly said, "It is quite all right, Burgoyne. I will attend to him."

She expected an argument, but Burgoyne simply nodded and said, "As you wish."

Selar reached down and took Xyon in her arms. He continued to whimper. Burgoyne watched her with curiosity. "Is there a problem, Burgoyne?" Selar asked with thinly veiled impatience, jostling Xyon slightly in a rocking motion. Xyon was still voicing his displeasure.

"Well . . . look at the way you're holding him."

Selar looked down at him. "What are you talking

about? I am holding him correctly. The head is supported, the back is in the proper—" She shook her head, stopping herself. "This is absurd. I am a doctor, Burgoyne. I have delivered children . . ."

"So have I. Ours."

Ignoring the interruption, she continued. ". . . and I think I have some passing familiarity with the proper way to hold a child." Xyon, apparently disagreeing, whimpered louder.

"From a purely technical, support-the-frame aspect, yes, what you're doing is fine. But he needs more than just to be held in such a way that he won't injure himself. He needs to know you're nurturing him. You should be holding him closer . . . cradling him . . . letting him feel the warmth of you. Let him sort of . . ." S/he smiled. "Let him sort of melt into you."

With an impatient sigh, but feeling that it wasn't worth arguing over, Selar drew the child against herself. To her surprise, he promptly snuggled against her, and his fussiness ebbed. She found the sensation oddly comforting.

"Very good," said Burgoyne.

Selar had almost forgotten s/he was there. For some reason, she suddenly felt extremely vulnerable. It was not a sensation she welcomed. "Perhaps . . . it would be best if you left now," she said.

"As you wish. And, Selar—if you change your mind . . ."

"I am afraid that I am rather resolute in this matter."

"Very well. Then . . . I shall see you." With that, Burgoyne turned on hir heel and walked out.

Selar found herself staring at the door long after it had closed. Then Xyon made a burbling noise that seemed to demand her attention, and she looked back down at him. Feeling him against her had quickly become so natural, she had almost forgotten that she was holding him.

He was looking up into her face with what seemed a boundless capacity for love. It seemed such a curious expression to see in a face that had a Vulcan cast to it.

Then she realized that he did indeed seem to be watching her without distraction. She shifted him slightly in her arms so that her left hand was free. She then raised her index finger and held it in front of Xyon's eyes. She waggled it slightly, and the finger promptly caught his attention. She moved it, first to the left and then to the right. His head didn't move, but his eyes tracked it with no problem whatsoever.

"Fascinating," she murmured.

ROBIN

IT WAS A CRISP MORNING, and Robin watched as her breath floated away from her mouth. She peered out of the tent, looking like an oversized snail as she did so. There was a scent of dew in the air, which she found extremely refreshing. She had forgotten what it was like to experience sharp changes in atmosphere, what with living in the isolated, recirculated environments of starships for so long.

She was also enjoying "roughing it," as it were. Naturally, she could have camped out with a far more elegant portable environmental stasis field. At full charge it would have lasted for two days, and kept the area around her in climate-controlled perfection. But on the occasions when she had gone camping with her father while growing up, he had expressed disdain for such modern trappings, and had insisted on such low-tech items as a collapsible tent. He claimed that was the only way to rough it, as his father had taught him and his father before him in turn, and so on through the years. When she had related this discussion to her mother, Morgan had simply shaken her head and muttered, "Ten generations of masochists." Robin, ignoring the dismissal by her mother, had packed the tent all the same. Now she was extremely glad that she had done so.

She crawled out of the tent, stretching and working the kinks out of her body. The air was sharp in her lungs, but for a stinging sensation, it was nevertheless a pleasant one. She used a portable generator to cook herself a quick breakfast. The generator was her one concession to modern convenience; she simply didn't have the wherewithal or the confidence to build a fire from scratch. Maybe next time.

She bathed quickly in a nearby river, then got the campsite cleaned up and her equipment packed up and stashed away. Then she pulled out her tricorder and consulted the map of the dig sites she had downloaded from the hotel's mainframe. One of them looked particularly interesting, and that was where she headed. As she walked, she whistled an aimless tune while her arms swung freely back and forth. She looked not at the ground but at the sky, the way that all truly free-thinking people should. It was indeed a beautiful day—the sky was the purest blue, the clouds thick and white. Maybe this entire vacation thing wasn't going to be so wretched after all.

And she kept on thinking that, right up until the ground gave way beneath her feet.

Robin let out a yelp of fear and clawed at the air, but there was nothing for her to grab onto. Instead she fell, her fingers grabbing at dirt as she plummeted past, and then she was in darkness, with absolutely no idea of how far there was to fall or how many pieces she would be in when she hit. She screamed at the top of her lungs, which was both embarrassing (since one would have expected better of a Starfleet officer) and futile (since there was no one else to hear . . . although at least that *did* diminish the embarrassment aspect somewhat).

It seemed to her as if she were falling for hours, but, in fact, it couldn't have been more than a few seconds. Robin hit the ground hard, landing on her back. Ordinarily, such a circumstance would have been disastrous, but she was still wearing her backpack; as a result, the blow was somewhat cushioned. It did serve to knock all the air out of her, but at least she was still conscious. She lay there for a few moments, gasping, still trying to sort out what in the world had just happened. High above her she could see the hole through which she had fallen, fresh morning light seeping through it.

"Ow," she finally managed to say. It was more to hear her own voice, and make certain that she was still capable of producing a noise other than a moan of pain. She sat up very carefully, concerned that she might have broken something and alert for the slightest hint of a fractured bone or some other catastrophic injury. First she rolled to one side, balancing on her elbow, and then she hauled herself to her feet. She was relieved that everything seemed to be functioning as it was supposed to.

She tilted her head back and called, "Hellooooo!" No response. Then again, that shouldn't have been surprising, since there wasn't a soul around.

After a moment to consider her predicament, Robin pulled out a palm beacon from her pack. There was a small clip on the shoulder of her jacket, and she placed the light in it and switched it on. That way the light was automatically pointing in whatever direction she was facing. She also took out her tricorder, trying to determine just exactly which way she should be heading.

The tricorder revealed a byzantine and confusing pattern of tunnels all around. This, she thought, was certainly not what she had been looking for when she had decided to visit assorted archaeological digs. She had already been to three of them, all very orderly and meticulous explorations involving searches for artifacts from Risa's prehistory. It was generally believed that there had been an ancient race of Risans eons ago, but their eventual fate had been obscured by the curtain of time that had been drawn across the world's past. Some even believed that there had been some sort of war; that before it had occurred, Risa had been a far more stable world, and the final battles of the now-departed race had caused the instability that had reigned until Risa had been made over once more.

She wondered now whether they had, in fact, lived in these underground caverns. Or was it possible that what she had discovered was some sort of getaway route? She had read of such things on other worlds. Means of escape crafted by monarchs who lived in uncertain times, enabling them to make a swift getaway if circumstances compelled them to do so.

Her eyes having had time to adjust to the darkness, aided by the flash mounted on her shoulder, Robin considered her options. She could simply sit there, waiting for someone to wander past and perhaps help her out. Or she could walk a bit, explore the caves she had literally stumbled upon. Perhaps they might even lead to another existing dig, enabling her simply to come out somewhere else. As long as she had her tricorder, she could not really lose her way. She marked it so that it would track where she was, and where she was going. That way, at the very least, she could retrace her steps with facility.

She started walking. The ground felt a bit spongy, but there was nothing to concern herself over yet. She continued to walk, taking readings off her tricorder as she went. Robin couldn't help but feel a measure of growing excitement. She was doing what she had wanted to do the entire time: have an adventure. Explore. Her only regret was that her mother wasn't with her.

She started to become a bit more concerned, though, as the ground grew more and more moist. She wondered if perhaps there wasn't some sort of steady water leak somewhere that might be turning the dirt into mud, making it tougher to slog through. Robin looked at her tricorder, ran a few more readings. Then she noticed an indicator flashing and punched up a closer scan on it.

Her eyes went wide. She was detecting something biological. There was some sort of life-form, and it wasn't simply nearby; it was practically on top of her. . . .

"Or I'm . . . on top of it," she suddenly whispered. And for the first time, she leaned forward and angled the light straight down.

An eye looked up at her, blinking against the light. Then more eyes, hundreds of them, shimmering and shivering beneath some sort of nauseating, gelatinous mass . . . which she was standing on.

She let out a shriek, yanked the flash off her shoulder and played it all around her. It was directly ahead of her, taking up the entire floor, and behind her as well. It was as if she were standing atop a huge jellyfish. It was watching her, and it did not appear to be happy to see her. Or perhaps it was, for reasons that were quickly making themselves apparent as it started to pull at her boots.

She couldn't go forward, couldn't go backward, and sure as hell couldn't stay where she was. With the path ahead uncertain, she decided the only thing to do was try and get back to where she had come from. Not that even that was necessarily going to be safe; it just seemed the best option of the three lousy ones handed her.

She pivoted and almost fell on the slick muck beneath her feet. She hadn't been imagining it; the thing really was pulling at her boots. It was trying to keep her in place, and it was all that she could do to yank her feet free. She started to run, and the area around her appeared to become more agitated. Whatever this monstrosity beneath her was, it didn't want to let her go.

Robin continued to run. Her one hope was that, if she kept moving, the thing might have a tougher time of slowing her down. That she would be able to skip across the surface of . . . of whatever this was, like a stone hopping across a lake surface.

It pulled at her, tried to slow her, and she kept moving. At one point she stumbled, skidded, and her hand went down into it, just missing one of the eyes that gleamed up at her. The moist, gelatinous mass immediately surged around her hand and started to work its way up her arm. With an abortive scream, she yanked free of it, her hand making a sickening popping sound, like a finger popped out of a mouth. She held up her hand and, in the brief illumination, saw foam between the fingers, as if the thing had been salivating over her . . . or even trying to digest her.

There was a low rumble around her, as if the creature was moving, shifting position. It threw her off balance and she toppled backward, landing with a loud *sploosh*.

If the sensation of her hand going into it was appalling, that was nothing compared to lying flat on her back in it. And this time it was moving quicker. When her hand had gone in, the movements had been slow, almost thoughtful, as if trying to comprehend this new creature introduced into its environment. This time, it moved with more certainty. She had barely fallen into it when it was already seeping over the top of her body, moving up and over her face. Her instinct was to scream once more, but then she realized what a fatal mistake that would be: the thing would come pouring into her mouth, and that would surely be the end of her.

She set her teeth fiercely shut, pushing everywhere she could at the thing, even though her hand kept passing through it. She finally managed to struggle to her feet, and this time, when she was in motion, she was determined not to let herself be slowed again. She felt as if she had no choice; if she let herself get caught once more, she was sure that the thing wasn't going to lose her again.

She ran as fast as she could, driving forward, determined not to slow down for anything. It was only at that moment that she realized she was no longer holding her tricorder. It had fallen from her grasp and was back there, somewhere, in the roiling muck. She had no choice; she didn't dare go back. It would be suicide.

She took her best guess, knowing that she might be losing herself even more as she kept running, right, left, left again, another right. All guesswork, and she had the hideous feeling that she wasn't going to see her mother again. She thought of all the things she wished she'd said to her, wished she hadn't been so damned stubborn. Why the hell hadn't she just stayed in the blasted resort to begin with? But no, no. She had to go off on her own, prove something. Well, she had proven something all right. She had proven that she could be a complete and total idiot.

She was positive her imagination was running wild with her. She was convinced that she was hearing the creature roar, moaning in fury, redoubling its efforts to try to drag her down. She knew that she was giving it too much credit. This creature, whatever it was, was undoubtedly a very simple-minded entity, incapable of doing anything except satisfying its immediate need. Unfortunately, right now its immediate need seemed to be centered on dragging her down, smothering her, and . . .

She didn't even want to think about that part.

She skidded slightly, but righted herself and kept going. She rounded another corner, was convinced that she had managed to double back on herself and lose herself even more, and then suddenly she saw a shaft of sunlight from just around a bend. She covered the distance in no time and, yes, there it was: the hole that she, like Alice in Wonderland, had fallen through.

The problem was that the creature had apparently located it as well. The space between where she was at that moment and the hole up ahead—or at least where the sun was coming in through the hole—was completely enveloped by the creature. The one place it wasn't occupying was the spot right where the sunlight was beaming down onto the floor. Instead, the creature had carefully circumvented it, leaving an isolated path of safety.

Obviously it could not tolerate the sunlight. Fine. If that was to be her one shred of advantage, then so be it. She had never stopped moving up to this point, because she didn't like her odds if she did. Now she almost skied across the remaining distance, sections of the creature rolling apart in waves on either side of her. She stepped into the "zone of safety," her feet on firm ground once more. Without this creature lining it, the floor was normal, craggy and rocky. She never thought she would be quite so happy to see sunlight as she was at that moment. Of course, she had no idea how long she was going to be able to stand there, but at least it was something. She could remain on that spot and shout for help until her throat went raw. At least it would beat being consumed by this . . . this whatever-it-was.

The moment she was absolutely stable, perfectly still . . . the creature went for her.

It was at that instant that she realized the thing was, indeed, intelligent. That it had, in fact, laid a trap for her, and she had walked right into it. Before she even had time to think about it, it was around her feet, moving up her legs, making a loud, slurping noise, like a child in the midst of eagerly devouring and savoring, all at the same time, an ice cream bar.

There had been any number of times in the past when Robin felt as if her mother was going to have her climbing the walls. Never, though, had it become literal.

In a heartbeat, Robin was climbing the walls.

When she had first fallen through the hole, the prospect of trying to climb back to the top never occurred to her. It was far too high, and there was no way she was going to be able to find enough foot- or hand-holds. Now, however, she had no choice. She grabbed hold of the wall and started to climb, as fast and hard as she could. Her fingers dug, almost on instinct, into nooks and crannies that she never would have seen before. She didn't look down, but she could sense the thing bubbling around down there. It was not, thank God, climbing the walls. But it was waiting for her to lose her grip, to plunge back down into it. And she had the nauseating feeling that if she fell into it again, she was not going to be getting out anytime soon—if ever.

Her right hand gripped a bit of outcropping, which then broke off. For one moment she was dangling there by one hand, her feet desperately seeking purchase. Then she found it, and flattened herself against the wall, gasping, steadying herself. Once she was certain that she had a firm handhold again, she continued to pull herself up. She was truly caught in a dilemma. On the one hand, she wanted to rush, to get up there and out of danger as quickly as possible. Also, she wasn't sure that her endurance, given the circumstances, was going to be up for a sustained climb. On the other hand, she knew that the more she rushed, the more likely she was to make a mistake. And this was one circumstance in which a mistake would prove costly, and even fatal.

Through gritted teeth, she muttered, "Let's have adventures. Let's go climbing. Won't that be fun? My God, what was I thinking?" Her fingers were being rubbed raw, and she was terrified that, if her fingers became blood-slicked, she would be unable to hold on.

Another foot up, and then another, and she was drawing closer and closer to her erstwhile entrance—which would, ideally, prove to be her exit. She wasn't bothering to call for help anymore; all of her focus was on keeping herself from falling. She could feel the sunlight on her face, the gentle breeze wafting down. Far below her, she could sense the thing still moving around, waiting for her to return.

Now, however, she was coming to the most dangerous aspect of her attempt to survive. The hole was above her and a little to the right. She was going to have to twist, turn fast, kick off from the wall, and lunge for the hole in desperate hope of grabbing the edges. She was not going to have the opportunity to make a second attempt.

She steadied herself, took several deep breaths . . . and then made the leap. One hand missed completely, but she snagged the edge of the hole with the other. Her sense of relief lasted for exactly two seconds, and then the uncertain ground she was gripping crumbled in her grasp, and she fell, straight toward the bottom.

BURGOYNE

BURGOYNE HAD BEEN TO BARS and taverns all over the Federation, and s/he was most curious to see what such an establishment on Vulcan would be like. Unfortunately, s/he had to comb the city for hours until s/he finally found what appeared to be the only one in town. The moment s/he entered, s/he promptly understood why: The Vulcan clientele was virtually nonexistent. The bar, which was called "Offworlds," catered to exactly that which the sign suggested: people who were from offworld. There were enough patrons there, certainly, but it was almost entirely people from worlds other than Vulcan.

Burgoyne sat down at the bar and watched the bartender go about his business. The bartender was Vulcan, and he mixed drinks with a quiet, straightforward efficiency. It bordered on the wretchedly boring to watch. The bartender turned to hir questioningly and said, "May I help you?"

"Scotch. Neat." S/he paused, and added with a smile, "It's the official drink of engineers everywhere."

"I was not aware of that."

"It was a joke," Burgoyne said.

"I was not aware of that, either."

Burgoyne was about to pursue the matter, but decided that it would probably be wise not to do so. The drink was placed in front of hir and s/he downed it in one shot. "Go again," s/he said.

The bartender had barely had time to turn away from hir, and now looked back with a mild gaze. "That is illogical. You consumed the drink in 0.09 seconds. Not only is it unlikely that you tasted it, but you have not permitted sufficient time for the traditional, less-than-salubrious influence of alcohol to take effect. You may wish to—"

Burgoyne squared hir shoulders, and there was an unmistakable undercurrent of warning in hir voice. "Which part was unclear? The 'go'? Or the 'again'?"

Without a word, the bartender poured another shot of scotch. Burgoyne was about to toss that one back, too, but something in the faintly scolding look of the bartender caused hir to hold up at the last moment and simply sip it. The bartender nodded slightly in approval and moved to another customer.

A voice from next to Burgoyne said, "Is there anything in the universe more boring than a Vulcan bar?"

"I'm beginning to think not," Burgoyne replied. "What the hell is wrong with these people?"

S/he turned and, to hir surprise, saw a Vulcan sitting next to hir. He was looking at hir with a sort of amused detachment.

"Sorry," muttered Burgoyne.

"No, you are not. One should never apologize for candor. It is illogical. Moreover, it is impolite. It assumes that another person cannot tolerate the truth . . . or, at least, the truth as you perceive it."

"All right," Burgoyne said evenly. S/he regarded the Vulcan thoughtfully. "But what are you doing here then?"

The Vulcan shrugged. It seemed a rather odd gesture on a Vulcan. "I have nowhere else better to be."

"I see." Burgoyne reflexively delivered the Vulcan salute of greeting. "I am Burgoyne 172. Peace and long life."

"Live long and prosper. My name is Slon."

"Hello, Slon." Burgoyne knocked back the remains of the scotch and caught the bartender's eye. This time s/he had merely to mouth the words, "Go again," and the bartender did not bother to dispute it. But Burgoyne could tell from the faint scowl that he did not approve. "I have never encountered a bartender who was reluctant to sell drinks."

"On Vulcan we believe in logic in all things. That would include imbibing."

"But what's the point of that? One drinks when one doesn't want to think logically."

"Hence the notable absence of Vulcans in the bar."

"Yes. I suppose the Romulans wound up getting all the distilling genes in the Vulcan gene pool."

"Romulans are not logical."

"No, but they make a hell of an ale. So what do you do for a living, Slon?"

"I am an attaché for the Vulcan diplomatic corps. A sort of aide. I am between assignments at the moment, but I spend a good deal of my time off-planet. And you?"

"I'm in Starfleet. An engineer."

"You are not in uniform."

"I'm . . . also between assignments." S/he tossed

back yet another glass. This time s/he didn't even have to catch the bartender's glance. He refilled it automatically, although s/he couldn't help but notice the slight shake of his head as he did so. Then s/he turned hir attention back to Slon.

Burgoyne felt as if Slon were dissecting hir with his gaze. "Are you quite all right?" s/he asked.

"I am fit. You are a Hermat."

"Yes."

"I have heard much of Hermats. Is what I have heard true?"

With a laugh, Burgoyne said, "How would I know what you have and haven't heard?"

"I have heard that you approach subjects such as sexuality with gay abandon."

"Interesting choice of words," Burgoyne said dryly. "I cannot speak for all of my people, but they have a tendency to . . . what's the best word . . . 'revere' it. I, on the other hand, approach the subject, and the practice, with somewhat more fervor. That, of course, is as opposed to Vulcans."

"Indeed. And what know you of Vulcans?" asked Slon steadily.

"That you . . ." Burgoyne stopped and looked down at hir glass. It was still full. S/he mentally chided herself; s/he was slowing down. Maybe s/he was getting old. "I'm sorry."

"Again?"

"This time I genuinely am. My understanding is that you typically don't like to discuss such matters with offworlders."

"I am not typical," Slon said. "Simply curious as to what an 'offworlder' might have heard of the topic."

S/he let out a deep breath. "Well . . . that you engage in the act only once every seven years."

"That is not true."

Burgoyne blinked at that. "What? That was what I was led to believe."

"You refer to the *pon farr*." Burgoyne couldn't help but notice that Slon was speaking in a slightly lower, *entre nous* tone of voice. Despite his claim to being atypical of his race, it was obvious that even he respected the delicacy of the matters at hand.

"Yes, that's right."

"Do not confuse the concept of Vulcan romance with breeding. The *pon farr* exists to guarantee the perpetuation of our species. But there is no mandate that requires we live in celibacy during the intervening times. We may not approach the subject with as much fervency as do other races, but . . ." Slon's eyebrows knit. "You are regarding me with a most curious expression."

"I'm still having trouble getting past 'Vulcan romance,' to be honest. It sounds like an oxymoron to me. Are Vulcans truly capable of romance?"

"Yes."

"But . . . you're not especially good at expressing such raw feelings," Burgoyne said, finding hirself intrigued by the discussion. "How do you convey romantic intent?"

"A variety of means, as with any race. One preferred method is the lyre."

"Oh, well, sure," Burgoyne said reasonably. "Going around and fabricating your intentions is standard for romance. Although I would have thought the renowned Vulcan addiction to honesty would have—"

"Not 'liar.' Lyre. L-y-r-e. It is a musical instrument."

"Oh. Sorry." Burgoyne flushed slightly. "A musical instrument conveys romantic interest?"

"In the case of the Vulcan lyre, it does so quite well. Its notes are virtual love songs in and of themselves."

"Is that what you use?" Burgoyne was not able to keep a slightly teasing tone out of hir voice. It was a tone that s/he knew all too well—reflexive and a bit suggestive.

"On occasion, if it suits the mood."

"And do you, Slon, have a mate to whom you were driven by *pon farr?*"

"No." Slon looked down at his empty hands, and it was the first time Burgoyne realized that he wasn't holding a drink. "No . . . I do not."

"Well . . . shouldn't you be due for that?"

"That is . . . apparently not going to occur in my case."

"Really? Why not?"

Slon looked at hir steadily. "I have a lack of interest in reproduction that no amount of genetic tradition can overcome."

"Ahhh," Burgoyne said, smiling. "I understand. Well, why not? Takes all kinds. Does your family understand?"

"They understand in that they are able to comprehend it. My sister seems more sanguine with it. My parents . . . less so."

"Moral indignation? From a Vulcan? I'm stunned."

"No," he said, shaking his head. "Not precisely. It is more that they simply consider it . . . illogical. A waste of material. My parents—my father in particular—consider me of solid genetic stock, and are displeased that my genes will not be perpetuated. He has said I am doing a disservice to my race on that basis. I offered to provide a genetic contribution that could be provided to a suitable recipient, but . . ." Once again, that odd shrug. "He said it was not the Vulcan way."

"I'm sure your race will survive without your contribution."

"Very likely so."

"So you yourself have no interest in romance at all."

Slon looked at hir with genuine meaning. "I did not say that. I find you most . . . interesting, Burgoyne."

"The famed Vulcan directness. At least people always know where they stand with you."

"That," deadpanned Slon, "is part of our collective charm."

"I can't say I'm surprised," Burgoyne said. "Vulcans by nature are an inquiring race, if you'll forgive my generalization. One doesn't have a philosophy based on logic unless one is willing to ask incessant questions about everything. And I've learned that a lot of people are curious about Hermats. Probably the only other race that generates that much sexual interest is the Deltans. 'Oath of Celibacy.' Silliest thing I ever heard. How can there be a race so formidable in the act of love that non-Deltans are driven insane from the sheer ecstasy of it? If you ask me, they're probably the worst lovers in the entire galaxy, and came up with this entire mystique to hide behind."

"Interesting theory. I had a friend at the University several years back who voiced the exact same opinion. I should convey your sentiments to him."

"You do that."

"I shall. He is allowed visitors every Thursday at the asylum where he presently resides."

Burgoyne stared at him. "What?"

"Oh, yes," Slon said, as if discussing utterly trivial matters. "You see, unlike you—obviously—he chose to field-test this theory. The results were . . . unpleasant."

"Un . . . pleasant?" asked Burgoyne uneasily. S/he was thinking about a time when s/he had nearly had an interlude with a Delta on a bet, until a last-minute summons back to hir shipboard assignment had forced hir to pass up the encounter.

"Very. He simply lies on the floor of his room most days, twitching spasmodically and occasionally gyrating his hips in a—"

"I get the idea. All right, I stand corrected," Burgoyne said. S/he shook hir head. "This has got to be one of the strangest conversations I've ever had, and I'm still a bit dumbfounded that I'm having it with a Vulcan in a bar."

"If it is my race that you find disconcerting, that is, naturally, something I cannot do anything about. If it is the location that daunts you . . . my residence is not far from here."

Although the steadiness of Slon's tone had not wavered, the meaning could not have been clearer. Burgoyne looked at him with interest. "Are you suggesting . . . what I think you're suggesting?"

"It would seem the logical thing to do," observed Slon.

"Bartender," Burgoyne said immediately.

The bartender materialized in front of hir. "Yes?" he asked, with that same faint disapproval.

"Check, please."

"Ah. I thought you were going to 'go again.' "

"I think I am, indeed," Burgoyne said, "but not with you." And s/he smiled invitingly at Slon, the alcohol giving hir a distant but nevertheless distinct and pleasant buzzing sensation.

Peter David

ROBIN

SHE'D FALLEN ABOUT TWO FEET when suddenly a rope was dangling right in front of her.

Robin reacted purely from instinct as she snagged the cord that had miraculously dropped in her face. Her grip wasn't immediately solid, and as a result she skidded a few feet down it, the rope tearing up her palms something fierce. She yelped, but also redoubled her efforts and managed to slow and then stop her descent. She dangled there, swinging back and forth, uncertain just how far above the gelatinous mass she was and afraid to find out.

And then, from above her, a voice called down, "Do you have a grip on it?" It was a strong voice, a masculine one. Of course, at that point, Robin would not have cared if the owner of the voice sounded as if he had been inhaling helium. As long as he was stopping her from falling, that was all that mattered to her.

"Yes!" she called up to him.

There was a pause. "Ah. You're a woman," came the thoughtful response.

Dangling as she was, Robin didn't exactly like the sound of that. "Do you have a problem with that?" she shouted. It would be just her luck that her potential savior was a homicidal maniac with a lousy social life who felt that all women deserved whatever happened to them.

"No, not at all," came back the reasonable reply. "Women tend to be lighter than men. I was just figuring that it was going to be easier pulling you up. Are you slim?"

"Yes, I'm slim."

"How much do you weigh?"

"108," said Robin.

There was a pause. "Really?" came the voice.

"Yes, *really!*" Robin said, starting to get irritated.

"You sound heavier."

"Oh, thanks a *lot!*"

"No offense. I just want to make sure I can do this. And I don't want any surprises. And some women tend to—not to be indelicate—lie about such things."

"I don't believe this," muttered Robin.

"So are you sure you're—"

"Yes! I'm 108! And in case it matters, I'm 5′ 6″, brunette, a Virgo, and I like reading children's poetry and taking long walks on beaches in light rain, okay?"

There was another pause. "What color are your eyes?"

"What?!"

"Just kidding. Hold on."

The rope lurched slightly, and then started to pull up steadily. She held on tightly, wrapping the rope between her feet for extra assurance. She could have sworn, in the fever of her imagination, that the creature below was making some sort of vaguely disappointed slurping noises.

And then, the next thing she knew, she had been pulled up and out into the sunlight. She blinked against it as she hauled herself the rest of the way to safety, getting herself clear of the crumbled ground so that more of it wouldn't open up beneath her. Standing several feet away, holding the far end of the rope, was her savior.

He extended a hand. "Here. Let me help you up."

She didn't react immediately. She was too busy staring at him. Damn, but he was one of the most handsome men Robin had ever laid eyes on. He had strong, chiseled features, and his eyes were ocean blue. His nose was slightly large, but the imperfection only seemed to add to his features rather than detract from them. He had thick eyebrows, and a mouth that seemed made for smiling, which he was doing at the moment and doing extremely well.

The hand remained extended, and she remembered only belatedly to take it. She winced as the firm grip ached against her still-injured palms, and he helped her to her feet. She was impressed by his strength: He had lifted her up as if she weighed next to nothing. Which, she reminded herself, she had told him she had. No use mentioning those extra pounds she had picked up since coming to the resort.

"Are you going to be okay?" he asked.

"Sure, sure . . . now."

"I take it you weren't exactly expecting to explore the subterranean aspects of Risa in that way," he commented, pointing at the hole.

"Definitely not," she said.

"Sorry that you hit a hot hole."

"A what?"

"A leftover from Risa's more unstable days," he said. "It used to be more geologically unstable than it is right now. There are a few areas where the ground just sort of separated, became unsafe, and created what would best be described as camouflaged crevices. Pretty hazardous."

"I should say so," said Robin. "They should put up signs to warn people off."

"You mean like that one there?" he said, and pointed. Sure enough, Robin had walked right past a sign informing anyone wandering into that area that they were about to enter treacherous ground, and would do so at their own risk. But Robin had been so busy looking toward the skies that she had been paying no attention at all.

"Wonderful," she muttered.

Her unexpected rescuer looked down at her boots and his brow furrowed. "What is that stuff on your feet?"

"What?" She looked down and saw traces of the gelatinous mass on the soles of her boots . . . and, more alarming than that, the bits of the mass were starting to move around on their own. She could swear that she was beginning to see traces of eyes developing on them.

Immediately Robin dropped to the ground and yanked the boots off her feet. Then she tossed them both into the hole. The young man watched in mute surprise as he saw what appeared to be otherwise perfectly good footwear disappear into darkness. "What did you do that for?" he asked. He didn't sound particularly upset or even mystified. Just interested.

"Trust me," she said flatly, "you don't want to know." She stretched her toes in her stocking feet.

"You're going to continue to explore like that?" he asked.

"Noooo . . . I've had it with exploring, if it's all the

same to you," she said with alarming heartiness. "Didn't occur to me to bring a spare set of boots, so I'm going to troop back to the hotel, where gelatinous masses are safely contained in dessert cups. Because frankly, if it weren't for you . . ." She looked at him curiously. "Say, where did you come from, anyway?"

"Same as you. Exploring," he said. "As I was passing by, I heard you grunting and moaning as you were climbing up from the hole. So I figured maybe you could use some help."

"Well, you figured correctly." They stood there, facing one another, nothing else immediately being said. She found herself drifting in his eyes. And suddenly, realizing that something fairly basic and fundamental had not yet been said, she announced, "My name's Robin. Robin Lefler. And, uh . . . thank you for saving my life."

"Oh, I don't know about saving your life. Saved you some inconvenience maybe—"

"No . . . you don't understand. There was something down there, it was . . ." She waved it off, not wanting to dwell on it. "Believe me, just . . . take my word for it. You don't want to know. You just—well, you just don't." She cleared her throat. "And you are . . . ?"

"Hmm? Oh!" He seemed moderately embarrassed, apparently realizing that he, too, had forgotten some basic social graces. "Viola. Nikolas Viola. Please call me Nik. My father and I, we're staying at the El Dorado."

"So are my mother and I."

"Ah." He nodded. "Let me guess: The two of you decided that it would be nice to have some time together. Get reacquainted, get to know each other, et cetera, so forth . . ."

"Ditto, ditto," said Robin with a laugh. "You got the same speech, too?"

"Oh, definitely," he said. "And then you'll never believe what happened."

"He found a woman."

Nik's eyes widened. "How'd you guess?"

"Believe it or not, I'm in exactly the same boat."

"I do find it hard to believe," Nik replied. "I mean, how could anyone not want to spend every available moment with you?"

She put her hand to her heart and fluttered her fingers as if she were seized with palpitations. "Oh. Oh, what a smooth talker you are, Mr. Viola. I think I'm going to have to be careful with you."

"No, you don't," he said cheerfully. "You could always give me enough rope and then watch me hang myself." And he held up the rope to demonstrate the possibilities.

"So . . ." She folded her arms resolutely. "I owe you my life, but you do owe me an apology."

"What for?"

"The weight thing. And keeping me dangling . . . literally."

"I suppose I do," he said. "How about if I give it to you over dinner? I have to warn you, my father will probably be there, along with his lady friend."

"That's okay," she told him. "I might as well get to spend some time with *somebody's* parent."

When Robin got back to the hotel room, there was no sign of her mother, which didn't surprise her. What did surprise her was that her bed did not appear to have been slept in. The thing was, she couldn't tell whether it was because one of the room 'bots had already attended to making it, or because she simply hadn't slept in it all night. Which meant, of course, that she had been somewhere else. Robin realized that she didn't even want to think about where that somewhere else was.

"Oh, ease up," she heard herself say scoldingly. "If she's out having a good time, who are you to criticize? The bottom line is, she was right and you were wrong. This place isn't bad at all . . . and that Nik . . ."

She caught her reflection in the mirror and couldn't quite believe it; she'd never seen herself grinning quite so stupidly as she was now. Good lord, was he having that much of an effect on her, so quickly? The truth was, it had been a long time since any man had paid any kind of attention to her. Granted, they had met in an exceedingly bizarre manner, but that was okay. "After all," she said, "when you meet someone while you're falling, there's nowhere to go but up." She then laughed merrily at her own joke, and congratulated herself on being able to joke about something that—only a short time before—had appeared to be her last moments on the planet.

She spent the rest of the day relaxing herself: Swimming, sunning, taking it easy. For a time she kept an eye out for Morgan, but after a while she stopped worrying about it. Instead she dwelt on dinner that evening. Nik was . . . quite a handsome man. There was no use denying that. And he was most attractive. And, well . . .

"Jamaharon?" asked a Risan who served drinks on the beach.

Robin looked up at him, squinting against the sun. "I'm sorry?"

"Well, you do not display a Horga'hn," said the rather attractive-looking young man, "but you have that look about you . . . that glow . . . that seems to indicate you are interested in *jamaharon.*"

"Is that a drink or something?" she asked in confusion.

He smiled. "In a sense. It is the act that provides the sweet nectar of life itself."

"Oh," she said, not understanding, and then *"Oh!"* as she suddenly realized. "Oh . . . you mean . . . uh . . . no. No, I'm not interested." She remembered now that a Horga'hn was a statuette that was displayed by any-one who wanted to have . . . well . . . *jamaharon.* "I'm not," she said.

"Your lips say no, but your aura says yes. However, I will leave you to your self-realization."

"That's very kind of you," she said as he wandered away.

Her aura? Her *aura?*

Under other circumstances, she would have assumed that the Risan was coming on to her. But she knew that wasn't the case here. These people were far too straightforward for such games.

Could it really be that she was giving off some sort of . . . of "interested" vibrations? And was it Nik that she was interested in? She had trouble believing it of herself. She wasn't accustomed to thinking in purely physical terms about people. She hardly knew Nik Viola, after all. For her, attraction stemmed from get-ting to know someone on a personal level, and the physical aspect tended to grow from that. It sim-ply wouldn't be like her to become so enamored of someone that her—what was it?—her aura would re-flect it.

Still . . . he was damned attractive. And he had saved her life.

"That's got to be it," she told herself. Her feelings for him were accelerated because they had met during a time of great personal jeopardy. She felt indebted to him for saving her life, so, naturally, everything she felt toward him was heightened. She was attracted to what he represented, namely her personal savior.

She would just take it slowly, that was all. If something did happen, well . . . this was the place for romance, after all. And if it didn't, well . . . that was fine, too.

"But it probably will."

She was so surprised to hear herself say that, she looked around the beach to see if anyone else had heard her. Not that the words themselves would have meant anything, but still . . .

No one had heard her. No one had paid attention. No one seemed to be studying her aura and making assessments on her interest in *jamaharon*. For that, she could only consider herself grateful. Then she lay back on the sand, worked on drifting to sleep, and only partly succeeded. The rest of the time she felt rather itchy, and the itchiness had nothing to do with sand in her bathing suit.

It was at that point that she resolved she wasn't going to make a big deal about it. Nik seemed like an interesting man, but he was just that: a man. They were going to go to dinner tonight, and very likely meet his father, but there was absolutely no reason to get worked up about it.

That was when she realized that she had been so disdainful of the entire notion of socializing, and even (God forbid) romance, that—despite her mother's urgings—she had not brought a single fancy dress with her. Quickly, she got her things together, so that she could race back to the hotel, change, and head out to the nearest clothing facility to find an appropriate outfit.

Somewhere buried in that train of thought was a substantial helping of irony, but she chose not to dwell on it.

BURGOYNE

As Burgoyne and Slon headed to the latter's home, they talked freely and openly. Burgoyne was surprised how quickly and easily s/he was able to relate to, and engage in conversation with, Slon. Hir experience with Vulcans had been so limited, and Slon was so much the opposite of Selar in every way, that s/he was having a bit of trouble making the adjustment. But s/he was reasonably sure s/he was going to be able to handle the transition, given time.

They stood at the door of Slon's apartment, and he gestured for hir to enter. S/he was totally relaxed, very much looking forward to the practice of hir favorite activity, unencumbered by angst or any considerations beyond simple pleasure. And Slon certainly seemed nice enough, and interested enough. Part of that might very well be, as Burgoyne had commented, simple curiosity. But that was fine, too. In fact, it was great. Everything was going to be great.

"You have been standing at the threshold of my home for nineteen seconds," observed Slon. "Most individuals are able to walk through a door in considerably less time."

"I know. But my feet don't seem to be moving. I . . ." S/he took a steady breath, tried to get hirself to proceed, and still was unable to do so.

"Burgoyne—?"

"I can't." There was a sort of amazement in Burgoyne's voice as s/he realized that simple truth. "I can't . . . do this. Damn her."

"I do not understand."

Burgoyne sank to the floor of the corridor, running hir fingers through hir short white/blond hair, as if some sort of answer could be forced from hir brain just by massaging hir head. "I can't do this," s/he said again.

"Have I said something—?"

"It's not you. It's me . . . and her . . ." S/he shook hir head. "You didn't ask me why I was here."

"I had thought you came here for the same reason I did."

"Not *here* here. Here, as in, on Vulcan. The truth is," and s/he took a deep breath—and then stopped. "Actually, the truth is far too involved to go into. Let's just say that there's someone else."

"You are involved with another person?"

"I don't think I am. That's the problem. She's rebuffed me repeatedly. She's made it clear to me that she doesn't want a romantic relationship. Because of that, I felt as if I were free to pursue what promised to be a most interesting evening with you. Except it's not turning out that way." There was genuine distress in hir voice. "What the hell am I doing to do about this? I can't go forward, I can't go back. I'm in a sort of romantic limbo."

"Fascinating."

"I'm so pleased," s/he said sarcastically, "that I can provide such fascination for you. But you'll excuse me if I'm less than ecstatic, considering where this leaves me."

"I did not intend to sound disinterested in your 'plight.' It is simply that, from what I knew of you, I did not think that you would pass up an assignation out of loyalty to someone who expressed disinterest in you."

"Oh, really. And what did you know of me before we met in the bar?"

"I knew that which my sister told me."

"And who would your sister b—" But then s/he stopped, as pieces suddenly tumbled together in hir mind. "Of course," s/he whispered. "Selar. Your sister is Selar."

"That is correct."

Still on the floor of the corridor, Burgoyne backed up as if s/he wanted to put distance between hirself and Slon. "She sent you. This was all some sort of . . . of setup."

"No," Slon said firmly. "That is not the case. She knows nothing of my seeking you out."

"Seeking me out?" S/he couldn't believe what s/he was hearing. "You came looking for me? How . . . how did you know where to find me?"

"There is a very small number of bars on Vulcan, as I am sure you have surmised. I was reasonably certain that you would be there . . ."

"Also based on what she told you about me?"

"That is correct."

"So what was all this?" s/he demanded, waving vaguely in the air. "Some sort of test to see whether I was going to be faithful to a woman who doesn't want to be with me?"

"No. I did not have a specific direction that I intended for this evening to take. I simply wished to get to know you, and in so doing, understand you."

"Well, you came pretty close to knowing me as well as someone can." To hir surprise, s/he actually smiled ruefully. "So do you understand me any better?"

"Somewhat. I think you are wrong, however."

"Wrong about what?"

"Selar. I think she does wish to be with you."

"Well, if that's the case, she's certainly doing an excellent job of covering it up."

"Yes. She is."

S/he stared at Slon, trying to figure him out. "All right," s/he said slowly. "You're her brother. You say you know her so well . . ."

"I do not know her 'so well,' or at least as well as you would wish. Selar has always been somewhat . . . guarded. Even more so than most Vulcans."

"But why?"

Slon sat down opposite Burgoyne. A Vulcan woman on her way to her own apartment passed between them without giving them a second glance, as if people sitting on the floor was something fairly routine.

"Have you forgotten," Slon told hir, "that you yourself tried to end your relationship with her shortly after the child was conceived? You spoke to her of the Hermat inability to commit to one relationship. You spoke of many partners . . ."

"I know, I know. But . . . I was concerned . . . because I really did feel something very unusual, even rare, for her. And I didn't know—"

"You did not know if your feelings were genuine or not. Whether you were behaving in a manner 'out of character' for you, and your species, due to the bond that was formed between you as a result of *pon farr.*"

"That's right, yes," said Burgoyne.

"Burgoyne . . . I am going to tell you things now. Some you may know, some you may not. But I think it reasonable to say that I know my sister as well as any, and better than most, and if you desire my insight, I will present it to you."

"I would indeed. I'd make one request of you before you start."

"And that would be?"

"With the understanding that we are simply going to talk . . . can we do this in your place? It's going to be a hell of a lot more comfortable."

"Very well."

They rose and entered the apartment in which Slon resided. Burgoyne stopped dead and looked around. There was practically nothing in it. No furniture, no possessions of any sort. Not even a light; the room was illuminated by moonlight. "Were you robbed?" s/he asked.

"No. I simply lead a minimalist life."

S/he peered into the adjoining room, which s/he took to be the bedroom. There was nothing there. "Where do you sleep?"

"On my back."

Realizing that they could just as easily have remained in the corridor, Burgoyne shrugged and slid back down to the floor. Slon followed easily, settling into a cross-legged position that looked quite contemplative.

"Selar," he began, "was joined at a very young age with a Vulcan male named Voltak. At the time of the *pon farr,* the urge that drives most of our race brought them together. However, during the initial amorous stages of their joining, while they were already bonded on a mental level and were in the process of doing so physically, Voltak suffered a massive heart attack and died. Selar literally felt him slip away. She not only experienced his loss, she sensed the finality of death, the blackness that awaits us all, the endless nothingness of—"

"I get the point," Burgoyne interrupted. "It was bad."

"Quite bad. The experience had an adverse effect on Selar. At a fundamental, psychological level, she associates the act of love, of being loved, of joining . . . with loss. With death."

"She's reluctant to be with me full time because she thinks I'm going to die while we're making love?" Burgoyne was unable to keep the skepticism from hir voice.

"No. It is a bit more complicated than that."

"I hope so, because if that's what it is, it's pretty stupid."

Slon frowned. "We are speaking of my speculations as to my sister's mental state, Burgoyne. There is nothing 'stupid' about it, and I do not appreciate the condescension."

"My apologies," Burgoyne said sincerely. "I know you're only trying to help. I'm sorry; it won't happen again."

"There is a reason I said 'loss' before 'death.' 'Loss' is the true stumbling block here. I believe that, consciously or unconsciously, she does not wish to let anyone become too close to her because she is afraid that person will leave her. The method of the departure— death, boredom, what have you—is incidental, secondary. She fears that she will lose anyone who becomes dear to her. She does not wish to take that risk. She considers it—"

"Illogical?"

Slon nodded. "So when she feels herself being pulled in that direction, it is her instinct to pull back."

"Which is why she's been running hot and cold."

Slon looked at hir questioningly. "I beg your pardon . . . ?"

"Don't worry about it," Burgoyne waved him off. "I shouldn't have interrupted. You were saying?"

"Yes. Indeed, as I was saying, when one is in a position where loss is undesirable to the point of obsession, then there is only one reasonable alternative. One must discard or push away someone before they can depart. In this way, Selar can guard herself from ever again experiencing loss by always being the one who initiates the separation. She can once again feel in control. Control is very important to her."

"Yes, so she's told me," Burgoyne said ruefully.

"It is one of the reasons, I suspect, that she became a physician. It made her capable of controlling the fates and fortunes of others. Healers do have a tendency to play God. They hold people's lives in their hands, and their decisions and skills affect whether people will live or die. It is a very heady sensation, so I am told. Selar prefers to be in control. She always has. That predates her union with Voltak. When she returned here due to the drive of *pon farr,* she was not—I can assure you—pleased. She was offended, even dismayed by being held a captive to hormonal impulses dating back thousands of years. She did not desire to cede control of herself for even a moment. Because of the loss of Voltak, that tendency has only become more pronounced for her. So, if she allows herself to enter fully into a relationship predicated on trust, she immediately runs into trouble. Her instinct is to demolish it before it can thrust her into a position of vulnerability."

"And what am I supposed to do about Xyon?" demanded Burgoyne. "I'm sorry to interrupt you, but what you're telling me doesn't bode well for our son in the least."

"Why do you say that?"

"Why? How could I *not!* Look at the scenario you've described for me," s/he said, leaning forward and extending two fingers. S/he ticked off the alternatives, one at a time. "You've outlined for me the psychological profile of someone who lives only in extremes. Either she is going to be so determined to control every aspect of his life that she is going to suffocate him, robbing him of any shred of independence that he might develop. Or else she is going to be so in dread that he will eventually leave her or reject her in some way, that she will reject him first. She will shunt him aside out of some deep-seated need to protect herself. A true parent, a real parent, doesn't adopt such extreme attitudes. Real life, a normal life, is lived in gray areas, in the middle. But you Vulcans don't think that way. It has to be pure logic for you, logic or nothing. You can't live lives that are normal blends of heart and mind. You operate solely through your mind and act as if the rest of the galaxy is inferior because the rest of us poor residents there burn with passions that you can only guess at."

"Your fervor is appreciated, if misplaced," Slon said easily. "I am not the enemy here."

"Technically speaking, you may not be. But you're here on her behalf."

"No. I am not. I told you, she is unaware of my presence here."

"Then why *are* you here? To convince me to give her another chance? Or to find some way to work matters out?"

"Matters will be worked out," Slon said calmly. "The only question is whether they will be worked out in accommodation with everyone's desires. I am beginning to think that may not be the case." He paused, and then added, "You are aware that Selar is not the enemy here, either."

"Then who is the enemy? Me?"

"I do not think she perceives you as an enemy. I think, in some way, she admires you your passion. Even envies you, as much as her nature allows her to do so. The situation is a tragic one, fraught with peril for all concerned. I ask you to consider carefully your next actions."

"I have been considering them, believe me." S/he shook hir head. "You know . . . she once told me she thought that, considering our personalities, we deserved each other. How's that for a ringing endorsement?"

"She may well be correct. Then again . . ."

Slon's voice trailed off, and the sudden silence caught Burgoyne's attention. "Then again what?" s/he prompted.

"It is nothing."

"Don't do that. Don't start a thought and then refuse to finish it. It's rude."

"I am simply wondering whether there is some aspect of self-flagellation in her actions."

"You've lost me," admitted Burgoyne.

"The loss of Voltak, considering the circumstances, would have hit anyone hard. But it may have hit her harder than most. She is, after all, a doctor. Her mate died in her presence, and she was unable to do anything to prevent it. As illogical as it may seem, it is possible that she is carrying with her some degree of guilt over the incident."

"You mean . . . she's punishing herself?" Burgoyne shook hir head. "You can't be serious."

"I am very serious. Perhaps she feels that she is not entitled to happiness. That she is, as you say, punishing herself for her inability to save Voltak. Every time some measure of contentment is within her grasp, she pushes it away. To move on, as it were, would give her closure on the wound, and she cannot allow herself that closure because she does not feel she deserves it."

"That," said Burgoyne, "would be a really screwed-up attitude to have."

"As you say," Slon said, offering no argument on that score.

Burgoyne was silent for a time. "That would indeed be a tragic state of affairs," s/he said. "But it's not going to dilute my intentions to do something about Xyon. I just . . . I wish I knew whether what I feel for Selar is genuine or a result of the bond that was forced upon me."

"I will tell you this much, Burgoyne, for what it is worth: I am no expert in such matters, and I have not undergone any sort of specific training. But it is my belief that what you and Selar share could not possibly have been manufactured from thin air. If you felt nothing for her at all, the bond of the *pon farr* could not create something from that nothingness. An intensity of feelings for a brief period of time, yes. That is well within the bounds of possibility. But it has been many months since you encountered each other in the blinding state of passion that was the mating ritual. There has been more than enough time for emotions to cool, for matters to return to what they were."

"It's more involved than that, though," said Burgoyne. "When Xyon was being born, that bond was still in force. I felt the sensations of the labor pains. You cannot begin to comprehend how agonizing that was for me. For Hermats, the birth process is almost entirely painless. It was something not only outside of my own memory, but beyond my race's physiology to endure."

"I do not doubt that. That, however, is the point."

"What is?"

"By the time your son was being born, you could *not* have shared that degree, that intensity of bonding . . . if you did not *want* to. Furthermore, it had to be two-way. On some level, you desired to maintain your connection to Selar—and she with you—far beyond the requirements dictated by the bond of the initial mating. She does want you, Burgoyne. Difficulties and traumas that she cannot easily release, unfortunately, bind her. And you want her. But your own nature as a Hermat makes you uncertain of your ability to commit, and she senses that uncertainty. Did you know that, after you initially approached her, she had decided to take you up on your offer to sire her child?"

"No, she didn't. She went to Captain Calhoun and asked him to 'do the honors,'" Burgoyne replied, unable to quite keep the sarcasm out of hir voice.

But Slon shook his head. "No. Before she went to the captain, she was going to approach you. And she was doing so out of a fundamental sense of attraction for you that was as pure and genuine as any—pardon the expression—'emotion' she had ever felt. But she saw that, after you had enthusiastically presented yourself as a mate to her, you were so undeterred by her rejection that you were already taking up with . . . what was his name? Oh yes. McHenry. She saw the two of you going off together."

"She . . . saw us?" Burgoyne didn't know what to say.

"Yes. Unsurprising—you made no effort to be discreet. It was almost as if you were flaunting it. Perhaps she was concerned on some level that it was a sign of insincerity on your part, and she was put off by the attitude."

"Certainly she can't fault me for that, though," Burgoyne finally managed to say. "It is my nature."

"Is . . . or was? After all," and to Burgoyne's surprise, there was a bit of a smile on Slon's face, "you could have had me. But you chose not to. It may well be, Burgoyne, that your nature has changed."

"Making me what, exactly?" S/he shook hir head, suddenly feeling discouraged. "As a Hermat, I may well no longer fit in with others of my kind. But I am hardly of a Vulcan disposition."

"That is true. You are unique. Do not be discouraged though, Burgoyne," said Slon. "There are worse fates than to be unique."

"Such as?"

"To be ordinary."

Burgoyne nodded and smiled at that. "That would be horrendous, wouldn't it?"

They were silent for a time, and then Slon inquired, "So, Burgoyne . . . what are you going to do?"

"See it through. At this point, I have no choice."

"One always has choices, Burgoyne. Whether one chooses to see them or not is, in itself, its own choice."

ROBIN & MORGAN

"SHAKESPEARE'S TAVERN" WAS ONE of the restaurants Robin had not yet had a chance to sample, and she was pleased that Nik had suggested it be the one they go to. The place was made up to look like an old English-style tavern, right down to waiters wearing Elizabethan togs and waitresses costumed as tavern wenches. There were decorations on all the walls, including texts from both the human and "original Klingon" folios. There were even gleaming swords of the period mounted on the walls. Robin figured that real taverns of the era were probably a lot more run-down and less pleasant, with the free-flowing alcohol helping to camouflage the fact that the food wasn't especially well-prepared. The Risa tavern, on the other hand, had an old-style look about it while maintaining the appropriate, modern-day levels of expectations. Most amusing of all were two actors who were assuming the role of Shakespeare, stalking the tavern while spouting off lengthy samples of the Bard's work. The reason there were two actors was that one was human, while the other was Klingon. Or at least an actor dressed up as a Klingon, for the owners had not managed to actually locate a Klingon who was willing to go along with the charade. The fact was that the true origin of Shakespeare's plays had become something of an issue between Klingon and Terran historians, both claiming that the other race had swiped the Master's work—and planet of origin— without so much as a by-your-leave.

As a result, in Shakespeare's Tavern, the human and faux Klingon would occasionally face-off against one another and emote in their respective languages. Robin hated to admit it, but the faux Klingon seemed to show far more passion for the Klingon text than the human did for the English.

Nik sat opposite Robin, pouring himself another glass of wine from the bottle that the wench had left on their table. He offered a refill to her, but she put a hand up, indicating that she was satisfied with what she had. He put the bottle down and smiled. "That," he said, "is a lovely dress."

"Oh, this?" She looked down in apparent boredom at the garment she had acquired mere hours ago. It was a blue satin off-the-shoulder ensemble. "Yeah, I almost forgot I packed it. And you don't look so bad yourself."

"Really?" He glanced at his own clothes. "Actually, I only bought this a few hours ago. Didn't have much in the way of stuff with me to impress a young woman. Wasn't really expecting, or looking for, romance."

"Me neither. Not to say that this is romance, what we have here."

"Oh, of course not. Much too soon. It's our first dinner, after all."

"I'm glad we agree on that."

With mischief in his eyes, he added, almost as an afterthought, "Now . . . we'll have to see how we feel about it after breakfast."

She raised an eyebrow in a mock-scolding manner. "My, my. Aren't we presuming facts not in evidence."

"Oh, my God. You're a lawyer. Check, please!" he said in feigned horror, pretending to look around for the waiter.

She laughed at that. "Actually, since we're angling toward asking about professions . . . I'm in Starfleet."

"Really?" He looked extremely interested. It was at times such as this that she wished she were capable of looking behind a man's eyes, directly into his mind. Did he *really* want to know about her profession? Or was he just pretending to listen while trying to decide what she would look like unclothed? And if the latter . . . should she be angry? Or flattered?

"Really," she affirmed. "I'm—I was—in charge of ship's operations aboard the starship *Excalibur*."

"Ah. Arthurian references. I'm a bit of a fan of that myself. So, are you on leave from the ship?"

"Actually, the ship is on leave from us. It blew up."

"Oh. I see. I'm . . . very sorry to hear that. Was anyone killed?"

"Amazingly, only one person. If it weren't for that person, far more would have been. Possibly all of us."

"He sounds very brave. What was his name?"

She looked up, slightly quizzical. "My, my. We're assuming, aren't we? I didn't say it was a 'he.' "

He hesitated only a moment and then smiled. "You

have me cold. I'm afraid I was egotistical enough to assume it was a man. Foolish, I know."

"I shouldn't scold you for it; in this case, it was also accurate enough. His name was Mackenzie Calhoun. He was our captain."

"Well . . . not to sound cold, but . . . don't they always say a captain is supposed to go down with his ship? So he would have just been doing his duty."

"I know," she sighed. "I know. But, believe it or not, somehow knowing that doesn't make it any easier." Quickly she forced the melancholy mood from her. It was hardly going to make the evening go any better. She cleared her throat and said, "So . . . what do you do? For a living, I mean?"

"I'm embarrassed to admit . . . I work for my father, actually. He's something of an industrialist, with his fingers into dozens of businesses. I run one of them for him: a rescue and salvage operation."

"And that's successful?"

"Oh, incredibly so," he chuckled, as if it should be self-evident. "There's always people in need of our services. And it helps my social life as well."

"Social life? How?"

"Well," he said cheerily, "if a date isn't going well, naturally you want someone who can rescue or salvage it. And that would be me." He paused, and then asked cautiously, "Would . . . my services be needed here?"

She shrugged. "Not so far. Then again, the evening's young. It could go downhill," she snapped her fingers, "just like that."

"You'll let me know if it does," said Nik amiably.

A throat was cleared near them, and both of them looked up. Robin was fully expecting to see another Elizabethan-clad waiter, but instead it was a well-dressed man who stood before her. He bore a remarkable resemblance to Nik, but was older and more distinguished, with his hair carefully cropped and shaped, and crests of gray on either side. "Am I disturbing you?" he asked.

"Hello, Dad," Nik said, and he was promptly on his feet. He was the same height as his father. "Robin Lefler, may I present my father, Rafe Viola. Dad, this is Robin Lefler."

"Charmed," he said, and bowed in a very old-world manner. He seemed ever so courtly.

"Pleasure to meet you, too."

"Do you mind if—?" and he gestured to an empty chair.

"By all means, Dad," said Nik, indicating that his father should make himself comfortable. Rafe promptly did so. "Robin is with Starfleet, Dad."

"Really." Rafe had a ready smile, but naturally Robin's metaphorical antennae went up. There was something in the way he said that that sounded a bit . . . confused. As if he couldn't understand why people from Starfleet would be wasting their time hanging out in a tourist resort. "How very interesting. Why are you not on a vessel somewhere?"

"There was a . . . bit of a mishap, Dad," Nik told him, glancing at Robin uneasily.

"It's all right, Nik," she said. "I've had enough time to come to terms with it. You don't have to tiptoe around it with me."

"Ship destroyed?" Rafe had a very direct way about him. He was a bit like Data, but without the rudimentary charm. Robin found it mildly disconcerting, but nothing she couldn't handle.

"Yes, that's pretty much what happened," she said.

"That's a shame. Waste of material."

She blinked at the apparent cold-bloodedness of that, but Nik told her, "Dad tends to think very much in terms of 'material.' Sometimes I think he's on a first-name basis with every molecule in the galaxy."

Rafe smiled at that, and Robin couldn't help but notice that he had a very appealing smile. "My poor son. Nik constantly has to go about making apologies for me. I freely admit I'm not always the easiest person to take. It certainly requires a good deal of patience."

"Don't be down on yourself, Dad."

"I'm not. Just being self-aware."

"Well, from what Nik tells me, you don't have anything to be concerned about. My understanding is that you've acquired some . . . company?"

"That's right. Apparently she's running a bit late, because she was supposed to meet us here." Just in speaking of her, his entire aspect seemed to change. Although the smile had been genuine enough earlier, now his whole face lit up. "She's quite a woman. Dark, mysterious. Everything she says, you feel that there's so much she's leaving unsaid. Truly, she's an endless lake of mysteries. . . ."

"Just waiting for the right swimmer, Dad?" asked Nik in a teasing tone.

Robin watched the two of them interact, and couldn't help but be a little jealous. Despite what had sounded like some initial trepidation from Nik regarding his father, she envied what she saw as a solid and relaxed relationship between the two of them. Naturally, she compared it to the relationship she had with her mother, and felt that the latter was somehow . . . lacking.

"Ah," said Rafe, rising. "Here she is now."

Nik got to his feet as well, and Robin turned and

looked in the direction that Rafe was facing. She froze in just that position, incredulous. Approaching them, having likewise frozen in midstep, was an all-too-familiar individual who looked equally surprised.

Robin sighed. "You know . . . you would think that I would have seen this coming."

Rafe looked from one to the other. "Morgan . . . Robin . . . do you two know each other?"

"Only all my life," said Robin.

"And I for not quite that long," Morgan added.

Nik looked puzzled, but Rafe understood immediately. "Mother and daughter," he said. They nodded simultaneously. He turned to his son and said, "Well, Nik, it appears that we have more similar taste in women than we would have thought. At least it saves me having to make introductions." As they sat, he added, "This is actually a pleasant bit of luck for you, Nik. They always say, if you want to see how the daughter's going to look in thirty years, look at the mother. Here's your chance."

"Actually, I have a funny feeling that, in thirty years, Ma's going to be looking better than I will."

"Isn't that a sweet thing for her to say, Morgan?"

"Oh, yes, Rafe . . . very sweet."

A waiter strode up to them. "Good morrow, lords and ladies. Is your food order to be . . . or not to be?"

"That is the question," Morgan said readily.

"Perhaps you'd be interested in Italian. See, on this side of the menu, there's the Montague specialties . . . and on the other side, the Capulets. We wouldn't recommend ordering some from each, though. They don't tend to get along."

"Why am I not surprised?" said Robin.

There was a sudden cry of battle from the middle of the restaurant. The human Shakespeare was facing off against the Klingon Shakespeare with great ire. "How dare you?" he was shouting.

"What's the problem?" the waiter called over. Robin tried to figure out whether this was simply part of the "show," or whether there was some genuine problem.

The human Shakespeare pointed accusingly at the Klingon. "He caved in my skull!"

"It looks fine from here," said the waiter.

Clearly annoyed, the human Shakespeare held up the shattered remains of a human skull.

"Alas. Poor Yorick," the waiter said mournfully.

"Can we go to a different restaurant?" pleaded Robin.

"Oh, Robin," her mother scolded her. "What happened to your sense of fun?"

"Maybe," Nik suggested, "it deserted her when she fell down a hole and nearly got herself killed."

Morgan turned and looked at her with undisguised interest. "You did?"

"Pretty much, yes."

"How very exciting!"

Robin couldn't quite recall the last time she'd seen her mother so enthused. Was that what it took to get a real rise out of her? A risk to life and limb? "Actually," Robin said, "that's more or less how Nik and I met. He saved my life."

"Well done, Nik!" said Rafe approvingly.

"Tell us all about it, Robin."

But then, before Robin could open her mouth, she spotted someone at the far side of the room, someone whom she had not been expecting to see . . . and yet, someone whom she had been wondering about from the moment she had had Morgan introduced to her as Rafe's significant other.

Montgomery Scott had just entered, alongside Mr.

Theodore Quincy, the El Dorado manager. Quincy was chatting animatedly, and Scotty appeared to be listening. But his gaze immediately fastened on Morgan. His face was, for the most part, unreadable, but Robin could swear that the edges of his mustache drooped ever so slightly. It was obvious to Robin that he was . . . annoyed? Hurt? He was definitely feeling something, but it was hard to tell what. Just as quickly as he had noticed Morgan and fixed his gaze on her, he looked away, shifting his attention once more to whatever it was that Quincy was going on about. They were shown to a table and spent the rest of the evening there. Every so often, Robin would steal glances over there to see if he was looking Morgan's way. But either he was far too crafty to be noticed, or he simply wasn't paying her any mind.

The only time that Morgan and Robin had to chat privately was when they opted to use the restroom. The moment they were alone, Robin said to her mother, "I thought you were involved with Scotty."

" 'Involved'? Robin, that's a very strong word, particularly considering this is simply a vacation."

"You went dancing with him!"

"No . . . I never said that. Scotty and I just talked, and then he turned in early. I went dancing with Rafe. Oh, don't look at me like that, Robin. I'm . . . having fun."

"Fun. Did you see the way Scotty looked at you when he spotted you sitting there with Rafe?"

"I hadn't noticed."

"Yes, you did."

"All right, I noticed. But what would you have me do, Robin? I ran into Rafe at one of the casinos, and he seemed charming, debonair. He seemed interested in talking about me."

"Really. And what was Scotty interested in talking about?"

"Engines. Machinery. Computer systems. He appreciates me for my mind, and considers me knowledgeable enough to be able to keep up with him. He told me how nice it is to be able to talk to an older woman who actually cares about the same things he cares about."

"Well, that sounds . . ." Her voice trailed off.

"I hope the word 'romantic' wasn't the one you were searching for, because I can tell you with utter conviction that it's anything but that."

"But he was so . . . sweet."

"Fine. You date him."

"I've got Nik."

"Have you?" She arched an eyebrow. "Just how much have you 'got' him? Have you and he—?"

"Mother!" Robin once again found herself astounded at the direction the conversation was going. "For heaven's sake! This is our first date!"

"I thought," said Morgan, washing her hands, "that you met when he saved your life."

"That wasn't a dating thing, though! That was a . . . a saving my life thing. So this is really our first date. And I'm sorry, but I just . . . well, I mean, Mother, I shouldn't have to explain it beyond that. It's only a first date."

"Don't sell a first date short, Robin," said Morgan, drying her hands.

"What do you mean by that?"

Morgan smiled enigmatically. "Where do you think you came from?" Shaking the last bit of moisture off her hands, she walked out of the restroom.

"That was more than I needed to know," said Robin.

THE JUDGE

THE INTERVENING WEEKS between Burgoyne's arrival and the actual time of judgment were not easy for Selar.

She endeavored to pursue her normal life's activities without any outward—or even inner—acknowledgment of what was going on. She was made aware, through intermediaries, that Burgoyne had filed the appeal, gone through various sources, and made a direct challenge for hir rights as the parent. It was a rather unusual situation for the Judgment Council to be confronted with and, naturally, being Vulcans, they approached it in a methodical, particular and—ultimately—logical manner. Such things, of course, took time.

Selar kept waiting for Burgoyne to show up again at her doorstep, to see the child once more. She was somewhat surprised, however, to receive a message early on in the process from hir. It was simple, succinct, and to the point: Burgoyne had no desire to create a series of confrontational situations. S/he felt it would serve no one, and was content to let the process unfold in the standard and accepted manner. S/he wished to make it clear that in no way did it indicate a diminishment of hir interest in Xyon . . . or, in a way, even in Selar herself. "Perhaps this will be an instance," Burgoyne concluded, "in which absence makes the heart grow fonder."

"I would not count on that," Selar said, but naturally there was no response, since the message was simply a recording. Selar shut the recording off and prepared to delete it from her computer files . . . and then, for no reason that she could really discern, elected to keep it. She told herself that perhaps, at some point in the future, it could be used as some sort of evidence. This, of course, did not explain why, every so often, she felt the urge to play the recording and just watch Burgoyne speak. It was an annoying thing for her to do, and she couldn't understand why she did it . . . even as she did it.

She only saw Burgoyne once during the intervening weeks. As Selar was rounding a corner one day, on her way home, she spotted Burgoyne emerging from a library. S/he didn't spot Selar, being apparently lost in thought. Selar intended to go on her way once Burgoyne was gone, but instead found her feet directing her—almost as if by their own accord—to the library. There she asked the curator what it was that Burgoyne was looking into.

"Ancient Vulcan traditions in general," replied the curator. "I do not know specifics." The vagueness was frustrating to Selar, but there wasn't really much more she could do about it. She wasn't about to start trying to duplicate Burgoyne's research and investigate which stores of information s/he had accessed. After all, just how obsessive was she going to be about this, anyway?

She continued to be impressed by Xyon's development. He seemed an exceedingly happy child. She found herself glancing at other small children as she encountered them in her daily activities, mentally assessing them and comparing them to her own. She couldn't help but notice that the Vulcan children seemed almost uniformly dour. The reason for this quickly became evident. When she was walking around with Xyon outside and he would be clucking or cooing, other Vulcans would glance at him, and her, with what could only be termed disapproval. She knew, intellectually, that they had every right to scowl. She knew what the Vulcan way entailed. Indeed, wasn't part of the entire point of her willingness to struggle with Burgoyne over custody precisely because of her dedication to that tradition? She knew that she should be as quick to discourage Xyon's burbling as other Vulcans were to make clear their own dissatisfaction with her. There were, after all, ways in which these things were done.

No Vulcan child learned overnight the discipline of logic and control. It took many, many years of teaching and reinforcement. But it was never too late to start. Yet, even though she knew that, Selar still had difficulty with the concept of silencing her child. How could she teach him what to be . . . if all she tried to do was stifle who he was? If nothing else, she did feel some degree of (inappropriate) smugness that, for all the "acceptable" dourness of their mien, the Vulcan infants seemed to be lagging behind Xyon in terms of dexterity and awareness. It enabled her to chalk off some of the clear sentiments expressed by others as a form of (equally inappropriate) envy.

Then, one day, she received word from the Judgment Council. It surprised her in a way; when nothing had happened after so much time, she had almost felt as if nothing was *going* to happen. It was certainly an illogical way to assess the situation, and upon receiving word from the Council, the folly of that illogic became clear.

An adjudicator had been assigned to the case. This came as a bit of a surprise to Selar, who had truly hoped that Burgoyne's claims would be rejected out of hand. But she quickly adapted to the situation. If this was going to be the way of it, then she would simply deal with it.

There would be no attorneys present; Vulcan law did not require it, and Vulcans traditionally disdained such options that were so prevalent in other cultures. The reasoning was that any capable Vulcan should be perfectly able to express his or her own case in the view of his or her peers. The humans had a saying about someone acting as their own lawyer typically having a fool for a client. That, however, stemmed from the notion that someone representing his or her self would be unable to view his or her own case or predicament in a dispassionate way. Obviously, that thinking did not apply to Vulcans, the most thoroughly dispassionate of individuals.

Burgoyne, being an offworlder, would be far more likely to make certain that s/he had an attorney present to state hir position for hir. That, however, was not the case; according to the information she'd received from the Judgment Council, Burgoyne had waived the opportunity for representation. It would just be Burgoyne against Selar, each putting forward their case to the best of their abilities.

Tradition, however, did dictate that participants in disputes could, and should, bring a companion along to provide counsel, support, and guidance. Selar intended to do just that. In a way, she felt a bit sorry for Burgoyne. S/he would have no one to be by hir side.

A bit sorry . . . but not very much.

The Vulcan sun was unconscionably hot that day, even taking into account the world's general tendency toward an arid climate. As Selar walked toward the center of the judgment grounds, she took a deep breath of the burning air and wondered briefly how she could ever have left Vulcan in the first place. This was her home, first and foremost. It had made her who she was, was a part of her no matter how far she might wander. She almost felt ashamed for having abandoned it in the first place.

Standing next to her in the judgment grounds' center was Giniv, her close friend. Giniv, with a saturnine face and slightly stocky build, had always been there for her and, frankly, Selar had never quite understood why. When they were quite young, Giniv had just attached herself to Selar, and Selar had never felt strongly enough about it to tell her to go away. So Selar had tolerated her presence, and that tolerance had actually developed into a form of friendship. Or at least as close to friendship as Selar ever let anything become.

"Will your parents be in attendance?" asked Giniv. They had not spoken for some time, merely stood there in the silence, waiting for others to arrive.

"They very likely would, had I informed them of the occasion," replied Selar.

"You did not tell them?"

Selar looked at Giniv with raised eyebrow. "I believe I just said that."

"Why did you not tell them?"

"To what end? To disrupt their lives for no reason? Certainly nothing will come of this. Burgoyne has made an appeal to the Vulcan Judgment Council. It is true that the Council is sending an adjudicator here to the judgment grounds to hear the case. But my conclusion—indeed, the only logical one—is that it is being done merely as a matter of form, and largely out of deference to Burgoyne's status as a Starfleet officer. The Council prefers to maintain solid relations with Starfleet at all times. Otherwise, they would likely have dismissed hir claims expeditiously."

Giniv considered the matter a moment. "What if you are wrong? What if matters are not as perfunctory as you believe they will be?"

"That will not matter. The fact remains that involving my parents would be a needless hardship for them."

Giniv made a noncommittal noise that caught Selar's attention. "You disagree?"

"I simply speculate as to whether you have not informed your parents because you do not wish them to meet Burgoyne. That you may be embarrassed in some measure because of your choice of mate."

"Burgoyne is not my mate," Selar informed her.

"S/he is the father of your child."

"That does not make hir my mate."

"What does it make hir, then?"

"An overly familiar acquaintance."

Clearly Giniv did not agree, but before she could pursue the matter, they were startled to hear a voice say, "Good morning, ladies. Hot day, isn't it?"

Burgoyne was standing a short distance away. Hir arms were folded, and s/he was studying Selar with an open and frank stare. The uninhibited nature of the scrutiny made Selar feel uncomfortable, but she was not about to admit that.

In the meantime, Burgoyne turned hir gaze to Giniv. "I am Burgoyne 172."

"Giniv," said Giniv. "I did not hear you arrive. That is surprising; my hearing is rather acute."

"That's because'a your ears'a are so'a cute."

Giniv stared at hir blankly, and then looked to Selar. Selar gave a very slight shrug.

"All right," said Giniv uncertainly.

"Burgoyne," Selar said, "it is not too late to withdraw your claim and avoid embarrassment."

The two of them, rather unconsciously, were circling one another like two stars.

"Are you concerned that you will be embarrassed?" Burgoyne sounded rather interested in the notion.

"I have no such concerns for myself. Allowing oneself to be embarrassed is an emotion. It is of no consequence to me. You, however, might feel differently."

"I feel that I'm doing what I have to do."

"As do we all, Burgoyne."

"How *did* you get here without my hearing you?" said Giniv, who apparently had not quite managed to work her way past that.

Before Burgoyne could respond, Selar said, "Burgoyne can move very quietly if s/he chooses."

"Thank you," said Burgoyne.

"It was not a compliment. Simply an observation." She inclined her head toward Giniv. "In case you are wondering, Giniv is here as tradition dictates. A trusted friend may be in attendance to witness the events when there is a dispute brought to the judgment grounds. I regret that you have no one of whom to avail yourself."

"Do you? I didn't know you cared."

"I do not wish hardship upon you, Burgoyne. You may or may not believe that, but it is true."

"Well, I appreciate that. But, you know, Selar . . . it is illogical to assume things."

"What do you mean by—?"

Then she saw someone else approaching. Her eyes narrowed. "Slon . . . ?"

Slon nodded slightly, walked over to Burgoyne, nodded once again and then stood by hir side. Selar looked from one to the other, her face visibly darkening. Her voice was so icy that, considering the heat in the air, it was surprising there wasn't mist coming from her mouth. "What," she said slowly, "is this about?"

"We made each others' acquaintance," Slon told her.

"In . . . deed." The temperature dropped another ten degrees.

In a low voice, Giniv said, "Did they—?"

"I neither know nor care," replied Selar, making absolutely no effort to keep her voice down. She was even more annoyed to see that Burgoyne was actually smiling. Presumably s/he thought she was annoyed by hir little "alliance" with her brother. Well, that was just another mistake on Burgoyne's part. One of many.

"You seem annoyed, Selar," Slon observed.

"You know better than that," she corrected him archly. "I find it curious that you would cast your alliance with . . . hir."

"I have cast no alliance with anyone," said Slon. "However, Burgoyne had no one to accompany hir through this experience. I saw no harm in volunteering my services in that regard."

"Your overwhelming compassion is duly noted, Slon," Selar said.

Giniv heard it first, but Selar and Slon both detected it moments later. Burgoyne took a few seconds longer, but in short order the sound had reached hir as well. It was the faint jingling of bells, as if a procession of some sort was heading their way. "The Judgment Council?" s/he asked. Slon nodded curtly.

"Who do you think has been assigned to it?" Giniv asked.

"There is no purpose to speculation," Selar said. In point of fact, she was wondering as well, but she was not about to admit to any sort of curiosity . . . or to anything. She was determined to play every aspect of the coming confrontation as coolly and sanguinely as possible. She was Vulcan. She wanted to bring her child up in the Vulcan way. Therefore, it was absolutely imperative that she remember, at all times, her own upbringing and training. Granted, no one could possibly think that a Vulcan child should be raised in anything approximating the situation Burgoyne would have to offer, but Selar was going to make absolutely certain that no one thought her anything but the ideal mother.

Burgoyne's nostrils were flaring. "Someone old," s/he said, sniffing the air. "Someone very old."

"How can you tell?" asked Slon, intrigued.

"The years surround her like a fine wine."

"Silver-tongued, isn't s/he?" Giniv murmured to Selar. Selar said nothing.

The group was approaching slowly in the distance, the tinkling of the bells getting louder. The judgment place itself was nothing impressive: A wide, flat area, paved with stone polished to a gleaming, pale blue. There were stone seats carved into surrounding rock from which spectators could observe what transpired. Dead center of the area was a pedestal upon which the person who stood in judgment would look down upon those who were being judged.

They drew closer still. There were a goodly number

of retainers, escorts, and guards, but it was clear just who was the center of attention. It was a wizened woman, walking in the exact center of the group. Selar, Giniv, and Slon recognized her instantly, and Giniv let out a most uncharacteristic gasp. Selar fired her a look that silently scolded her for the breach of etiquette, but she understood exactly why Giniv had reacted in that way. Truth to tell, it was all that Selar herself could do to restrain her surprise.

"Who is she?" asked Burgoyne.

"That is not simply a she, Burgoyne," Slon said. "That is living history."

The Vulcan woman known as T'Pau made her slow way to the center of the judgment place. Everyone stood in respectful silence, and even the bells began to diminish in their jingling until all was quiet.

Selar was reasonably certain that she had never seen such an elderly Vulcan in her life. Her skin looked drier than the driest deserts of the world, and she moved with the air of someone who was concentrating every moment on not inadvertently falling and snapping a bone like a rotted twig. And yet, for all her apparent frailty, the woman seemed to radiate power. When she spoke, there was nothing the least bit feeble in her voice. It was deep and quite strong, with the occasional over-enunciation of Vulcans schooled in the planet's ancient dialects.

"We have the two people in question?" she inquired. But there was something in her voice that did not sound very much like a question, but rather an order. As if to say that, if the people of the hour were not present, then there were going to be some rather serious consequences.

"I am Selar," she said formally. "I am summoned. I am here."

"I am Burgoyne 172. I am summoned. I am here." They had both walked forward so that they were now a short distance from T'Pau. Even with the elevation, she was barely an inch higher than either of them. Nevertheless, she seemed to be looking down upon them from an almost dizzying height.

For a time, nothing was said. T'Pau simply stared at the two of them, her gaze swiveling from one to the other and back again. She was heavily robed, and the day was dry, even sweltering, but she did not appear to show any signs of the heat.

"Thee has . . . a dispute." she stated finally. "There is a child. A half-breed. Yours . . . and yours," and she nodded to both of them.

"I can present medical documentation, T'Pau, indicating a preponderance of the child's genetic structure is Vulcan," Selar started to say.

However, she only got as far as "I can present—" before T'Pau silenced her with nothing more than a look. "I did not ask you . . . did I?" T'Pau said.

"No, T'Pau."

"The offworlder knows to wait. Why does thee not?"

Selar felt herself beginning to color slightly in her cheeks. But, with long practice at hiding such things, she took control of her chagrin. She said nothing in response. The absence of a reply appeared to be exactly what T'Pau desired. She waited a time more before continuing. "There is more to a Vulcan . . . to any living being . . . than the body," she said. "There is . . . the *katra* . . . the soul. Does he have the body of his mother . . . but the soul of his father? That . . . we cannot determine. Even a mind-meld will not determine such a thing, for we speak of matters . . . beyond the mind. Beyond our ability . . . to know.

"Where . . . then . . . does that leave us?" T'Pau paused a moment and regarded each of them in turn. "Speak to me," she said to Selar.

"The child was born of my need," said Selar. "The child is Vulcan. Whatever contributions his father may have made . . . a way must be chosen in which the child can be raised. That must be the Vulcan way. Whatever instincts come from his Hermat 'heritage,' they are ways that lead to impulsive behavior and lack of self-control. Xyon's best interests can only be served by maintaining him fully in an environment that is conducive to those teachings and that development. Burgoyne desires to have him half the time. That is unacceptable. A choice must be made for Xyon here . . . now . . . as to what his life's path will be. He cannot be exposed equally to two cultures and told that both apply equally to him. As his Vulcan parent, I must choose the method in which he will be shaped. And that way . . . is the Vulcan way. Here. On this world."

She continued to speak, laying out her case point by point for many minutes. She kept waiting for T'Pau to interrupt, to ask her a question or challenge something that she was saying. But T'Pau did nothing except listen. Her face was utterly inscrutable, her eyes like two dark stones set in her face, showing about as much compassion as a rock might feel. Then again, she was T'Pau. Her mind could have been a roiling fury of tumult, and one would not have known it to look at her.

When she had concluded, T'Pau then turned to look at Burgoyne. "And thee . . . ?" was all she said.

Burgoyne took a deep breath, and then coughed slightly. Taking a deep breath on Vulcan was not quite as easy as it appeared; for offworlders, the heated air could be very trying on the lungs. Selar wondered if

Burgoyne's time on the planet had made the adjustment any easier for hir.

"Xyon is mine as well as hers," Burgoyne said.

And then s/he stood there.

Selar and Giniv exchanged a puzzled glance. They waited for Burgoyne to continue, but nothing more was forthcoming. Even Slon looked a bit surprised.

T'Pau arched an eyebrow. "Is that all?" she inquired.

"Madam," Burgoyne said with a slight bow, "there are only two oratorical paths open to me. The first is to explain the shortcomings I feel characterize Selar's mothering techniques . . . and Selar as a person, in general. I . . . was prepared to do so. But I find now that I cannot. I would rather not. So that path is closed to me. The only remaining avenue is to argue for my rights as—in this case—the father, although, admittedly, the concept of 'father' is one that my own race does not quite recognize. Even if I did that . . . it would not matter, would it?" S/he paused, and when T'Pau did not respond immediately, s/he prompted again, "Would it?"

"No," T'Pau said slowly, dragging one syllable into three. "It would not. Because you are an offworlder, you have no truly recognized rights in this matter. When it comes to matters of who is the proper guardian for a Vulcan child, the answer according to law is a Vulcan. There is no disputing that."

"Then why are we here?" Slon blurted out. Despite his veneer of stoicism, he seemed a bit annoyed. "Was all this just . . . just some sort of ritual?"

"Rituals," T'Pau told him, "are the very essence of society. The Judgment Council did not consider the offworlder's claim to have merit on its face, but was willing to assign me to hear the plea and judge accordingly."

"With all respect, T'Pau," Slon said, squaring his shoulders, "that does not seem fair. Your mind was already made up."

"Has the offworlder lost the power to speak for itself?" asked T'Pau.

"Hirself," Burgoyne corrected reflexively.

T'Pau leveled a gaze at hir. "You are male and female . . . and neither. 'It' is the proper word. We have no use for semantic games on Vulcan."

Burgoyne's jaw twitched reflexively—in contained anger or mortification, Selar could not tell. But she was surprised to discover that she actually felt some small degree of pity for Burgoyne. She had no idea why she should. After all, it was Burgoyne who had decided to press the matter. Everything that had occurred, s/he had brought on hirself. Selar's conscience should have been perfectly clear.

For a long moment, nothing was said. It was as if something was waiting to spring, some invisible beast of prey that no one was capable of perceiving, but which was lying in wait there all the same.

"If that is all that remains to be said on the matter," T'Pau said finally, "then the course is clear. My judgment—"

"That is all that is to be said . . . but not done," Burgoyne suddenly interrupted.

T'Pau clearly did not appreciate being cut off in the middle of a sentence. Her face darkened, but rather than verbally castigate Burgoyne, all she said was an icy, "Yes?"

"I claim the *Ku'nit Ka'fa'ar.*"

"What?" Selar looked blankly at Giniv, who seemed equally puzzled. The words were confusing to her. She recognized them as ancient Vulcan, but she was not fluent in that particular aspect of their tongue. She couldn't make out the meaning of them. "S/he claims the what?"

Slon likewise appeared perplexed. Even the ceremonial bell-bearers who circled the judgment center were baffled.

Only T'Pau understood. And she did not appear to appreciate it at all.

"Offworlders," she sighed. "Half-breeds. I have some small experience with both . . . and always, always, very little goes smoothly with either. You truly seek the *Ku'nit Ka'fa'ar?*"

"It is a ritual, T'Pau," Burgoyne said evenly. "Only moments ago you spoke of the importance of rituals. The *Ku'nit Ka'fa'ar* has never been officially repudiated. You've never turned your backs on it in any sort of formal manner."

"Because it is a ritual that is obsolete . . . that has not been used in millennia. . . ."

"The specifics of it may be moot . . . but it still exists. And the *Ku'nit Ka'fa'ar* makes no mention of offworlders . . . only parents."

"At the time, there were no offworlders, so there is no reason for them to be mentioned in the description of the rituals, one way or the other."

"True," said Burgoyne. "But silence in the matter implies consent. Because offworlders are not specifically forbidden . . . we are implicitly allowed. No one here is disputing that I am, in some measure, Xyon's parent. This qualifies as a dispute under the *Ku'nit Ka'fa'ar,* and if you are the civilized society that you claim yourselves to be, you must honor it."

Even from where she was standing, Selar could practically feel daggers flying from T'Pau's eyes into and through Burgoyne, but the Hermat simply stood there, patiently, as if s/he had endless amounts of time to do so.

"She may refuse," T'Pau said finally. "She has that option."

"Yes," Burgoyne said. "She may. In which event, the child goes with me automatically. You know that."

"That is correct."

"That is correct?" Selar had gone from not understanding what she was hearing to not believing what she was hearing. "T'Pau . . . what is Burgoyne talking about? What is the *Ku'nit Ka'fa'ar?"*

T'Pau did not seem particularly anxious to answer, but she did so anyway. "The forging of our society to the philosophies of Surak . . . was not an easy process. There was . . . resistance. It is natural that such would be the case, for we were a barbaric and warlike people. That was our way of life . . . and there was no desire to change it, even though Surak showed us the way. There were many tribal leaders who resisted as well, for their strength and power derived from our barbarism, and they feared—rightly so—that they would lose their leadership if a new belief system took hold. Surak's philosophy . . . destroyed as much as it created. Tribes, families were split apart, as some followed him while others remained behind. And the children—particularly young children—presented a dilemma. In many instances, one parent would desire to follow the teachings of Surak, while another fought to maintain the old ways. From these disputes came the *Ku'nit Ka'fa'ar* . . . the "Struggle for the Way."

Selar suddenly started to get an uneasy feeling. " 'Struggle' in what sense?"

"These were barbaric times, remember. One's worth

was measured not in the ability to think, but in the ability to defend by force of arms. The parent who was stronger . . . was considered the parent who was worthier."

That was when Selar understood, and she could see from Giniv's expression that she likewise comprehended. And from Slon's next words, it was clear that he got it as well.

"You cannot be serious," he said, although it was unclear whether he was addressing Burgoyne or T'Pau. "This . . . this is not a challenge in a mating ritual, where individuals are not in their right mind and the only way to settle matters is by trying to bash each other's heads in. These are rational, thinking people, and there has to be some other way—"

"There isn't," Burgoyne said, and s/he sounded a bit regretful. S/he looked sadly but with conviction at Selar. "I wish there were."

"Selar," said T'Pau, and from the sound of her voice, she wasn't simply speaking, but rather making a pronouncement. "The challenge of the *Ku'nit Ka'fa'ar* has been made. So as it was in the ancient times . . . so is it still, as we remember who we are and the times that forged us. The challenger believes that *its* philosophies and intentions for the raising of your child together are preferable to those that you would impart to it. You must display strength of mind through strength of sinew, or, in failing to do so, forfeit your child's future to the other parent."

"This is insane," Selar said. "You are telling me that it has gone beyond merely splitting our time with the child. That it is now all-or-nothing."

"That is correct."

"That if I do not fight Burgoyne . . . I lose Xyon."

"That is correct," T'Pau said again.

"Insane," Selar repeated. "I will appeal this to the—"

"There is no appeal. There is none who knows the rituals better than I, and none will contradict me," T'Pau told her, and her eyes were as cold as the depths of space. "This is what matters have come to, Selar. The challenge has been issued. Accept it, and fight for your child. Refuse . . . and the child goes with the off-worlder. Choose . . . now."

MORGAN

"I DINNA LIKE 'IM."

Morgan had been lying out on the beach, sunglasses shielding her eyes. It was, of course, yet another glorious day on Risa. Rafe had been lying next to her, and they had been idly holding hands and chatting about nothing of any major consequence. All in all, it had been extremely pleasant. Then, commenting that he had promised to spend time with Nik, Rafe excused himself and padded off across the sand. Morgan watched him go, rather pleased. He certainly had a good look about him when he was walking away.

So she was understandably startled when the familiar voice with the even more familiar brogue spoke from about a foot away. She peered over the sunglasses and up at Scotty. From the angle at which she was looking up at him, his body was in silhouette, and it seemed as if he was blotting out the sun.

"I beg your pardon?" she said.

"I'm tellin' ye as a friend . . . ah dinna like 'im."

"Odd way of saying hello, Scotty."

"Hello. Ah dinna like 'im."

"Would the *'im* in question be Rafe?"

"Aye."

She stared up at him for a few moments. "Are you going to sit?" she inquired.

"Are ye gonna reply to muh question?"

"Question? Was there a question in there? I just heard a statement. You said you didn't like him. Which, oddly enough, doesn't factor in all that much, considering that you're not the one who's seeing him. Why don't you like him—and furthermore, why am I bothering to ask you why you don't like him, because it's none of your business!"

"Hey, Scotty!" called several guests as they walked past. Scotty tossed off a salute to them and turned back to Morgan.

"Ah'm making it muh business," he said.

"How very considerate of you. Do you do that for all the guests?"

"Ah would like t'think," Scotty said, "that we'd moved a bit beyond th' greeter-and-guest relationship."

"Have we?" Her eyebrows puckered in surprise. "To be honest, Scotty, I wasn't getting that impression at all." She stretched, and then stood. She couldn't find it in her heart to be annoyed with him; deep down, he really was sweet, and he certainly meant well. He was just . . .

Jealous?

How charming. How utterly charming.

"You're jealous," she said.

Scotty looked utterly taken aback. His mouth moved, but no words came out of it. And then, to her surprise, he turned and walked away. For a moment, Morgan toyed with the idea of letting him just storm off, but something made her follow him. She caught up with him quickly, her towel slung over her back. "Truth hurt, Scotty?" she asked.

"What do ah look like t'ye?" he demanded, without even looking at her. Little sprays of sand were being kicked up in his wake. "Do ah look like a schoolboy?"

"No, but you're acting like one."

"Ah'm acting like a friend who's concerned about ye, and all ye come back with is that ah'm jealous. What kind of codswallop is that?"

"It's the truth, Scotty, at least so far as I see it."

"Then ah'm afraid ye aren't takin' much of a look at it at all." Finally he stopped and faced her. "Morgan . . . ah won't lie to ye. I'll never lie to ye. I think you're a fine woman, and a damned attractive female. Setting aside that ye look like a woman from days past . . ."

"A former lover?"

"Ach, no. No," and he smiled faintly at the memory. "She had her attentions focused elsewhere, poor thing."

" 'Poor thing,' meaning that she didn't have the good sense to be enamored of you?"

"No, 'poor thing,' meanin' that the affection she felt was somewhat unrequited. It wasn't about me at'all, and why do ye keep doin' that?"

"Doing what?"

"Makin' it seem that every bloody thing in the world has to do with me? I warn ye about this fellow—"

"Rafe."

"Aye, Rafe. I warn ye about him, and suddenly ah'm 'jealous.' " He made finger quotation marks around the word. "I talk about Christine, and ye think ah'm talkin' about some lost love. Damn, but ye can be a most aggravatin' woman, Morgan. Has anyone ever told ye that?"

"Only on days when I was awake," she said ruefully.

"Morgan . . . unrequited crushes, jealousy and such—those are all activities of the young. For the likes of Robin and ye."

"The likes of me?" Morgan laughed at that. "Oh, Scotty, believe it or not, I'm a bit older than I look."

"Perhaps, but not by much, I'd wager."

"You have no idea how much I'd like to take that bet. But go on."

He sighed, as if he was anxious to divest himself of a great weight. "All ah'm trying to say t'ye—and ah think ah'm not havin' a great deal of success—is that when one gets t'be muh age, one tends t'leave b'hind all of the excess crap of youth. Ah say what ah mean 'cause that's what ah mean t'say, and there's no deep, ulterior motive. No hidden agenda. That's simply the way it is, that's all."

"All right. All right." She looked out at the "ocean" lapping up against the beach. Utterly manufactured, of course, with great wave machines propelling it toward the shoreline, but that didn't make it any less pleasant. Since she was in her swimsuit, her feet and legs were bare, and she took a few steps toward it so that the water would lap up around her feet. "Fine, Scotty. You've got my attention. Why is it, then, that you don't like Rafe?"

Scotty pursed his lips for a moment and then said, "Ye know what humans are? Human beings, at their core?"

"I have my own opinions on it, but I suspect you have an answer already in mind, so go ahead."

"Machines," he told her. "Finely tuned machines. Probably one of the most sophisticated machines around. Do ye know how ah figure out what's wrong with an engine?"

"I further suspect you're going to tell me that as well," she said evenly.

"Ah don't have to run diagnostics. Ah don't need 'em to tell me that somethin's wrong. Y'see, ah know every sound an engine makes. Ah feel it, right down to muh bones. So when something is off with an engine, ah just . . . know it. And once ah know, ah study it and look it over and see with muh own eyes where the problem is. And ah don't just do that with engines. Ah can do that with any sort of machinery. Ah just have a sense of these things."

"And you're saying that you can look at a person, and know something's wrong with that person, using that same intuition."

"That's exactly right," he said. "Ah just know it. Even when ah don't know why ah know it . . . ah still do."

"But, Scotty, isn't it possible—just remotely possible—that the way you perceive certain other people might be shaped by considerations that have nothing to do with the people themselves?"

"Is it remotely possible? Ah suppose so. But ah don't believe that's th'case in this instance."

"Why not?"

"Because ah could tell somethin' was up with 'im, that's why. From the moment ah first saw 'im. He felt . . . wrong. He came by the Engineering Room, and ah did muh usual greetin' business. The moment ah shook his hand, somethin' felt . . . off. As if he was not happy to see me there."

"That's silly, Scotty. Who could not be happy to see you?"

"Ah have no idea. Ah kept trying to figure out if he was some old enemy from the original *Enterprise* . . . someone who'd managed to survive, just as ah had managed."

"Scotty . . . your imagination is running wild. Don't you see that? Rafe is just a man . . . a good man . . . a handsome, supportive—"

"All right, all right, ah get the idea." He looked down at the water, which was starting to lap at the toes of his boots. "And ah suppose ah haven't been exciting company. Ah can see where ye'd be interested in him."

"Oh, Scotty," she said in surprise. "How can you think that?"

"Because ah was foolish t'think that ah knew what ye wanted," he told her candidly. "Maybe ah'm just too cynical or too tired or too damned old . . . but ah should have realized that ye'd be interested in romance. Me, ah was just so happy to have someone to talk to that seemed to have a brain in their head—particularly after dealing with the know-nothings who run this place—that ah gave no thought to where yer interests might lay. The day before ye hooked up with Rafe, ah remember . . . we went for a long walk on the beach, and all ah did was tell ye how the artificial wave machines worked. What a romantic time that must have been for ye."

"Scotty, to be honest, I wasn't really intending to look for romance."

"Don't lie t'me, Morgan," he said, sounding a bit scolding. "Ye can lie t'others, and even t'yerself. But never t'me."

"Sorry," she apologized, and meant it. If there was one thing that this fellow seemed to have in abundance, it was pride.

"It's just that . . . well . . . ah hadn't really been lookin' for romance muhself. Not that there haven't been opportunities, ye understand. After all, ah am loaded with charisma," he said modestly.

"That goes without saying."

"Aye, but ah thought ah would say it anyway. Women have come through here, and don't think ah'm not aware when they're givin' me the once, twice and even three times over. But at muh age, ah tend t'be more interested in what's above a woman's neck, not below it."

"But romance doesn't have to be solely a matter of what's 'below the neck,' Scotty. Although, please, don't misunderstand: Our time together has been wonderfully engaging. I mean, the chat about phase coil replication alone was enough to keep my head whirling for hours."

"Are ye makin' fun of me, now?"

"No, I'm quite serious. It's just that . . . well . . . sometimes . . ." She smiled. "Sometimes a woman is more interested in looking at the stars than discussing how to navigate them. You see?"

"Aye."

They were silent for a time, and then Scotty said, "He's coming."

From the way that he'd said "he," Morgan knew instantly to whom he was referring. She turned and, sure enough, there was Rafe heading toward them. No longer in bathing attire, he was still dressed casually, and he looked rather amused that Morgan was talking with the engineer.

"Well, well," he called over to them. "Nik was otherwise occupied, so I thought I'd come back and pick up where we left off . . . and here Mr. Scott has already picked up where I left off."

"Just chattin'. Ye needn't worry," Scotty said diplomatically.

"Oh, I wasn't worried at all." He drew up so that he was alongside them, without making any attempt to step between the two of them. "I wasn't aware that your duties ever really took you out of your personalized bar, Mr. Scott."

"Ah, muh 'duties' are fairly loosely defined," Scotty assured him. "Ah can come and go as ah please. The management here is quite accommodatin'. Probably comes from muh not needin' th' work."

"And yet you choose to remain here. Interesting. And you feel fulfilled?" asked Rafe.

Scotty eyed him with obvious suspicion. "The way ye just said that . . . makes it sound as if ye had somethin' else in mind."

"Yes, Rafe, I must admit it sounded that way to me, too." The gaze of Morgan's dark eyes played over him.

Rafe did not seem the least nonplussed. "Very simple. I have a rather large business endeavor. And from everything I've heard and read, Mr. Scott, you are a rather talented individual. My company could use a man like you. We're doing work on computer systems that make the work of UFP scientists—even those at the Daystrom Institute—look primitive in comparison. Although I admit, of course, that Daystrom was a genius, back in the day—"

"Really. Poor fellow was comin' apart at the seams, last ah saw 'im."

Rafe appeared momentarily startled, and then smiled politely. "Yes. Of course. Foolish of me. You do tend to go back quite some time, don't you?"

"Aye, that's right. Ah do."

Rafe studied Scotty a moment more and tilted his head thoughtfully. "Mr. Scott . . . I think you have something to say to me. Am I wrong?"

Before Scotty could reply, Morgan put up her hands, one against each of them. "Gentlemen . . . I don't think this discussion is going to get anyone anywhere."

"Ah was just thinkin' the same thing. If ye will excuse me . . . ah believe ah've said everything ah can, or should, say on the matter. And ah have other guests to attend to." He bowed graciously to Morgan, taking her hand suavely and kissing her on the knuckles. But she saw that his gaze was focused not on her, but on Rafe. Oh, yes, Scotty was making it abundantly clear that he had serious reservations about Rafe Viola.

Were they founded? Morgan didn't think so. The piece of information Scotty was missing in all of this was that Morgan had lived quite a few lifetimes, and was not remotely what one would term "naïve." She knew her way around the universe, and had met all types. Scotty might fancy himself the worldly-wise type, honor-bound to watch out for the delicate sensibilities of less experienced females. But that didn't make his perception of things correct, and since Morgan knew that, she could respond accordingly to his stated paranoia. Simply put, she knew better than he did. She knew it, and he didn't. Based on that alone, there was no reason she should accord any great weight to his concerns . . . at least, not to the extent that it outweighed her own judgment.

Scotty thought himself in a better position to judge than Morgan was. Morgan knew better. Of course she wasn't going to tell Scotty that she knew better, or why. There were some things she just didn't feel the need to share.

Still . . .

Rafe looked to her, clear puzzlement in his eyes as he watched Scotty walk away. "Would you mind telling me what that was all about?" he asked.

"Nothing extraordinary. He talked. I listened."

"And what did you two talk about?"

"About how nosy you are."

He laughed at that . . . but there was just the slightest hint, Morgan thought, that he didn't find it the least bit funny. But then the momentary doubt was gone, replaced by her endless confidence that she knew exactly what she was doing.

SELAR & BURGOYNE

"YOU CANNOT BE SERIOUS," Giniv said, standing to one
side with Selar. She kept casting glances in Burgoyne's
direction. S/he was standing at the far end of the judgment grounds, engaging in a series of stretching exer-
cises. Slon was speaking to hir in what were clearly
low and urgent tones, but it was difficult to see whether
Burgoyne was paying any attention to him at all. "You
are not going to fight hir."

"I do not see a good deal of choice being presented
me," Selar replied. She was no more sanguine about
the notion than Giniv. "But the alternative is that I hand
my child over to hir. You do not seriously expect me to
do so."

"It did occur to me."

Selar looked at her with barely contained surprise.
"It . . . occurred to you? How could it?"

"You do not seem the type to fight, Selar, but you seem

even less the type to mother," Giniv said reasonably. "Given these two observations, it seemed reasonable to—"

"I am not giving up my child."

"You make it sound a matter of pride."

"It is, to some degree," Selar said thoughtfully.

"One would have thought it far more appropriate to be a matter of love."

Selar frowned at her. "What would you have of me, Giniv? Burgoyne has sought refuge in the old ways. I cannot deny them, nor can you. I will simply have to . . . attend to this." She let out a steady breath. "There is one fortunate aspect of this, at least. Unlike a challenge at *pon farr,* it is not a battle to the death."

"Are you certain?"

"Yes," nodded Selar. "Even in the ancient times, no advantage was seen in the death of one parent or the other . . . to say nothing of risking the death of both. The losing parent was expected to abide by the decision made by force of arms . . . and, hopefully, contribute in some way to his or her child's future. At least, that is how T'Pau explained it to us just now when we spoke privately of the matter."

"I see. So you are saying that no one has ever died in this mad endeavor?"

Selar hesitated and then said, "Not . . . precisely. There have been a few instances. Bad falls, mistimed blows to the head. It is not an exact science."

"Selar!"

"I have no choice," she said tightly. "Burgoyne is not walking away from this matter. I cannot. It is settled. The traditional weapons are being brought from the city. Ideally, within a few minutes, the matter will be settled."

"Or you will be dead."

Selar nodded. "That would settle it."

Slon cast a glance in his sister's direction, saw her in conference with Giniv, and then turned back to Burgoyne. "When I steered you to the Vulcan archives," he told Burgoyne, "it was simply to enable you to familiarize yourself with Vulcan law and tradition on the matter," he said. "I did not anticipate that you would embark on such an obscure path."

Burgoyne stretched, catlike, extending each finger of both hands individually. Each one seemed to grow an inch as s/he did so. "That is the interesting thing about me. I tend to do the unexpected."

"This is not a game, Burgoyne."

"I hope I don't appear to think it is."

"No. But you do not seem to fully appreciate the consequences of your actions. Weaponry is unpredictable, and this is not some choreographed or rehearsed bit of business. One or the other of you could die."

Burgoyne did not answer immediately. Instead, s/he was busy stretching one of hir legs back and over. There was a faint cracking of bone, a small sigh of relief from Burgoyne, and then s/he started working on the other leg. "I would venture to guess that we will both die," s/he said. "You will, too, I'd wager. Although frankly, I'm having my doubts about that T'Pau. She looks like she'll outlive us all. Instead, the planet might crack apart and she'll still be going about her business."

"I certainly hope you are having fun in this matter, Burgoyne, but I am most certainly not."

"That's no surprise. I don't think Vulcans would know how to have fun if—"

"Burgoyne." Slon's tone was sharper than he had intended. He steadied himself and said, "I am asking you to call this off."

"No."

"This is not a logical course."

"No, it's not. It is totally illogical," said Burgoyne, ceasing hir warm-ups and stretching exercise. "But I'm not the one who came up with it. Your people did. And they came up with it at a time when your entire race was, frankly, a lot more interesting. No offense."

"I could not take offense," Slon said reasonably.

"No, you couldn't, could you? Just another one of the things that makes Vulcans, occasionally, rather boring." S/he regarded Slon with open curiosity. "Do you really, truly think that Xyon—that *any* child with my blood in him—could conceivably be happy here? Here on this world where joy, love, anger—all the things that give life its meaning, its juice—are actively discouraged?"

"It is not about matters of blood. It is about matters of breeding. To that end, yes, I believe that Xyon could indeed know happiness here."

"I disagree. And do you know why? Because I think your whole damned race has completely lost touch with the notion of what happiness is. The closest you come to being happy is when you're not feeling happy . . . or unhappy . . . or anything. You strive for nothingness."

"We strive for balance."

"Same thing."

"No. It is not. You do not understand us, Burgoyne."

Burgoyne nodded. "I can easily believe that."

"You think us emotionless, passionless, heartless. We are not. There are members of religious orders on other worlds who take oaths of celibacy, as do the Deltans when they are offworld. This does not render them incapable of passions. It simply means that they contain them, bottle them. But the passions are there nevertheless, and should be neither ignored nor discounted."

"I used to believe that. But when Selar cold-bloodedly walked off with my son, I decided I was wrong. No one who had any feelings, even contained, could have done such a thing."

"You are wrong, but not in the way you think."

"What are you saying?" asked Burgoyne.

"I am saying," Slon told hir patiently, "that if you thrust Selar into a position where she must fight on her own behalf, or on behalf of her child—"

"Our child."

"—that you may get more than you bargained for. If you mistake her apparent lack of passion for actual absence of passion . . . you could get yourself killed."

"Are you saying that I should be afraid?" Burgoyne said with a smile.

The smile faded from hir face when Slon said, with absolute seriousness, "I know I am."

Selar and Burgoyne faced each other, with T'Pau in the middle. She was no longer standing upon the elevated rock, but was instead on the ground, looking at one and then the other. Even though she was shorter than either of them, she seemed to loom over them.

"Combat will begin with the *lirpax*," she intoned. "If both survive . . . it will continue with the *ahn-soon*."

"Survive?" Giniv spoke up. "This is not supposed to be a battle to the death."

"If all matters went as they were supposed to," T'Pau replied, "we would not have this situation."

The Vulcans bearing the traditional bells shook them, and the tinkling floated over the area. As they did so, two stepped forward, each bearing fearsome-looking weapons. They walked forward in matched strides, and laid them at the feet of Burgoyne and Selar, respectively.

It was a staff, about three feet long. Selar picked it up, hefted it experimentally. At one end was a large bludgeon, padded but still formidable. At the other end was a curved blade, but there was no cutting edge on it. It had been blunted, although it was still intimidating enough; one could seriously injure another if it was used with enough force.

This was the *lirpax*, a modified version of an even more devastating weapon called a *lirpa*, which Selar had only seen in museums. An actual *lirpa*'s edge was razor-sharp, and there was no padding on the bludgeon. The *lirpax* was designed to stop and stun; the *lirpa* was created to kill.

She saw that Burgoyne was hefting hirs experimentally, sweeping it through the air. S/he twirled it around a few times, swung it back and forth.

And then s/he tossed it aside. It clattered across the polished ground and rolled to a stop at the far end.

T'Pau looked at the discarded weapon, and then turned her flinty gaze on Burgoyne. "Is your *lirpax* inadequate in some way?" she inquired.

"I don't like the weight of it," said Burgoyne. S/he bowed slightly. "No offense. I know, I know . . . you can't take any offense."

"You wish another brought?"

"No. I'll be fine without it."

Selar's eyes narrowed. "What do you think you are doing, Burgoyne? What do you hope to prove? If you wish to provoke sympathy—"

"That would be an error on my part; yes, I'm quite

cognizant of that. I know what I'm doing," Burgoyne said easily. S/he was reaching down and removing hir boots.

"Is there some purpose to this?" asked T'Pau.

"Just trying to be comfortable." Hir boots removed, hir toes stretched individually in much the same way that hir fingers had. S/he took a few steps back and forth, balancing on the balls of hir feet.

"It is obvious why you are doing this," said Selar.

"Is it? Enlighten me."

"So that, when you lose, you will be able to claim that it was because you did not wield a weapon."

"I wield my body and my mind. Those are two weapons right there. Overdependence on weapons outside of those tend to make me sloppy. I can't afford sloppiness right now."

"If this is your choice, it will be honored," T'Pau said.

Selar could not quite keep the irked tone from her voice. "What of my choice," she said, "not to battle an unarmed opponent?"

"If thee chooses not to battle . . . then thee forfeits," T'Pau said.

"Then I do not really have a choice."

"No," affirmed T'Pau.

For a moment, Selar considered tossing her own weapon aside, to show that two could play at that game. Then she saw Burgoyne extend hir fingers, saw the claws on the ends of each finger, and decided that that plan of action might not be such a good one. She gripped the *lirpax* more tightly and set herself.

T'Pau stepped away, clearing herself from the area of combat. She looked stonily from one to the other, and then she barked an order for them to begin.

Selar approached cautiously, learning the wielding of

the *lirpax* as she went. The entire business had an air of unreality to it. She felt as if she were dreaming, her consciousness thrust into a primitive ancestor. She swung the *lirpax* cautiously this way and that, learning what it took to maneuver the weapon without losing control of it. If she kept it too close to her body, that would allow Burgoyne to get within striking distance. If she swung it too far, she risked overbalancing and allowing it to fly out of her grip.

Immediately she saw the cunning of Burgoyne's casually tossing the weapon aside. The *lirpax,* like the *lirpa,* was designed to thwart an attack by someone using a similar weapon. There were certain moves, defenses, thrusts, blocks and countermoves, all of which would come naturally with two identically armed combatants. But Burgoyne was empty-handed. That meant the attack could come in any form. S/he was not aided by the weapon, but neither was s/he hampered by it.

Burgoyne moved comfortably, cautiously. S/he continued to maneuver on the balls of hir feet, arms hanging loosely. S/he feinted slightly with hir upper body, but it did not even seem a serious fake. It seemed to Selar as if s/he was toying with her, and if Selar were capable of allowing herself irritation, she would have felt it now.

Selar felt hampered by her own upbringing. She was trying to see logic in Burgoyne's movements, even though they appeared random. It was likely that very randomness was the plan. Burgoyne knew that Selar sought order, logic, and sense in everything. So s/he reasoned—correctly, it seemed—that Selar would spend so much time overthinking and analyzing the situation that she would be vulnerable to attacks that bordered on the arbitrary. To a certain degree, s/he was right.

Which meant that Selar had to make sure that s/he turned out to be wrong.

At which point, Selar let out a most unVulcan, bellowing challenge. Until that moment an utter silence had fallen upon the place of judgment, and the noise was so unexpected that it momentarily froze Burgoyne in surprise. That was precisely what Selar had hoped to accomplish.

She came in fast, driving forward with the blunt-bladed end, swinging it like a scythe. Burgoyne backed up, hir feet padding noiselessly on the gleaming floor, and s/he seemed to elongate, pulling hir stomach in and just avoiding the swish of the blade. Selar swung it back and forth, like a deadly pendulum, and Burgoyne backed up all the way to the edge of the arena.

"To step beyond the borders is to lose," T'Pau informed hir from a safe distance.

Whether Burgoyne had actually intended to step out of bounds or not was unknown, and now would never be known. S/he stopped an inch shy of stepping out, and then leaped high. Selar tried to bring the weapon up and around to swing up at hir, but the weight of the bludgeon at the other end impeded such a quick shift in the way she was gripping it. Before Selar could readjust, Burgoyne was sailing over her head, and s/he swung hir right heel down and around, slamming it against the side of Selar's head. Selar went to one knee, pain exploding behind her eyes. She heard Burgoyne land, heard the quick shuffle of feet, and swung the *lirpax*'s bludgeon end around in a desperate guess as to where Burgoyne was going to be coming from.

She guessed correctly. The cudgel end struck Burgoyne squarely in the stomach, and the Hermat stumbled back, gasping, having left hirself momentarily open and not having gotten away with it. Selar struck again, this time slamming Burgoyne in the upper right shoulder with such force that Burgoyne backed away. Hir right arm was hanging limply at hir side, and s/he was desperately flexing hir fingers, trying to restore feeling.

Selar swung the *lirpax* up like a lance and charged with the bladed end, and it was only at the last moment that she realized that Burgoyne had tricked her. Burgoyne was not as injured or even as semi-helpless as she had thought. Burgoyne moved to one side with the grace of a dancer, and hir perfectly functioning right arm snared the *lirpax* just under the joint of the blade. For just a moment it was immobilized, and Burgoyne lashed out with hir left foot, taking Selar just under the chin. Selar staggered, almost losing her grip on the weapon, but then she rallied and swung it around. Burgoyne released hir hold on it, lest s/he be thrown to the ground, and Selar chanced a kick to the side. But it was a clumsy move, for Selar was anything but an experienced hand-to-hand combatant, and Burgoyne dodged it easily. Moreover, the outthrust leg left Selar completely off balance when it didn't connect, and Burgoyne snagged her ankle, braced hirself and threw. Selar landed heavily on her back, clutching the *lirpax*.

Burgoyne dropped down atop her, gripping the *lirpax* on either side, and tried to wrench it from Selar's grip. However, although she was unaccustomed to fighting, Selar still possessed the pure strength that was her heritage. Selar slammed the *lirpax* up and the staff caught Burgoyne square across the face. Burgoyne lurched, hir head swimming, and Selar struck again with the same move. Selar's hope was to get Burgoyne to release hir hold on the *lirpax*, whereupon she could shove the Hermat off herself and perhaps even pin hir to the floor.

It did not work out that way, however. With an infuriated roar, Burgoyne slammed the *lirpax* to one side, the bladed end crashing against the hard rock-ground. Crashing . . . and breaking. The sound of snapping metal reverberated through the thin air, and suddenly the *lirpax* had a jagged end where once a blunted blade had been.

The ramifications of the moment were suddenly clear to Selar, and, for just a moment, she hesitated. That was more than enough for Burgoyne, who suddenly released the *lirpax* and—with one quick move—cupped hir hands and boxed Selar's ears.

For one of such sensitive hearing, it was as if two small bombs had suddenly exploded in her head. Selar let out a most inappropriate cry, losing her grip on the *lirpax* altogether. Burgoyne yanked it out of her hands, reversed it, and suddenly the jagged and lethal blade was directly above Selar's face. One thrust downward would cleave Selar's skull in half.

"Surrender," whispered Burgoyne.

"Never," Selar shot back.

Burgoyne froze, hir eyes glittering with momentary triumph. But s/he didn't move. S/he simply stood there, as if paralyzed.

Selar took the opportunity and speared out with her foot, catching Burgoyne squarely in the knee. Burgoyne went down, the *lirpax* tumbling away from hir. Instantly both of them were on their feet, facing each other, hands poised.

"*Kroyka!*" shouted T'Pau, the air reverberating with the strength of her command. Immediately Burgoyne and Selar took several steps back from one another. Selar studied Burgoyne carefully, looking for some sign of stress due to the heat or the thinness of the Vulcan air. But Burgoyne gave no indication at all that s/he was the least bit hampered by the unforgiving climate. Hir eyes were glittering with excitement, hir lips drawn back to display hir fangs.

"Step back and rest," ordered T'Pau. They did as she commanded, and Giniv stepped in close to Selar.

"S/he had you. Dead to rights, s/he had you."

"I am most aware of that, Giniv," Selar informed her, not sounding particularly pleased to acknowledge it. "But in order to complete the victory, s/he would have had to kill me. Or at the very least, pound me into unconsciousness, which may have had the same result."

"But s/he did not."

"You sound almost disappointed."

"Do I?" Giniv looked at her with polite bemusement. "I did not intend to. I simply found hir choice not to do so . . . fascinating. If you died, after all, it would solve hir problem."

"Leaving hir to explain to our son the circumstances of his mother's demise."

"I do not think s/he was thinking that far ahead."

"It does not matter. The moment is past. I must attend to other difficulties."

"You could have killed her." There was a faint sound of scolding in Slon's tone.

"Yes," said Burgoyne. It was only now that s/he was out of Selar's immediate line of sight that s/he allowed any of the exhaustion to show on hir. S/he felt as if s/he were running uphill through mud. Hir breathing was labored, and hir eyes, lips, and throat felt completely dried out. S/he couldn't help but feel as if hir tongue was swelling up to twice its normal size. S/he leaned against a rock, steadying hirself.

"But you did not."

"Would you have preferred that I did?"

"Of course not," said Slon. "But you must understand that you are dealing with someone who is not only a mother fighting for her child, but a being of pure logic. She will do whatever is necessary to thwart you."

"You're saying she would kill me."

"We are a passive race, Burgoyne. It goes against our philosophy, our grain, to take such extreme steps. But you have thrust her into an extreme position. There is no telling what she will be motivated to do, particularly if she sees you as an implacable foe." He paused and studied Burgoyne. "Why did you not kill her? As I made clear, I did not desire that you do such a thing. But it would have, from your point of view, been the logical thing to do. So . . . why did you not?"

"Because," Burgoyne said, drawing in as deep a breath as hir aching lungs allowed hir to. "If I did that . . . then she would never love me."

Slon was about to respond to that when T'Pau called firmly, "It is time."

"Perhaps she has an important social engagement after this," Burgoyne said, casting a glance over at the Vulcan noblewoman. "I keep trying to picture her in the throes of some mating lust. I'm not having much luck."

"You may be more fortunate than you know," Slon told hir.

Burgoyne took one more breath that came out raspy in hir chest, and then s/he walked forward to the middle of the arena to face Selar. One of the Vulcan attendants was affixing a leather strap, about four feet long, to Selar's left wrist. He gestured solemnly for Burgoyne to step forward, which s/he did. He tied the other end of the strap to Burgoyne's right wrist.

"The ties that bind," commented Burgoyne. Selar said nothing, which didn't surprise Burgoyne in the least.

The other attendants were slipping a heavy glove onto their untethered hands. Burgoyne turned hir hand over to inspect the glove thoroughly. Each of the fingers of the glove was padded, and there was a sizable weight sewn into the middle. It felt like a thick, metal cylinder of some sort, and when Burgoyne curled hir fingers around it, it gave hir fist a remarkable amount of heft. It served as both an advantage and disadvantage to Burgoyne, the latter of more significance than the former. On the one hand, it increased considerably the power of hir punch. On the other hand, it covered up the claws on hir free hand, and besides . . . in terms of pure strength, Selar probably exceeded hir, so all it did was make Selar even more formidable than she already was.

"It is inconceivable to me," Selar said in a low voice, "that you have brought matters to this. As if a show of strength will make any difference, will give any indication of who is the better parent."

"I never wanted to be the better parent. Just *a* parent. But you had to shut me out."

"It was for your own good, as well as Xyon's. The child cannot grow up confused."

"We all grow up confused, Selar. All of us. The only thing you Vulcans have going for you is a racial belief that you're somehow the only ones who absolutely know what's going on. Well, guess what? In the final analysis, you're as clueless as the rest of us."

"Very warm words. I shall embrace them forever," said Selar.

T'Pau ordered them to begin once more, and they closed in combat for what would be the final time.

ROBIN

"I CAN'T BELIEVE I'M DOING THIS. I really can't," said Robin as she and Nik headed for the small, glimmering building that housed the Black Hole ride. It was night, and a cool breeze was wafting in from the distant shoreline.

"What I can't believe is that you haven't tried it yet," Nik replied. She had to admit that there were times when Nik could seem like nothing so much as an overgrown child. Which, she further had to admit, could either be annoying or charming, depending upon how one chose to look at it. She opted for the latter. "You said you went on the ride into the sun."

"I know, I know," she admitted, rolling her eyes. "I can't believe I did that, either. I suppose it's just that . . . well, when you've been in real life-and-death situations, thrusting yourself into something that simulates it, just for a quick thrill—"

"Don't knock quick thrills. They can be far more intense than slow thrills, and they've got . . . got . . ."

"Got what?"

"Half the calories?" he finished hopefully. "Let's hurry; there's no line."

She rolled her eyes, but picked up the pace at his urging, as he pulled on her arm.

They got to the entrance to the ride and stopped short. There was a sign posted outside the entrance to the simulator that read, "Under repair."

"Oh, well, that's that," said Robin cheerfully.

Nik made absolutely no attempt to hide his disappointment. "That is so very unfair!" he complained.

"Well, at least now we know why there's no line. Come on, let's—"

"Hello!" Nik called out, and then, more loudly, *"Hello! Is anyone here?"*

For a moment there was no response, and Robin was more than happy to try to depart. That was when, with a rush of air, the simulator door opened. Just to add a bit of panache to the moment, mist came billowing out. Robin was suddenly worried that the thing was on fire or something, but then a figure emerged with no particular sign of distress. She recognized him instantly.

"Scotty!" she said.

"Ach. Hello, lassie," he replied. He was holding what Robin recognized as a neuron flux detector. Then he looked slightly contrite as he said, "Ahhh, yes. Ye dinna want me t'be calling ye 'lassie.' Muh apologies."

"Why don't you want him to call you that?" asked Nik.

"It's stupid. It's . . ." She sighed. "When I was a kid, my father read me a book called *Lassie Come-Home.* It was about a collie, and the family couldn't afford to keep her, so they found her another home. But the collie kept coming back, until finally they decide to keep her. And it never made any sense to me. How could a disobedient collie be considered anything other than annoying? 'Hey! Collie! You've got a new home! Stay there! How is the word "stay" in any way unclear?' " She laughed slightly at that in a self-deprecating way. "I suppose, even then, I was getting ready for a life in Starfleet, where the chain of command is so important and you just obey orders, dammit."

"I suppose you're right." Then, in an embarrassed voice, Nik said, "Uhm . . . what's a collie?"

"A magnificent dog," said Scotty. "When I was a wee lad, ah had one for a brief time. Beautiful thing. Although ah never called it 'Lassie.' "

"Why not? I'd've thought it would be a perfect name, considering."

"Aye, if it'd been a girl. What with it being a male and all, ah thought 'Laddie' more appropriate. He ran off, though, with some little bitch. Never saw 'im again. Ah well. So." He turned his full attention to Nik. "Ye'd be Robin's young man, ah take it."

"Well, that . . . is a work-in-progress. Nik Viola," and he stuck out a hand. "We met earlier when my dad and I first arrived."

"Ah, yes. Your father," said Scotty in an oddly non-committal tone. "A most interestin' fellow. Offered me a position with your company, he did."

"How exciting! Are you going to take it?"

"Ahh, at my age, laddie, ah dinna take well to the notion of a full-time boss. Ah like settin' muh own hours and bein' not truly answerable to anyone if ah dinna feel like it." He shrugged. "Ye canna teach an old dog new tricks, I suppose."

"Could we stop talking about dogs, please?" Robin

inquired. She glanced into the simulator. "So what's wrong with it?"

"With the ride? Nothin', now. Ah have it straightened out." He looked with faint irritation back at the ride, as if there was something within that was personally offending him. "Some computer core glitches that should not have occurred. Ah dinna understand it . . . and that fact alone is enough t'have me a bit worried. Or at the very least, annoyed. I dinna like the notion that computers are pulling surprises on me in muh old age."

"Well, that's going to happen," Nik said pleasantly. "After all, that's what humans do. Surprise each other, constantly. And the closer computers come to duplicating the human brain, the more likely they're going to be to pull a few surprises on us."

"Ye say that as if it's a good thing," Scotty said dryly. "Ah'm still not certain what the attraction of this contraption is. Those miraculous holodecks they have these days would render such quaint notions as 'thrill rides' obsolete, wouldn't ye think?"

"Not necessarily, Mr. Scott," said Nik. "The bottom line is that people like things that are unique, things they can't find anywhere else. The fact that something is hard to find can be more enticing than the thing itself. People will come to Risa to do things they don't do elsewhere, and if that means riding an old-style simulator ride, well . . . they'll try it for the novelty."

"Ah suppose ye have a point," he admitted. "Well . . . it's fixed, in any event. If ye two would care to try it; ye'd have the whole thing to yourselves."

"You're sure it's fixed," Robin said uncertainly.

"What, a wee bit of genuine uncertainty, and now ye have cold feet?" Scotty said in a mocking tone.

Galvanized into action by his words, Robin stepped

into the simulator ride. Nik was right behind her, but when she turned back she saw that Scotty had stopped him and was murmuring something into his ear. She thought that rather odd, and when Nik finally did climb in next to her, she said, "What was that about?"

"I'm not sure," he admitted. "He said, 'Be good to that little girl.' Did he think I was going to hurt you or something?"

"Oh, I wouldn't worry about it," she said with a shrug. "He's got some old-style ideas. But, y'know . . . who's more entitled?"

The simulator itself was designed to be evocative of a shuttlecraft. Naturally, however, it had more seats. The view screen made it look as if the shuttle was inside a hangar bay, which was mildly disconcerting for Robin, since it made her feel—just for a moment—as if she were back on the *Excalibur.* The "shuttlebay" launch door was open and a starfield was visible through it, although when Robin studied it for a moment she realized that it didn't look right. Obviously, it was not an actual array of stars; the computer had just formed a particular grouping that some designer somewhere had decided was going to be aesthetically pleasing.

"Think we can find a seat?" he joked.

"Shouldn't be too difficult." She sat down dead center in the shuttle, providing the best view of the front screen. He sat next to her, and after a moment his hand strayed over and rested on her lap. She didn't do anything to move it off.

The voice of an unseen "pilot" said, "Shuttlecraft *Magellan* to bridge. Requesting clearance to depart to explore space anomaly."

And from the bridge came the response, "Bridge to *Magellan.* Cleared for departure."

The shuttlecraft jolted ever so slightly, which immediately annoyed Robin. Shuttles simply didn't jolt, unless the helmsman was incompetent. There was no reason for it. But then she reminded herself that the audiences for these rides were not people who had extensive familiarity with the realities of shuttles. They were for audiences who spent most of their time planetside. The extra little "push-off" would give them the additional feeling that they were being propelled into space.

Nik draped an arm around her and she nestled back into it as the "mission" played itself out. From a technical point of view, it actually made a certain degree of sense. The narrative of pilot to bridge, and the ongoing pilot's log, indicated an investigation into a spacial anomaly that might, or might not, be a black hole. The readings were too indeterminate for the long-range sensors, and a closer look was required. Naturally it was a very "dangerous" mission, since the slightest miscalculation could cause a precipitous tumble into a black hole's gravity well, and before they knew it they could be spiraling down over the hole's event horizon. In theory, that would be pretty much the end of that. This, of course, was not going to be the case. Robin knew that intellectually. Yet she found it interesting that part of her was reacting with a sense of concern. The simulation felt realistic enough to her that it almost seemed as if she really was going out on some sort of a survey mission. Once more she started thinking about the departed *Excalibur,* and it saddened her.

Nik put his other arm around her, looking at her in concern. "Are you all right?" he asked.

"I'm fine. I'm just . . . thinking about things."

"Anything involving me?"

"No. Sorry," she admitted.

"Well, then . . . we'll have to change that."

"What do you—?"

He answered her question before she could finish it as he brought his lips down upon hers. They had kissed before over the previous days, but that was as far as it had gone. She had not wanted to rush matters, and besides, there were . . . other issues for her. Other places, other people being carried around in her head, including one particular scarlet face that she could not erase from her consciousness.

But here, in the "shuttle," she felt to some degree as if she was in accustomed territory. She was starting to relax into the familiarity of it, and with the relaxation came the ability to enjoy the emotions that were bubbling within her.

His hands began to move across her as the shuttle continued its "mission," and her instinct was to resist. But the things he was doing, the places he was touching, felt so good, and the first instinct was washed away by a desperate need to surrender to what she was feeling. Robin had always been a creature of impulse, with a tendency to then second-guess herself endlessly. This time, however, she was determined to do anything other than second-guess.

Even so, as their lips parted for a moment, she whispered, "This is crazy . . ."

"What makes it crazy?"

"We'll get caught . . . the ride'll break down or something . . ."

"That doesn't make it crazy," he said softly. "Just risky. And adventurous. But . . . if you tell me to stop . . . I'll stop."

He paused for a moment, waiting for her to speak.

The recorded "pilot" suddenly called out, "We're getting some sort of readings . . . it's time to probe further."

"Well?" prompted Nik.

She smiled, and said in a voice that felt choked, "You heard the man. It's time to probe further."

Within moments the shuttle had run afoul of the black hole, but neither Robin nor Nik was paying the least bit of attention. Their clothes were scattered around the interior, their glistening skin pressed against one another, Nik still in his seat and Robin facing him. Their breath came in short gasps, their names were whispered in each other's ears, the blood was pounding through the both of them. Suddenly the "pilot" called an alarm. "Oh . . . my God! It's . . . it's right in front of us! Trying to pull away . . . full reverse thrusters!"

"No . . . no reverse . . ." Robin moaned.

"We can't resist . . ." the "pilot" shouted. "We're . . . we're going in . . . !"

The world seemed to stretch and pull around them, like taffy, and Robin felt as if all her senses were over-loading. The sensory apparatus of the simulator was more than just visual; it managed to stimulate all the sensory nerves, to convince the brain that everything around them was in the grip of some greater, over-whelming force. As it so happened, for Robin Lefler that was exactly the case. And she let herself be carried away with it, away and down into the heart of the black unknown, calling out, crying out and not caring who heard. . . .

When the door cycled open, Scotty was standing there with arms folded, watching with curiosity. Robin and Nik stumbled out, and they looked extremely disheveled. Their faces were flushed, and Robin's hair looked a bit damp. "Are ye all right?" asked the engineer.

"Fine," Robin managed to gasp out. "We're . . . we're fine."

"Are ye sure?"

"Oh, we're sure. Fine. Better than fine," said Nik, with a glance toward Robin.

"Was it operating correctly?"

"Better than correctly. It was . . ." She cleared her throat, steadied herself by leaning on Nik's arm. "It was . . . very intense."

Scotty stroked his chin thoughtfully. "Funny. Ah would've thought that a Starfleet veteran would consider it more of a routine jaunt . . . putting aside, of course, the preposterousness of getting out of a black hole. Hard t'believe that anything ye experienced in there is more stimulating than what ye've done on a bridge."

"Ohhh, you'd be amazed," said Robin. She and Nik walked away, arm in arm, leaving Scotty to shake his head and mutter something about "tourists."

Once they were away from the simulator building, Nik turned her around, took her in his arms and kissed her. She insinuated her body against his and held the kiss passionately for what seemed forever. But when they parted, he was looking at her a little oddly.

"I'm just curious," he said.

"And did I sate your curiosity?"

He laughed. "I meant . . . curious about one thing. When you were . . . and we . . . you know . . . I thought you shouted out something like, 'Oh, Cwan.' What did that mean?"

For just a moment she froze, and then—feeling a dizziness behind her eyes—she said, "Uh . . . no. No, I was saying, 'Oh, come on.' To myself. To encourage myself to relax."

"Oh." He didn't quite appear to understand. "Do you usually shout encouragement to yourself during those times?"

"Uhm . . . yes. Yes. Always. So . . . got any plans for the rest of the evening?" And she steered him quickly off into the night.

BURGOYNE

BURGOYNE TOOK A STEP BACK, which was exactly the wrong thing to do; all it did was pull the strap tight and bring Selar a step closer to hir. Selar, for her part, didn't hesitate. She snagged the strap with both hands and pulled as hard as she could. If she had been struggling with another opponent, it would have yanked him right off his feet. But Burgoyne was both barefoot and sure-footed, and despite the smoothness of the ground beneath them, didn't budge so much as an inch.

They stood there for a moment, facing each other, the strap taut between them. And then Burgoyne lunged straight toward Selar. Selar tried to sidestep, but there was simply no way she could avoid the charge. The two of them went down in a tangle of arms and legs.

Burgoyne's throat was exposed and, seizing the opportunity, Selar tried to clamp the Vulcan nerve pinch on hir. She wasn't certain if that was in the rules. If it were, then she would win; if it weren't, it would buy her time and breathing space. But the glove on her hand was too thick, and she wasn't able to get a proper grip. She tried to bring her other hand up, but Burgoyne was alert to the strategy now, and s/he kept Selar's hand at bay by the simple expedient of extending hir own arm away from hir, so that Selar's arm was likewise kept away.

Selar swung her gloved fist as fast and as hard as she could. She was slowed in speed because of the weight of the glove, but what she lacked in velocity, she made up for in impact. Burgoyne's head snapped around, and for a moment hir eyes crossed slightly. Selar struck hir again. Burgoyne rolled over onto hir back, dazed, and Selar whipped the leather strap around, trying to snag Burgoyne's throat with it.

Burgoyne got hir fingers up there fast, intercepting the strap before it could settle around hir neck. S/he ducked hir head down and out and scrambled to hir feet. Selar thought s/he was going to try to pull away, but she was mistaken. Without slowing hir forward motion in the slightest, Burgoyne rolled and yanked hard on the strap. Selar was yanked completely off her feet and hit the ground violently.

Burgoyne did not hesitate. S/he drove forward with hir powerful legs and swung hir gloved fist in an uppercut, just as Selar was trying to get to her feet. It knocked her back, and the only thing that stopped Burgoyne from putting a quick end to it was Selar's legs, coiled like two springs, which caught Burgoyne's chest and managed to shove hir back. Ironically, it was Burgoyne's own backward motion from the enforced retreat that brought Selar to her feet.

Suddenly Burgoyne started to run. Not just run:

sprint. S/he turned hir back on Selar and started dashing all over the arena. With Selar attached to her by the tether, she had absolutely no choice but to follow. She tried to bring Burgoyne up short, but Burgoyne already had a head of steam going and wouldn't be slowed. Burgoyne dashed to the edge of the arena and then started running as fast as s/he could along the perimeter, Selar being hauled haplessly behind. The Vulcan had to run just to keep up, and even then she wasn't able to, as Burgoyne outsped and outdistanced her. Soon the inevitable happened: Selar missed a step, tripped herself up, and sprawled. And still Burgoyne didn't diminish hir efforts, continuing to pull and yank Selar along behind as if wrestling with a mule. Selar tried to get up, tried to get to her feet and continue in desperate fashion after Burgoyne, but she kept falling, grunting every time her knees would bang into the ground.

It was torture to watch as Burgoyne relentlessly pulled Selar along. Slon looked away, unable to continue seeing it. Giniv flinched, and she likewise wanted to look anywhere but in front of her. Even the attendants seemed to wish that they could be elsewhere. Only T'Pau, face utterly inscrutable, never shifted her gaze from the proceedings.

And suddenly Giniv called out, "Stop! Stop this! Selar, surrender!" For that was all it would take. One or the other of them either had to be unable or unwilling to continue the battle. Once that occurred, the dispute would be settled.

T'Pau fired Giniv a stony glance, but if there was any look that was filled with more anger or disgust than T'Pau's, it was Selar's own.

"Never!" she shouted, and then she threw herself flat

on the ground, concentrating all her mass and weight as if she were a recalcitrant human child, refusing to take another step and frustrating her parents' best efforts to get her to budge even a little further.

The move caught Burgoyne slightly off guard, but only slightly. S/he skidded to a halt, and suddenly s/he backflipped through the air in a move of such astounding agility that even Slon gasped (although he quickly stifled the inappropriate sound). With a thud, Burgoyne landed squarely on Selar's back. Quickly, s/he looped the strap around Selar's throat, going for the same strategy that Selar had attempted earlier.

Selar couldn't get a breath as the strap constricted around her. She grunted, coughed, tried to pull in air, couldn't. She sensed the world starting to black out around her, and then the pull of the strap lessened ever-so-slightly on her throat. "Surrender," Burgoyne whispered in her ear. And for just a moment, Selar considered the notion.

But then an utterly inappropriate, but thoroughly understandable, fury overtook her, and Selar grunted, "Never." Before Burgoyne could reapply the suffocating tightness of hir hold, Selar—with tremendous effort—managed to turn herself over so that she was facing Burgoyne. She struck Burgoyne once, twice, three times on the side of the head with the weighted glove, and Burgoyne's eyes seemed to be swimming in hir head. That was when Selar clamped down on Burgoyne's throat with her gloved hand, and with the other hand snagged Burgoyne's exposed shoulder and applied the Vulcan nerve pinch.

Nothing happened.

Selar's eyes went wide; all the training in the world could not have prevented her from revealing the surprise she felt. The muscles beneath Burgoyne's shoulders had bunched themselves into something that almost felt like a protective grouping, pure muscle control shielding the key nerves from suffering the obstruction of blood flow that would send Burgoyne into unconsciousness. Now she had no choice. Both hands gripped Burgoyne's throat as s/he continued the pressure of the strap on Selar's own.

But Selar realized bleakly that Burgoyne had the advantage. Selar could barely stop her head from swimming, and she felt the strength ebbing from her. The fact was that Burgoyne was simply better built for fighting than Selar, was in better shape, was . . .

. . . was going to win. Burgoyne was going to win, and Selar was going to lose her child. A blackness settled upon Selar then, a feeling of utter helplessness such as she had never known.

"You win."

The words had been Burgoyne's.

Selar couldn't quite believe it. No . . . she flat out *didn't* believe it. She thought it was some sort of trick, another strategy on the Hermat's part. But no . . . Burgoyne was releasing hir hold, pushing hirself away from Selar, and there was no spring in hir movements, no grace. S/he seemed tired and worn and just as aching and frustrated as Selar herself was. When s/he had spoken, the words had been thick and raspy, but s/he repeated—apparently just to make sure there was no mistake—"You win."

"What?" Selar was surprised at the huskiness of her own voice, and she was having trouble getting a breath, thanks to the stress that had been put on her own larynx.

"I couldn't hold off the nerve pinch forever," Burgoyne said, sounding annoyed with hirself. Hir voice was unsteady, but growing in strength with every moment. "I've been dropped by it before. I developed a technique to resist it, but I can't do it indefinitely. I'd rather surrender to you than be knocked cold by you. It's more . . . dignified." She brought hir gloved hand up and pulled the glove off.

"Are you . . . sure . . . ?"

Burgoyne looked at her with undisguised astonishment. "You'd rather we kept fighting?"

"No."

"Then that's it," said Burgoyne.

"Release them," T'Pau ordered.

But Burgoyne did not wait. Instead, hir claws popped out and s/he sliced through the strap with ease. S/he got to hir legs unsteadily and then, without a word, turned and started to walk away.

Selar, much to her own amazement, called after hir. "Burgoyne . . . if you . . . if you wish to visit Xyon from time to time, you can—"

Burgoyne did not turn back to look at her. S/he did stop walking, though, and squared hir back. "Do not say that," s/he said. "Do not say such things . . . for they are not true. Because you will be there, and you will not want me there, and that will be clear to our child. I would rather not be in his life at all, than to let him grow up watching two parents who clearly do not like each other. Tell him . . . tell him his father is dead. That is preferable."

"Burgoyne, such extreme measures are not—"

"Then tell him that I simply abandoned you both, so that he can hate me with the same enthusiasm that his mother does."

"Burgoyne," she said softly, "I do not hate you."

But s/he did not respond. Instead, s/he simply walked away, leaving only a field of Vulcans behind hir.

* * *

This time Burgoyne was not the least bit surprised, as s/he sat in the bar, to find that Slon was by hir side. He eased himself into the chair next to hir, and they simply sat there for a time, both staring forward and at nothing. The bartender, by this point, knew better than to argue with anything that Burgoyne said, and simply continued to bring hir scotch, neat.

"I know she did not win," Slon said finally.

Burgoyne did not reply immediately. Indeed, s/he took so long that for a moment Slon wondered if s/he had heard him. But before he could repeat the comment, Burgoyne abruptly said, "Perhaps. But, you see . . . I knew she could not lose."

"What do you mean?"

"I think . . ." S/he licked hir lips, trying to find the right words, "I think . . . I was able to handle a loss better than she. Because, without the child . . . I'll still have my love for her. And him. But Selar, without the child, would have nothing. No concrete result of her biological need to perpetuate her species. No pleasant memories of love, since she would deny herself those. No . . . nothing. Why do that to her? To anyone?"

"You love her?" Slon was clearly having trouble understanding it. "So that is why you let her win?"

"There was no winning in this business. That's what it took me a while to understand. For all I know, that's what Vulcan parents learned eons ago when the idiotic tradition was first begun." S/he shook hir head. "I had thought it just foolishness. Now I'm beginning to wonder whether there wasn't some reason to the rhyme after all."

"But do you still feel that Selar will not be a good mother? If so . . . how can you leave Xyon with her?"

"I don't know that I ever felt she would be a *bad* mother. Just that I would be better for him. I still would have been happy if both of us worked together. I felt we had enough of a relationship that we could build upon. . . ." Hir voice trailed off. This time, without even looking at the bartender, s/he tapped the bar in front of hir. The bartender, without hesitation, produced another glass of scotch and almost put it in Burgoyne's hand. "You know what? Dwelling on it is pointless. Selar won. I . . . did not. I leave this business, and the future of our son, to her. I can only hope that everything will turn out for the best. And as soon as I know what the best is, I will be sure to let you know."

"Where will you go? What will you do? Will you return to your homeworld?"

"My homeworld?" At that, Burgoyne laughed unpleasantly. "You don't seem to understand, Slon. Odd, considering your business is diplomacy. I went to any and all lengths possible in order to secure support for my claims. I got none. Instead, all I managed to do was get myself perceived as . . . an oddity. Even a freak, if I am to use the less generous phrasing. My people do not understand any sort of drive to take care of young ones. Hermat child care is done very systematically, and not for a very long duration."

"Why not?"

Burgoyne waved off any further inquiries. "It doesn't matter. There's no need to go into it, really. The point is . . . I have managed to make myself somewhat notorious, even infamous, as far as my society is concerned. But, of course, I've no real place in Vulcan society. I would not say anything as melodramatic as that I'm a Hermat without a world . . . but there is nowhere that I am truly comfortable. At least, not for now. We Hermats have a notoriously short attention span, however. Before you know it, I will be accepted without comment among my people. They will have no awareness, or very little care, as to why I was something of an outcast for a time. In the interim, I have acquired a most pleasant domicile on Earth. I had originally thought that it would be where Selar, Xyon, and I would reside. It turns out I was wrong. Very well: It isn't the first thing I've been wrong about in my life, and will likely not be the last. It's a bit roomy for one person, but I'm sure I'll make myself comfortable. And after a time, I'll ship out on another starship . . . and try to put all this far behind me."

"And you really want Selar to tell Xyon that you died? Or abandoned them?"

"Slon . . . believe it or not, you're not making this easier on me. What I would like to do, ideally, is just accept what happened and move on. I cannot do that if I dwell endlessly on those things that I have no involvement with or control over. Do you understand?"

"I think I do," nodded Slon.

"Really?"

"No."

Burgoyne laughed at that, although there was not a good deal of humor in it. "You know what? I don't think I do, either."

At that moment, a firm hand clamped down on Burgoyne's shoulder. Burgoyne turned and looked at the owner of the hand. It was a tall, muscular Vulcan, and there were several others of similar build accompanying him. They were wearing uniforms that were not familiar to Burgoyne, but, nevertheless, s/he immediately comprehended the nature of these newcomers. "The authorities?" s/he inquired of Slon, speaking out of the side of hir mouth.

"That is correct," said Slon, clearly having no more

idea why they might be there than did Burgoyne. "Is there a problem?"

"You are Burgoyne 172?" rumbled the Vulcan who had his hand on Burgoyne's shoulder.

"Just missed hir. I'm Burgoyne 181. If you hurry, you can still catch hir."

The Vulcans exchanged looks with one another. At this point, the eyes of everyone in the bar were upon them.

"Ah. Right. Humor-impaired. Very well, then," Burgoyne said slowly, as if addressing a child, "Yes. I. Am. Burgoyne. 172. Now, would you care to tell me what the problem is? I have to warn you, I'm not in the best of moods."

"You will come with me."

"Sorry. You're not my type, and I had a glorious evening of self-pity lined up. I really don't know that I can get out of it."

"You will come with us," amended the Vulcan. He had no more sense of humor than he'd had moments before; he was just listening to Burgoyne less.

"And why am I going to do that?"

"You are to be questioned in connection with the disappearance of the child Xyon."

The languid air that Burgoyne had been effecting immediately evaporated. S/he sat straight up, brushing the Vulcan's hand from hir shoulder. "Xyon? Disappeared?"

"That is correct."

"Where's Selar?" s/he demanded tersely.

"At her domicile. We are to take you to our headquarters—"

"The hell you are," shot back Burgoyne. "You're taking me to her. Now. That is where we're going, and any other destination isn't being tolerated."

"You are not in a position to make demands."

Burgoyne's lips drew back, hir fangs fully bared. "The only position you're going to be in is prone if you don't get out of my way."

Immediately Slon was between them, and his voice was calm and unruffled. "Gentlemen," he said coolly, "I am the brother of Selar. In her absence, I feel qualified to speak for her and in the interests of my nephew. If your intent is to speak to Burgoyne, it can be accomplished in any venue. Certainly logic dictates that it be done at the venue that will cause the least amount of difficulty to get to. Your headquarters, while no doubt comfortable, appear to be problematic. The residence of the mother is where Burgoyne desires to go. If, for the sake of argument, we grant that Burgoyne is, in fact, not responsible for the child's disappearance, then forcing hir to go somewhere other than the scene of the crime—when Burgoyne's role in this is merely that of victim and concerned parent—is certainly most illogical."

The Vulcan guardsmen looked at one another, then the one who was clearly the higher-ranking of the two simply nodded. "Very well," said the first one. "We shall proceed along the lines of your suggestion. We shall go to the residence of the mother."

"Good," Burgoyne said.

"After that, we will proceed to our headquarters. For further interrogation."

"And here I thought this was going to be a dull evening," said Burgoyne mirthlessly.

MORGAN & ROBIN

"EXTENDING OUR STAY?"

"That's right, Robin," said Morgan matter-of-factly as she tidied up around the room. "I've talked to the resort management about extending our stay. Why? Does that present a problem?"

Robin sat on the edge of the bed, looking a bit perplexed. "Not . . . a problem exactly. I just wasn't expecting it, that's all. And, you know, you could have discussed it with me first. I mean, I might have some thoughts on the matter."

"I didn't think it was necessary, because I didn't think you'd object too strenuously." She walked over to her daughter and cupped her chin. There was a knowing smile on her face. "After all, you and Nik have . . . hit it off."

"I don't know what you're talking about, Mother," Robin said with absolutely no conviction in her voice whatsoever. And then, in spite of herself, she giggled. She actually giggled. She couldn't believe that the sound was coming out of her mouth. As if trying to force it back down her throat, she put her hand up to cover her lips.

"Ohhh, yes. Yes, I can see that you don't."

"Mother! You're embarrassing me."

"You're letting yourself be embarrassed, Robin. It's not exactly the same thing." She ruffled her daughter's hair affectionately. "Was it nice?"

"Yes, it *was* nice, if you must know. And . . . thank you."

"What are you thanking me for?"

Her hands were folded neatly in her lap, and she kept squeezing her fingers together as she spoke. "Because," she said very softly, in a self-conscious manner, "I wouldn't have had the nerve to ask about extending the stay just so I could spend more time with Nik."

Morgan crouched opposite her, her eyes alight with amusement. But what she said then surprised Robin. "I hope you're not thinking of this continuing past our leaving Risa."

"What? Well, I . . . I hadn't thought about it one way or the other, really," Robin lied, badly. Trying to cover for the uncertainty in her voice, she continued, "And even if I were, for some reason . . . what would be so wrong with that?"

"Robin," sighed Morgan, "let me give you some remarkably helpful advice: The sort of relationship one experiences in these types of situations isn't necessarily, well . . . real. It's very intense, and often very passionate, but once you leave the site of the encounter, well . . . passions tend to cool. Quickly. Very quickly, sometimes. Take it from someone who's made that mistake on one or two or ten occasions."

"Ten?"

"Well, that may be a slight exaggeration, but not by much. I would love to tell you that one learns quickly from experience. That's not always the case, unfortunately. Sometimes you find yourself making the same mistake repeatedly just because you've convinced yourself that, this time, it couldn't possibly go as wrong as it did last time. People can be very strange, Robin."

"So I've noticed. So . . . are you sure that Nik and Rafe are staying longer?"

"Yes, definitely. Rafe said something about taking care of some business and exploring some options on Risa. I can't pretend to know what he was talking about but . . . as you know . . . one should never question why good fortune has come to you, because . . ." She paused expectantly.

"Good fortune will start questioning why it came, too," Robin said by rote. "You said that to me when I was so little. It's amazing what people remember."

"So," Morgan leaned forward, "tell me the details."

"Mother!"

"I want details," Morgan said with an impish grin. "Come on. When you were an infant, I'd stand there looking into your crib and think, 'I can't wait until she's all grown up so I can re-experience vicariously the thrill of the early days of romantic exploits."

"That's what you thought about when I was in my crib?" said Robin incredulously.

"Absolutely," Morgan deadpanned. "Why? What else could there possibly be to think about?"

SELAR

SELAR STOOD AT THE CRIB SIDE, staring into the empty bed as if she could somehow force Xyon to return through sheer mental effort.

Her mind whirled back to the moments after she had returned from the judgment. Every muscle in her body had ached, and she was walking with a slight limp. She kept telling herself that all her physical distress was temporary and could be easily dealt with via simple relaxation techniques. When she limped in the door, T'Fil, the nurse, was seated in a chair and cradling Xyon in her arms. She took one look at Selar's banged-up condition, immediately returned Xyon to his bed, and set about cleaning up Selar's wounds and bruises. Selar offered a token protest, but otherwise let T'Fil go about her business.

When she was done, she said, "If you desire that I stay the night . . ."

But Selar shook her head. "That will not be necessary. I appreciate your efforts in this matter. I could have tended to it myself, of course, but . . . having you tend to it was beneficial."

T'Fil inclined her head slightly in acknowledgment and then let herself out. Selar leaned her head back on the chair and wondered distantly what it would be like to be able to be genuinely happy about the outcome. Or, indeed, genuinely happy about anything. It was somewhat ironic. Here she had won . . . and yet, in some rudimentary way, she found herself envious of Burgoyne.

She drifted off, and in her slumber, she heard some sort of distant thumping noise. She did not react to it immediately, so exhausted was she. Despite all that she knew about dealing with stress, even Selar had to admit that the pressure of the last weeks had been formidable. Now that it was over, she wanted nothing but to escape into a total lack of sensation.

But then slowly, excruciatingly slowly, the fact that there was a noise in the other room filtered from her subconscious to her conscious mind, and Selar roused herself to wakefulness. Despite the typical Vulcan down-to-the-second awareness of time, she was uncertain just how much time had passed between the sound and her reaction. She got to her feet and headed into Xyon's room. Frighteningly, she somehow had a feeling of what she would see even before she walked in.

The crib was empty. There was no sign of Xyon anywhere.

A human mother might have called out Xyon's name . . . a futile display since, of course, Xyon could not possibly respond. Moreover, it would simply fill the void that his absence had created, for it was painfully obvious to Selar that someone had absconded with the child.

She went to the window, found it open. There did not seem to be any sign of forced entry; truthfully, she could not be certain whether the window had simply been left open, or someone had shoved their way in.

No. Not just someone. Instinctively, immediately, she knew. "Burgoyne," she whispered. She didn't want to believe it, but it made an awful, terrible sense. Burgoyne had not been able to deal with the loss of Xyon. Whether it was out of love for the child, or a sense of humiliation that Selar had defeated hir, Selar couldn't know. And to think that, in some small way, Selar had believed that Burgoyne had deliberately lost the battle out of a feeling of love, misplaced or otherwise. Obviously, Selar had been wrong. Burgoyne loved nothing but Burgoyne, that much was now quite clear.

She immediately informed the authorities. Blocks were put up at the local spaceports. That could not provide a one hundred percent guard against Burgoyne slipping away with the child on a private vessel, but it would certainly prevent any departure on a commercial vessel. A search was also conducted throughout the city, although Selar didn't really have any genuine hope that it would yield anything. Burgoyne was simply too crafty, too capable. S/he had probably gone to ground somewhere, holding Xyon tightly to hir breast and laughing over how s/he had managed to pull a fast one on Selar. . . .

The front chime sounded at the door. With effort, Selar forced herself to turn away from the crib and walked on unsteady feet to the door. "Yes," she called.

The door slid open and her eyes widened as she saw Burgoyne standing there, looking nothing but concerned. There were guardsmen on either side of hir, and standing just behind Burgoyne was Slon. *Was he part of this somehow?* The question slammed through her mind, but she couldn't believe it was possible. Her own brother aiding in the kidnapping of her child? She had never been close to him, but she could not believe that even he would stoop to such a thing.

She was rather surprised, however, when the first words out of Burgoyne's mouth were, "Where is he?"

She blinked in confusion, but then she understood. "Of course. You would naturally take an air of aggressive concern in order to obscure your own guilt."

"My guilt? You're crazy." Burgoyne wasn't even looking at her anymore. Instead s/he was walking around the main room, hir nostrils flaring. "I've nothing to feel guilty over."

Selar moved alongside him, limping slightly. "That is another natural reaction for you to have. You do not feel guilty because you believe that you were perfectly entitled to take—"

"I took no one," Burgoyne said flatly. S/he still wasn't even bothering to look in Selar's direction. It was as if she didn't exist. "And frankly, the thought that you believe I would is a bit disheartening."

"How would you know? You have no heart."

That got Burgoyne to look directly at her. A long moment passed, and in that moment Selar saw a world of hurt pass through Burgoyne's eyes. But when Burgoyne spoke next, it was in a voice that was surprisingly soft and sad.

"Of all the lousy things you've ever said to me . . . that was the worst." Then s/he went back to what s/he was doing.

Now Slon stepped forward. "Selar . . . tell us what happened. Exactly. The authorities here told us, but I would rather hear it from you."

In quick, broad strokes, never taking her eyes off Burgoyne and hir curious theatrics, Selar told her brother precisely what had happened. He listened to every word, his face a mask of concentration. "There is another possibility, you know," he said as he stepped out of Burgoyne's way. The guardsmen were watching hir carefully, clearly not certain what s/he was doing, but not wishing to interfere.

"And what would that possibility be?" Selar said with barely concealed sarcasm.

"T'Fil. The nurse."

"That is absurd."

"No. It is not absurd. It is, in fact, logical."

"It is not logical—"

"Consider," said Slon, stroking his chin and speaking in a slightly singsong tone, as if he were a detective analyzing a case. "It is possible that she is not in her right mind. That some chemical imbalance, perhaps, is causing her to act in an unprecedented or peculiar fashion."

"Slon," Selar began, with just the slightest hint of impatience.

But Slon was not listening. He was far too caught up in the possibilities that he was putting forward. "You may not wish to acknowledge it, Selar, but it does make eminent sense. Consider the following potential chain of events: T'Fil has desired for some time to abscond with Xyon. When you return from the judgment, tired, injured . . . she sees her opportunity."

"This is foolishness."

"No, Selar," Slon said, sounding a touch offended. "It is logic. Deduction. While ministering to your needs, she finds a way to put you to sleep. A drug, perhaps, or even a subtle application of the mind meld . . . possible if you were not prepared for it. She then goes back into Xyon's room, removes the child, and departs the house. She does this secure in the knowledge that if anyone is to be a suspect, it shall be Burgoyne. Why not, after all? It is Burgoyne who has fought you, challenged you. Burgoyne is the off-worlder. Burgoyne is the 'frustrated father.' Burgoyne . . ."

"Suggests that you keep your voice down, or you're going to wake Xyon," said Burgoyne. S/he had seated hirself on the couch and was looking rather pleased with hirself.

"What are you talking about?" demanded Selar, but there was a slight sign of hope on her face.

For response, Burgoyne simply pointed downward. S/he said nothing further, but instead folded hir arms and sat there, sphinxlike. Selar hesitated a moment, then got down on her hands and knees and looked where s/he was pointing.

Xyon was under the couch. His eyes were closed, and he was sleeping peacefully.

"Xyon!" Selar was unable to contain her reflex response, and Xyon's eyes fluttered open. He blinked several times and then focused on Selar's face. He smiled amiably, utterly oblivious to the consternation (albeit controlled consternation) that he had caused. Selar reached under the couch, and he batted playfully at her hands as she scooped him out and up, balancing him on her leg.

"Of course," said Slon, unperturbed, "another possibility is that he was under the couch."

"How did he . . . ?" She looked at Burgoyne in confusion. "How did you . . . ?"

"I scented him. I'm not on Ensign Janos's level when it comes to olfactory skill, but I have my moments. Particularly when I'm searching out my own flesh and blood." Burgoyne smiled at Xyon and reached out to touch him under the chin. Selar automatically started to move Xyon back so that Burgoyne couldn't touch him, but then clearly thought better of it and kept him close. Xyon made a soft, cooing sound as Burgoyne's finger stroked the soft underside of his chin.

"Gentlemen," Slon said briskly, picking up the momentary slack, "I believe your services will not be required here any more this evening."

The Vulcan guardsmen nodded slightly, and one of them said, "Doctor . . . the next time you report a child as missing, you may wish to check under all available furniture to make certain he is not merely hiding."

"I will see to that," Selar assured them, still looking with polite confusion at her child. The guardsmen then let themselves out.

"He is developing quite well," Slon observed. "I have never seen a Vulcan child of such tender age balance his head—indeed, his entire body—with such confidence." He turned to Burgoyne and said, "We are somewhat long-lived as a race, and tend to develop far more slowly in the early years."

If Burgoyne heard what Slon said, s/he didn't indicate it. Instead, s/he was looking at Selar. "Do you think it possible that perhaps—just perhaps—you owe me an apology?"

Selar took a deep breath. "I apologize, Burgoyne, for believing that you had anything to do with the disappearance of Xyon."

"Accepted."

"However—"

Burgoyne looked to Slon with resignation. "There had to be a 'however,' of course. She could not leave well enough alone."

"However," Selar continued, "I do not see how it is possible that Xyon got under the couch. Is it possible that someone was attempting to take him away, but stopped short when I began to awaken and simply tossed him under there for—"

"I believe I have a simpler explanation," Burgoyne commented. "Put him down."

"Down?"

"On the floor."

"Burgoyne," Selar said impatiently, "I am not about to—"

"Selar, please, for once in your life . . . just do something because I ask you to. Not because it's logical, not because of any reason other than that I'm asking you to take me at my word. Please."

Selar, shaking her head, placed Xyon on the ground. It was, she knew, a pointless endeavor. The child was far too young—far, far too young—to do anything other than simply lie there. Within several months, he might be capable of turning himself over, but that was some time down the line. . . .

Xyon was lying on his back, and stayed that way for exactly two seconds. And then he rolled over.

"Fascinating," said Slon.

For her part, Selar could not believe it. This was something that Vulcan children simply could not do. But if that was surprising, what happened next was positively stupefying. Xyon drew his back legs up into a crouch and brought his tiny fingers down in front of him. With a slight grunt, he managed to push himself back so that his hands and feet were giving him equal balance. The posture was vaguely simian . . . or, Selar realized, quite akin to Burgoyne when s/he was moving at high speed, using all four of hir limbs.

"This is not possible," Selar said with such certainty that it seemed likely Xyon might actually vanish into thin air.

Xyon stubbornly refused to acknowledge the preposterousness of what he was doing. Instead, he added to his impossible feats by moving forward quite quickly. There was some awkwardness to the movement, but there was no questioning his capacity for locomotion. He cruised around the apartment, pulling himself up every so often to get a better look at something that might have caught his fancy. As this happened, Selar simply watched as if she was viewing the activities of some alien species that was of no relation to her at all.

"Not . . . possible," she managed to get out.

Amazingly, it was Burgoyne who sounded eminently calm. "It is indeed possible," s/he said. "You see, Hermats don't live quite as long as Vulcans. But more than that—our biology and developmental processes are different from yours."

"Different, yes, I can accept that, but this . . . ?" She reached for Xyon and picked him up, but this time he actually squirmed in her grasp. She quickly put him down and watched as Xyon pulled himself up with more speed and confidence than he had before and started to clamber around the living room once more.

"Why shouldn't this be the case?" asked Burgoyne. "On earth, newborn horses stand within minutes of birth. Baby Hortas are capable of feeding themselves in no time at—"

"This is not a Horta, not a horse. This is a Vulcan child, and Vulcan children simply do not . . ." Her voice trailed off as she moved quickly to stop Xyon from scaling a cabinet. He emitted a petulant wail and, unable to deal with what she was seeing, she brought

Xyon into his room and placed him in the crib. He howled indignantly. Selar ignored him as she walked back into the living room. Burgoyne was perched on the edge of a chair, and Slon was near the door. "Vulcan children," she said, picking up from where she'd left off, "simply do not do this sort of thing."

"This is not merely a Vulcan child. This is—"

"I know what he is, Burgoyne," she said with an annoying bit of sharpness in her voice. "That has been driven home to me very thoroughly by the—"

Slon cleared his throat loudly and pointed. They looked where he indicated, although Selar had a sick feeling that she knew what she was going to see. She was right. Xyon had clambered out of his crib and was joyfully bounding across the floor. It was hard to believe that, only minutes ago, he had been feeling his way with his new method of locomotion. Now he was moving with utter confidence.

Without a word, Selar walked back to him, picked him up, and carted him back into his bedroom. This time she did not come out quite as quickly as before. When she did re-emerge, her arms were empty. "He is asleep," she said flatly, closing the door behind her.

"You made sure of that, did you?" Slon asked.

"Yes."

"Made sure?" Burgoyne didn't quite understand.

"Careful and subtle use of the mind meld," Selar told hir. "Nothing intrusive." She sat down on the chair, her hands neatly placed in her lap. "Perhaps, Burgoyne, it would now be best if you left."

"And what about Xyon? Are you ready to handle a child with his peculiar . . . attributes?"

"Nothing has changed. He is a Vulcan, and will be raised as a Vulcan."

"Nothing has changed? Nothing has *changed?*" Burgoyne laughed at that. "You reported a child missing after he hauled himself out of his bed, months before a Vulcan child should be capable of such an action. And you think that nothing has changed? That, Selar . . . is illogical." With that, Burgoyne walked out, still laughing softly and shaking hir head.

Slon remained behind a moment, standing at a respectful distance. "Are you all right, Selar?"

"Of course I am, Slon. The dispute is settled. I have my child. He is not missing. Nothing else need be said."

"Then . . . I shall say good evening to you."

"Good evening, Slon."

Slon walked out, leaving Selar to the quiet of her solitude. She sat there, trying to sort through her conflicting thoughts. At that moment, she heard a faint but persistent scratching at the door of Xyon's room.

She closed her eyes and said firmly, "Nothing has changed." But she wasn't at all sure who she was saying it for, because there was no one there to believe her . . . including herself.

SCOTTY

THE COMPUTER CORE was truly a magnificent achievement, and even though he had not installed it, Scotty had done so much work on it that he'd come to take something of a proprietary interest in it.

Stretching several stories high, the core was what kept not only all aspects of El Dorado running, but also a number of other, smaller resorts. Everything, from the hotel climate to the wave generator, had its instructions filtered through this one place. So the fact that everything was not as it should be was extremely irritating to Montgomery Scott. It was, naturally, also of concern to Theodore Quincy, who was following Scotty around as he took readings, making small talk and in most ways—if not all—serving as far more of a distraction to Scott than a help.

"It's good to know it wasn't just my imagination," Quincy was saying. "A glitch here, a glitch there. Indi-

vidually, they seem like nothing. But when you com-
bine them, well . . . that's when the trouble sets in.
That's when you get a true overview of just how things
are."

"Aye, Mr. Quincy, ah know." He was studying the
readings off one of the check stations.

Quincy's voice echoed slightly in the cavernous
room. "May I ask why you felt the need to come down
here? After all, we have any number of access ports in
the resort itself."

"Aye, ye do. But ah happen to be a hands-on sort of
fella. Mr. Quincy."

"Thomas, please, Scotty. I don't know how many
times I've asked you to call me Thomas."

"Ah'd wager it's quite a few. Very well—
Thomas . . ."

"Yes, Scotty?" Quincy replied genially.

"Would ye get the hell outta muh way?"

"Oh. Sorry." He stepped aside and let Scotty get to
another section of the core. Scotty rechecked the readings and then started climbing up the utility ladder built
into the side. "So, Scotty . . . how goes matters with
that rather charming woman? What was her name?
Morgan Primus?"

"Aye, Morgan is her name. As for how things are
goin'," He shrugged. "Ah canna tell ye. Ye can ask
her . . . and her beau, Mr. Viola."

"Now, now, Scotty," he said as Scott walked around
one of the feeder cores and he followed him. "If you're
really interested in her, you shouldn't just step aside.
You should fight for her."

"Fight?"

"Yes."

"For a woman?"

"Exactly."

Scotty stared at Quincy as if he'd just grown another eye. "What would be the purpose of that? There's always women. Lots of women. One is very much like another."

"That's where I think you're wrong, Scotty."

"Do ye? Do ye think I'm wrong?"

"Definitely."

Scotty looked stricken for a moment. "Oh, no! That would bother th'hell out of me . . . if ah cared." Then he went on about his business.

But Quincy seemed disinclined to let it drop. "You can't fool me, Scotty. The fact is, the only female you ever felt comfortable with was the *Enterprise*. And you never had to fight for her. In fact, when you had to stand there and watch her be blown up, years ago, that sent you into a tailspin of mourning that you've never quite recovered from."

Scotty snorted derisively. "And where did ye come up with that harebrained idea?"

"James Kirk's autobiography."

That gave him pause. "Oh," he said softly, and was silent for a few moments. He even stopped consulting the readings on the computer core, which simply thrummed away on its own for a time.

Scott moved up a rampway that led to the upper levels of the core. Quincy followed, but made the severe mistake of looking down. He gripped the railing unsteadily. Scotty glanced where Quincy was looking and, truthfully, couldn't entirely blame him for his momentary swirl of vertigo. The area where they were standing was indeed quite high, and the only thing that stopped them from plummeting down into what a more fanciful individual might have considered a bottomless drop was the rampways and catwalks upon which they were standing.

Scotty walked over to him, leaned over and let go a large wad of spit. Then he watched with interest as it disappeared into the bowels of the computer core. "Quite a drop," he said cheerfully. "Perhaps ye shouldn'ta come along, ye think?"

"I am the manager of the El Dorado," Quincy told him, trying to stitch together his flagging resolve. "I am responsible for all aspects of the operation . . . even the somewhat dizzying ones. I just . . . well, I've never actually stood all the way up here, and it can be . . ."

"Nauseating? Vomitous?" Scotty suggested. "Vertiginous, maybe?"

"Scotty . . . please . . . you're not helping," said Quincy, and he sounded so pathetic that Scott couldn't help but ease up on him. "I just . . . wasn't prepared."

"Ah, well, that's the difference between us. Ah prepare for everything."

"I see. So . . . how long do you think it's going to take you to find the computer problems and fix them?"

"A week," Scotty told him.

"A week! Can't you get it done any sooner than that?"

"I'll try," Scotty sighed heavily. "But ye know . . . it's not as if ah have a reputation as a miracle worker."

"You do! You absolutely do!"

"Ach! Ah do? Well, then," Scotty said lightly, "ah will have to do all ah can t'live up to that reputation, won't I?"

He started tracing the logic circuits, and was beginning to feel a slow crawl of apprehension, even as he gave no hint from his manner that anything was amiss. He was becoming convinced, however, that the computer problems were not simply random occurrences. Something, or someone, was not only causing them, but also making it difficult for Scotty to track exactly what was happening. His frustration level was beginning to rise; he felt as if he were battling some invisible enemy.

To try to calm himself down, so as not to fly off the handle while he worked, he started talking to Quincy, although he didn't actually look in Quincy's direction. "Ah suppose," he said slowly, "that there's something to be said for what ye said before. Ah mean, what Captain Kirk said. Ah have to admit . . . when ah saw 'er blown outta the sky, well . . . Ah knew the captain did what he had to do, but that didn't make it any easier. When ah watched her go, it was like somethin' inside me died along with her." He continued monitoring the neuronet impulses and noted, with interest, that the polarity of the neutron flow had reversed. "And now ah've wound up here, dislocated from muh time, dislocated from . . . muhself. It figured that Morgan would be th' first woman t'stir me back to what ah was, because she looks like . . . I dinna ken how to say it . . . a figure from the past. Makes me almost wonder whether what ah feel for her is genuine . . . or just a ghost. Then again, sometimes ah wonder whether ah'm a ghost as well. Ye know what ah mean, don't ye, Mr. Quincy. Hope ah'm not bending your ear too much.".

Then he stopped. Checked the readings he was seeing. Double-checked them and couldn't believe it.

"Mr. Quincy," he said, his voice trembling with a combination of confusion and anger, "ah find it hard to believe . . . but ah believe you're bein' robbed blind. Someone has been—"

He turned to face Quincy just in time to see the man tumble over the railing. Scotty gasped and lunged for Quincy, but it was too late; the El Dorado manager was gone, tumbling end over end toward the bottom of the computer shaft, hundreds of feet below. Even as he fell, the full truth dawned on Scotty, an instant mental flash photo developing: Quincy's head had been at an odd angle, indicating that his neck had been broken before he fell. Someone had silently, effortlessly, come up behind him and snapped his neck without Scotty noticing, or Quincy managing to get out so much as a single word of warning.

And even as Scotty's mind processed that information, he came to the inevitable conclusion that the exact same thing was about to happen to him.

From the corner of his eye, he caught the movement of someone who seemed to be there. Once upon a time, young Montgomery Scott would have stood his ground, relied on his fists and determination, and been reasonably certain that if he went down, he would go down fighting. But that was many decades ago, and even if he had been in his right time, he was still beyond his time for such things.

There is a moment when each man knows that it is his time to go—and let it be on his own terms. This was such a moment for Montgomery Scott.

He did not hesitate. With a movement that would have been admirable in a far younger man, Scotty vaulted the railing, hurling himself into space. Within seconds he had vanished into the dimness of the shaft, nothing but a huge drop yawning beneath him.

His assailant—or at the very least, the one who would have assailed him had he remained where he was—stood there for a long moment, staring down into the pit and seeing nothing of the man who had thrown himself into it. "Die fighting or die not fighting. Same thing either way, I suppose," he said to the emptiness around him. "At least you don't have to wonder anymore, Mr. Scott. The matter is settled: You're officially a ghost."

SELAR

IT WAS THE TAUNTING that attracted Selar's attention. It was, after all, a most unusual noise to hear on Vulcan. Indeed, the sound of it made Selar realize just how quiet life in the city was. That was . . . unusual. She had grown so accustomed to a fairly steady chatter of voices back on the *Excalibur,* wherever she went. There were people laughing, talking, voices raised in argument or anger, happiness or sadness, a constant stream of background noise. On those occasions when she would go to cities on far-off worlds, she would find the same thing. By contrast, Vulcan seemed to exist under a muffling blanket.

She stopped in her path and turned her attention to the source of the sounds. Other Vulcans passing her on the street cast brief and vaguely impatient glances in the direction of the taunting voices, but otherwise ignored them. Selar, on the other hand, felt the need to see what was happening. The noises were coming from just around the corner up ahead. She rounded it quickly, and then stopped.

She saw a small group of Vulcan schoolboys. Whoever was their teacher when it came to logic, decorum, and deportment was apparently not doing their job, for these boys were acting in a most inappropriate manner. They had formed a loose circle, and were calling out insults. "Freak," they were saying, and "Misfit," and "Thin blood." There was someone in the middle of the circle, another boy, and he was trying to push past them. Because there were so many of them and only one of him, they were easily thwarting his attempts to get past them. He was becoming more and more agitated, running into them with full force. But he was not making any headway. They would shove him back, shove him down, and continue to shout out their contempt for him.

What could this child have done? Selar wondered, even as she moved forward quickly. She drew near them and called out, sharply but firmly, "What do you think you are doing?"

This drew the boys up short. They looked up at her, and one of them said in utter deadpan, "We are speaking with one of our classmates."

"This is not speaking. It is torture. Furthermore, it is unworthy of being called Vulcan."

"So is he," said the boy, pointing in an accusatory fashion.

She looked where he was pointing. In the midst of the group was one boy, the one whom they had been apparently berating. For just a moment his face had been twisted in raw anger and humiliation. But then, when he saw that an adult was looking at him, he drew himself up straight. It was as if a shroud passed over him. The only indication of the turmoil within him was his trembling lower lip. Apparently aware of how it was betraying him, he sank his teeth into it to still it.

At first glance there was no hint as to why the others would be picking on him the way they had been. But then Selar was able to pick out a few telltale signs . . . the shape of the brow, the fainter complexion. The child was a half-breed . . . part Vulcan and, unless she was mistaken, part human.

"This is a private discussion, ma'am," he said stiffly.

"This is not a discussion. This is a beating. You should all of you . . . *all* of you . . . be ashamed of yourselves. The reason for it is not relevant."

"It is relevant," one of the boys said reasonably. How absurd, she thought, for a bully to be explaining the logic of his actions. "He is . . . not one of us."

"In what sense is—no," she abruptly said. "I will not argue the merits, or lack thereof, of your contention. That would be foolishness. Instead, I will simply point out that no one should ever undertake any action without considering what the desired outcome will be. You feel your classmate is not 'one of' you. By engaging him in this violent pursuit, what did you think to accomplish? Did you hope to convince him to depart Vulcan? Did you hope to kill him? What was your goal?"

The boys looked at each other in discomfort. "We . . . did not have a particular goal in mind. We simply desired to—to—"

"Show your contempt?" Her voice was nearly dripping with sarcasm. "Is that what you desired to do? In a manner similar to the way that I am now addressing you?"

"Yes," said another one of the boys evenly.

"That is not acceptable."

"With all respect, ma'am," said the boy whom they had been tormenting, "this is not your concern."

"I am making it my concern," Selar said firmly. "Come with me. Now."

"But . . ."

Her eyes narrowed. "Now."

Clearly realizing that it was pointless to argue with an adult so determined to thrust herself into other people's business, the boy cast a glance at the others, who were still blocking his way. They parted silently and he walked past them. The moment he was clear of them, he began to walk away very quickly. Selar paused long enough to say to the others, "You are to give great consideration to the inappropriateness and illogic of your actions," and then she moved off after the swiftly departing boy.

"Wait," she called after him, but the boy quickened his pace. Selar almost had to break into a run to overtake him. Seeing that the woman was bound and determined to catch up with him, and knowing that the only way to avoid it was to break into a sprint, the boy instead slowed down so that Selar drew alongside him.

"What do you wish to say?" he asked, not really sounding as if he wanted to know.

"What is your name?"

He stopped altogether and turned to face her with his arms resolutely folded, as if to say that he was not going to provide her with a scintilla of information more than he absolutely had to. Apparently his name was not among those pieces of information he felt any need to share.

"Very well," she said when it became clear that he was not going to volunteer his name. "Why did those boys behave that way toward you?"

"They hate me." He said it so matter-of-factly, so without any passion at all, that it was disconcerting to

Selar—all the more so because the child's emotions were perfectly readable upon his face. Yet he was containing it all.

"Why would they hate you?"

"Because I am half-human."

She hesitated, and then said, "Is your mother human . . . or your father?"

"Does it matter?"

"I . . . suppose not. Listen—"

He took a step back from her and said sharply, "Thank you for helping me. You did not have to. It was a kindness. I do not know why you did it; I do not much care. I am leaving now. Please do not try to stop me." Then he headed away from her, walking rather than running.

She stood there and watched him go, feeling frustrated that she was not in pursuit of him, but unclear on what she would do if she did manage to catch up with him again. Then something else occurred to her, and she turned and quickly retraced her steps. Within moments, her longer stride had enabled her to catch up with the other children who had been tormenting the boy. They saw her coming. Children on every other planet in the Federation would probably have tried to bolt. But these boys were able to discern that the longer-limbed Selar would likely be able to overtake them without much difficulty, and so they simply stood there. Trust Vulcan children to react in a logical, rather than a childish, manner. But that did nothing to explain their earlier actions.

"Do you wish to speak with us?" the biggest of them—who had been one of the more vicious in taunting the boy—inquired.

"I want to know why you were harassing that boy."

His eyes narrowed, and he seemed to assess her for a moment. "Do you have a half-breed of your own?"

It was all Selar could do not to be staggered by the incisive question. When one got down to it, of course, it seemed a logical deduction to make. Nevertheless, it still caught her off guard. She rallied so quickly, though, that the boy did not see an instant's hesitation or even reaction on her part. "I suggest you answer the question," she told him, "unless you desire to have me accompany you back to your parents' homes and inform them of your actions."

"I think they would likely approve," said the boy.

"Would you care to find out for sure?"

It was an interesting moment of gamesmanship, but ultimately it was the boy who wilted. Not overly, nor in a big way, but it was clear that he had suddenly lost his taste or interest in trying to show just how tough he actually was. "He is a half-breed. He was . . . pretending to be a Vulcan. We did not like that." The others nodded in a most sullen manner.

" 'Pretending' to be a Vulcan?" She wasn't quite sure she was hearing him properly. "What do you mean, 'pretending'?"

"He is not one of us. He pretends to be—tries to act like us, behave like us. But it's . . . it is . . ." He seemed to be casting about for the word.

One of his friends supplied it. "Insulting," he said tersely.

" 'Insulting'? The boy has Vulcan blood in him. That entitles him to respect."

"Perhaps. But it doesn't entitle him to act as if he is the same as us."

She couldn't believe what she was hearing. She crouched so that she was on eye-level with them. They stared at her, sullen, annoyed that this adult had chosen to stick her nose into their business. "Have you learned nothing of the acceptance of others?" she asked. "Infinite Diversity in Infinite Combinations. Does that mean anything to you?"

"IDIC celebrates individual life forms, coming together into one great life form, all of us part of the whole. That . . ." the boy pointed in the general direction of the young Vulcan boy Selar had assisted, "is not an individual. He is a half-breed, a mix, neither here nor there. He is not one of us, but acts as if we cannot tell the difference. As if we are stupid. But we are not stupid; we are Vulcans. And he is not. Not really."

"Yes, he is. He is Vulcan."

Another of the boys stepped forward. He spoke in a slightly lower voice than the others, sounding almost professorial. "If one looks out the window at the morning, and sees a sun blocked by clouds, would you say that it is a sunny day, considering that the sun is up there, and only obscured? Or would you say that it is a cloudy day?"

"A cloudy day, I suppose. But that is not the point—"

"Yes, it is," said the pedantic lad. "The Vulcan philosophy, the Vulcan mindset . . . these shine out through the quadrant like a beacon of reasonableness and rational thought. And the . . . the confusion and disorderly conduct that comes from a human mind, that is the cloud, blocking the golden glow of the sun. When the sun is gone, only that which obscures it is left, and that is what is commented on. A half-breed is not Vulcan, cannot ever be Vulcan, because all his best qualities are going to be diminished by that which is undesirable."

"Humanity is not undesirable. True Vulcans see worth in all races, including humanity. Perhaps most particularly in humanity. We made first contact with them, and they are now one of the dominant species in the United Federation of Planets."

"Yes. We know." The boys shared a look of mutual incredulity. "Most . . . illogical."

"It is not illogical," Selar said, suddenly feeling rather old and, even more, rather tired. "When you are older, you will understand that."

"Perhaps that will seem to be the case," replied the boy. "Then again, it is sometimes the case that one's reasoning faculties become impaired as one gets older, due to various illnesses. What may seem like understanding may simply be a deterioration of common sense."

Selar stared at them for a long moment, and then said, "Your behavior . . . is inappropriate. Wholly inappropriate. If you refuse to comprehend that, then there is nothing that I can say."

"And you have said it rather well," replied the boy. With that, the Vulcan youths headed on their way. Naturally, there was no chortling or self-satisfied snickering as they did so . . . but there could have been.

Selar was sitting in her living room, repeating the incident with the half-breed Vulcan boy and his charming classmates. Xyon sat across from her, watching her with wide eyes as she finished the narrative.

"I never though of my people as snobs before," she said after a long silence.

"They are not snobs. They are children. That's all," Xyon replied.

"But I cannot simply ignore what they did, how they acted. That is what you are going to be faced with." She sat forward, her fingers interlaced. "What am I to do? About you? About this situation?"

"Why are you expected to do anything?" he asked reasonably. "The situation is what it is. I am what I am.

The decisions have already been made, the path chosen. There is nothing left but to walk it."

"I do not agree. If—"

There was a chime at the door. Selar started to rise, but Xyon had already hopped off the couch and was padding over to the door. "You look tired, Mother. Let me attend to it. Open!" he called.

The door slid open and the Vulcan boys poured in. Their voices were loud, almost deafening, so much so that Selar had to clap her hands to her ears to cut out the pain.

"Freak!" they shouted "Misfit! NonVulcan! Impure!" They circled Xyon, howling at the top of their lungs, their derisive laughter filling Selar's head, filling every molecule of her being. She could no longer see Xyon, for the other boys had completely obscured him from view. Their chanting, their derision, became louder and louder, even though the increased volume seemed impossible.

And then came the shrieking.

And the blood, thick and green, flowing across the floor.

The boys fell, one by one, or screamed in a most unVulcan way, or tried to run but failed as Xyon pounced upon them, snarling. Despite his Vulcan ears and the elegant curve of his eyebrows, his lips were drawn back and the distinctive fangs of a Hermat were visible. Small claws extended from his hands, and he ripped at the throat of another boy even as he howled his fury and indignation.

Selar tried to shout to him to stop, but even though her mouth was moving, no sound was coming out. Blood splattered on her, oddly cold to the touch.

"Xyon!" she cried out with no voice, and again, "Xyon!" The surviving boys dashed for the door, and

Xyon was right after them, charging out the door after them. *"XYON!"* she called out once more, and this time she found her voice, so loud that she herself was startled by it.

She heard a pitiable wailing, and it jolted her from her sleep.

She sat up on the couch where she had drifted off, and was on her feet even before it had fully registered on her that she had been dreaming. She blinked against the low light as she staggered into the next room, where Xyon was calling out. It was the middle of the night, and Xyon had been, until now, a remarkably sound sleeper, so she could only assume that she herself had been responsible for awakening him. Small wonder: If someone shouted her name at the top of their lungs from the next room, that would certainly awaken her as well.

Moments later she was leaning over the newly customized crib . . . the one she had fitted with a force field, strong enough to contain the child but gentle enough that contact would not hurt him in the slightest. She disliked restricting him in any way, but she really had no choice. She couldn't risk him just climbing out of the crib any time he chose and getting into trouble.

She stared down at him, watching him as he slept peacefully, his chest rising up and down steadily. She knew that what she had seen in her dream wasn't going to happen. . . .

Except . . . it might.

"It will not," Giniv said confidently.

Selar was pacing the room as Giniv sat there, watching her, looking slightly bleary-eyed. That was understandable, considering that Selar had summoned her there in the middle of the night without any explanation beyond, "I require someone to converse with."

"I did not say it *will*," Selar pointed out formally. "I said it might."

"Very well, if you feel the need to split hairs . . ."

"No. Just a need for accuracy."

Giniv stopped her immediate gut reaction before it got out, and instead said, with customary control, "It might not happen."

Selar turned to face her. "Ah. So you are saying it might."

Giniv closed her eyes to block out the annoyance, and in doing so almost drifted back to sleep, so she opened them once more. "Selar . . . this is a pointless exercise."

"I am looking for reassurance, Giniv, and so far you are not providing it."

"I apologize most sincerely, Selar, for not living up to your expectations or requirements. May I go home now?"

As if she had not spoken, Selar continued to pace. She began ticking off comments with her fingers. "Vulcan children are capable of great cruelty. We have seen that. Worse; rather than admitting wrongdoing, they appear determined to defend their bigotry with frightening erudition."

"They are simply children, Selar. They will learn better as they get older."

"Will they? Or will they simply grow up into arrogant snobs who are more skilled at concealing or denying their intrinsic arrogance?"

At this, Giniv's eyes narrowed. "Is that what you are saying we are as a race, Selar? Arrogant snobs?"

Selar stopped pacing and covered her face with her hands. "I do not know what I am saying."

Giniv settled back in the chair. "At last. Something upon which we can concur."

"What are my choices here, Giniv? Realistically, I mean. Look at the speed with which Xyon is developing. If he maintains this pace, he will be ready for school, for social interaction, at a far earlier age than other Vulcan children are. He may continue to grow and develop at an accelerated rate. This will give children further cause for taunting him. Worse, if he is not capable of handling such treatment with equanimity, the results could be disastrous. He could lash out, hurt someone, even . . ."

"Kill someone?"

Selar nodded.

Giniv shook her head. "I do not accept that, Selar. It will not happen."

"How do I know that?"

"Because you will not let it! You will train him. You will teach him. You will impart to him your wisdom, let him know what is right and what is wrong. You will teach him control, as any Vulcan mother does with her child."

"The parents who taught those children apparently did not do their job sufficiently. I saw no control in that instance. I saw only cruelty. Needless, heartless cruelty."

"What are you saying here, Selar?" she asked. "What is the point you are trying to make? What alternative are you presenting? Thus far, you have simply tossed out a string of utterances that border on the hopeless. You are underestimating yourself. You are not allowing for the possibility that you will be a superb mother who will be perfectly capable of raising an equally superb child. Battering yourself in this manner is counterproductive."

"I am simply—"

"Concerned, yes, I know. And because you are concerned, you will behave in an appropriate manner and raise your child accordingly. I would expect nothing less of you."

Selar ceased her pacing and sat in a chair opposite Giniv. "You are quite certain of that?"

"I am positive. Absolutely positive."

And in a very quiet voice, Selar said, "And if I am wrong . . . or if I am unable to do my job sufficiently . . . and a child's taunting words die in his throat because my son, in a childish fit of rage, killed him . . . what will you say to that?"

"I will say," Giniv told her, "that at the time when the decisions were being made, and the efforts at childrearing were being put forward, you acted in a logical fashion. What could be asked of anyone other than that?"

"What indeed," mused Selar.

Except that she was coming to her own conclusions on the subject . . . and they were conclusions that did not appeal to her at all. They were disconcerting. They were bothersome. They were even painful. However . . . they were also logical. And that was the worst aspect of all.

Peter David

RAFE

RAFE WAS WALKING PAST the Engineering Room when he noticed, to his surprise, Morgan emerging from it, looking a bit puzzled. He walked toward her briskly, and it was obvious that she was greatly lost in thought because she didn't hear him until he hailed her by name. "Oh. Rafe, hello," she said, not with a lack of enthusiasm, but certainly in a distracted manner.

"Is something wrong?" he asked.

"Well, I . . ." She looked once more toward the Engineering Room.

"Should I be jealous?" he said teasingly, kissing her on the forehead.

"No, no, not at all, it's just . . . well, I wanted to talk to Mr. Scott. I feel as if there are . . . things that we should be saying to each other, or things that I wanted to say, or . . ." She shook her head in frustration. "Damn him. I can't remember the last time a man actually had me confused. I'd forgotten the sensation, and I can't say I appreciate the reminder."

"Then why bother yourself over it?" He draped an arm around her. "Come. Why don't we—"

"It's not a question of bother, Rafe. It's that Scotty is really a good man at heart, and I'd like to talk to him about . . . things. But he's not there."

"That shouldn't be a surprise. It's not as if he's under house arrest, unable to wander away from that one place."

"I know that. But they haven't seen him around for most of the day now, and frankly, that's got me a bit alarmed."

Rafe scratched his chin, giving the matter consideration. "Perhaps you want to talk to that manager fellow. Quincy, I think his name is. He might be of some help."

"I asked after him, but they haven't seen him around, either."

"Well, there you go!"

She looked at him blankly. "There I go where?"

"They're probably off together somewhere."

"Why didn't I think of that? What a lovely couple they make, too," she said dryly.

"Now, that's not what I mean, and you know it," Rafe said in a faintly scolding tone. "There's probably business that needs to be attended to. Perhaps they're touring some other facility, or having meetings in other resorts. It could be any one of a dozen things. No need to suspect foul play."

For a long moment she was silent.

"Is something wrong, Morgan? Did I say something—?"

"I never said I suspected foul play," Morgan said, her eyes narrowed.

"Well, I . . . I thought it was implicit in your concerns. You did say you were 'alarmed.' What would give you reason for alarm if not a worry that something . . . unfortunate . . . had occurred? Foul play, an accident . . . whatever you'd want to call it. I don't really want to get tangled in semantics."

"Neither do I. I'm sorry, Rafe. You're probably right," she sighed. "Two problems: I'm a mother, and I've been around for . . . a bit. So I tend to excel in dreaming up worst-case scenarios of all manner. There's no need to inflict any of them on you, though."

"Tell you what," Rafe said, "I have a thought. Let's have dinner tonight, the four of us, back in Shakespeare's Tavern. The place where all four of us first met. Do you think Robin will be up for it?"

"Don't you mean, do I think Robin and Nik will be up for it?"

"Yes," he laughed, "they have become somewhat inseparable, haven't they?"

"You shouldn't make fun. I think it's sweet."

"I wasn't making fun, and I think it's sweet, too."

They chatted for a bit longer, and then he kissed her gently and they went their separate ways. When he returned to his hotel room, Nik was already there, emerging from the shower with a bathrobe draped around himself. From long practice, Rafe could tell that something was bothering him. "Problem?" Rafe asked.

"You could say that. I had to kill the manager and the engineer. Tossed them down a computer shaft."

This brought Rafe up short. "Why did you do that?" he asked calmly.

"They had the damned poor luck to show up when I was working at the computer core." He'd been toweling his hair dry, but now he lowered the towel. "I'd been trying to do what needed to be done at remote consoles, but that annoying Scotsman built in safeguards without realizing what he was guarding against. Damn him, even his safeguards had safeguards. The only way to get things done was at the core itself."

"Had they seen you?" asked Rafe. He sat in a chair on the far side of the room.

"Oh, please," said Nik disdainfully.

"If they didn't see you, then why did you feel the need?"

"Because they might have seen me. And because the Scotsman had caused us some inconvenience, and because the Quincy person was just annoying. Did I need more of a reason than that?"

"No, no. I just wanted to make certain that you had not acted precipitously. So the transfer of funds is in place, then?"

"Processing even as we speak. By tomorrow morning, every credit will be shifted over into your private accounts."

"Good," said Rafe, nodding approvingly. "We'll want to stay to see that nothing goes wrong. But, by tomorrow afternoon, we'll be long gone."

"I'll miss Robin," Nik said, looking a bit saddened. "She's . . . very exciting."

"The mother is most intriguing, but the daughter is nothing special. When you've lived long enough, you'll understand that. Which reminds me . . . we'll have dinner with them tonight. Now," he raised a cautioning finger, "don't kill them. That would be most impolite."

"I'll try to restrain myself," said Nik, and went to comb out his hair.

BURGOYNE

LIFE IN NEVADA had been rather quiet for Burgoyne, and s/he had decided that was the way s/he liked it. Perhaps there was something to be said for the Starfleet philosophy of taking time off after the destruction of a vessel. It was a time of thought, of introspection. It was . . . peaceful. Burgoyne realized that it had been a long time since s/he had truly known peace.

One day was very much like the next for hir, and even that was welcome. After all, working in engineering, every day had presented new challenges, new obstacles, and new crises. S/he had begun to think that s/he required that constant stimulation, as if s/he was incapable of settling into some sort of routine. But s/he was rather pleased to discover that that was apparently not the case, for nothing could have been more uniform—even boring—than the existence that s/he was presently living, and it wasn't bothering hir one bit.

S/he would get up in the morning . . . have breakfast . . . meditate. There was a cool lake not far from the house—one that had not been there as recently as fifty years ago, but thank heavens for land reconstruction. S/he would go down there in midmorning and paddle around. Float there, arms outstretched, the sun beaming down upon hir, and hir thoughts would fly a million miles away to Vulcan, as s/he wondered what Selar and Xyon were up to. S/he discovered that, with the passage of time, the sting lessened just a little bit. Only a little, but at least it gave hir hope for the future.

S/he would spend the balance of the day simply walking around the desert. The thing that was most impressive to hir was that s/he would see new things every day. Hard to believe, since one would think that a desert was unchanging, one day to the next. But s/he would find endless fascination in discovering that, for instance, some new bit of green growth was fighting its way into existence on some rock. S/he would stop by every day to see how it was doing, rooting for it in its struggle to assert its own existence. *I am here. See me. I will not be defeated,* it seemed to say to hir, and s/he wondered just how much it reflected hir own situation.

And in the evenings . . .

Well . . . s/he didn't like the evenings, actually. They were a difficult time for hir. Not terribly so, not insurmountable in their discomfort. But somehow, when the sun was down and it was just hir and the darkness, that was when the solitude would begin to sting hir a bit. That was when s/he wished s/he had an adult to play with . . . or a child to dandle on hir knee.

"It's for the best," s/he told hirself. In fact, s/he told hirself that several times a day . . . which was an improvement, considering that s/he used to tell hirself that several times an hour. So it was true, s/he was getting better at handling the hurt.

Why had s/he done it?

S/he didn't know. S/he had gone over and over everything that had occurred, and still had been unable to make sense of it in hir own mind. S/he supposed, when it came down to it, it had to do with pride. Selar simply seemed to have so much more of it than Burgoyne. Not that Burgoyne thought little of hirself; quite the opposite. But Selar was so intensely prideful that it seemed to be one of the overwhelming aspects of her character. As they had struggled there, under the hot Vulcan sun, two different futures spun out for Burgoyne in hir imagination. One of those futures showed Burgoyne without Selar and hir child. Oddly enough—or perhaps not oddly at all—that future looked very much like the one s/he was living right now. It wasn't so bad, really. Not really. S/he was surviving just fine, and, indeed, even enjoying the time to hirself. S/he was becoming reacquainted with all that s/he liked about hirself, and that was quite a bit to like.

The other future showed Selar without her child, and more . . . without her pride. Rightly or wrongly, Burgoyne was certain that Selar would not bounce back quite so quickly from a pride-shattering defeat. She had walked into that place of judgment certain that logic and tradition would carry the day. She had had no warning whatsoever, not the slightest inkling, that tradition was going to work against her. That an ancient rite of battle was going to be thrown in her face, that she was going to have to go toe-to-toe and slug it out for the right to raise her child the way she saw fit. For Burgoyne, Xyon was on the line. For Selar . . . everything was on the line.

There was never any doubt in Burgoyne's mind that Selar would give Xyon a good home. It was just that s/he was certain that s/he could give him a better one. But s/he found that s/he did not want to destroy Selar in order to do that.

"Do you still love her?" Slon had asked hir. The truth was, s/he didn't know anymore. If s/he did—and it was indeed possible that s/he did—it was obviously unrequited. It couldn't have been more clear to Burgoyne that Selar felt nothing for hir at all. Burgoyne had simply been . . . a means to an end.

Well . . . that was the crux of it, wasn't it? Because when they had been together, Burgoyne had felt like it was anything but that. S/he felt that Selar and s/he had connected at a far more basic, spiritual, emotional level, and had always assumed that Selar had not wanted to acknowledge it simply because the concept of emotions was anathema to her. The things that Slon had told hir about Selar went further toward explaining what Selar's mindset was like. It had helped. It just hadn't solved it.

There really wasn't much point to dwelling on it anymore. And yet, Burgoyne couldn't help but do so, as one tends to pick at a scab. The hurt would fade. The sting would pass. But there was always going to be some part of Burgoyne that found itself wondering . . . what if?

S/he had stumbled upon a piece of poetry in hir reading that summed it up for hir: "For of all sad words of tongue or pen, the saddest are these: It might have been."

And then, one day, it all changed.

Burgoyne was walking back from the lake where s/he had been swimming. As always, there was no one around, and so Burgoyne had not bothered with clothing of any kind. S/he was allowing the gentle, warm wind to dry hir for the most part, with a towel slung over one shoulder that s/he had been lying out upon while sunning hirself on a rock near the lake.

As s/he approached hir house, however, scents began to waft down the wind to hir. Hir nostrils flared, and s/he stopped where s/he was, balancing hirself on hir toes without thought, as if poising hirself to make some sort of an attack on whoever was there. All of hir defensive instincts were kicking in.

There were two scents coming to hir from the house. S/he recognized both of them.

S/he gasped, unable to trust hirself that what s/he thought s/he was detecting was genuine. But s/he was so eager to believe it that s/he tossed caution aside entirely. S/he gave no thought to the fact that s/he was nude, or that s/he might be running into some sort of danger. Instead, s/he barreled straight toward the house, moving with absolutely no noise across the desert surface other than the occasional clicking of hir extended claws, which were giving hir traction and additional speed.

S/he burst into the house and stood there, eyes wide.

Slon stood and blinked in very mild surprise. "My apologies," he said. "I was unaware that you were going to be so informal."

S/he paid no attention to his obvious discomfiture, or hir own undress. Instead, hir attention was riveted purely on the child, who was sitting up on the couch next to Slon. Xyon took one look at Burgoyne and made gleeful, cooing noises, his arms spinning in little circles.

He remembers me. That had been the most difficult thing for Burgoyne to come to terms with: that Xyon was not going to have any recollection whatsoever of his other parent. That Burgoyne was going to be a nonperson to him. But that was clearly not the case, at least not yet. It was painfully obvious that Xyon knew ex-

actly who s/he was. Burgoyne went to him and picked
him up, holding him tight against hirself, gasping at the
warmth, the pure, vital life of him. Xyon burbled, and
then began to slap at Burgoyne's small breasts. Burgoyne didn't understand why at first . . . but then s/he
comprehended. "He wants to nurse," s/he said with understanding. "He wants me to breast-feed him."

"If you say so," Slon said.

"I . . . my God, I don't have anything . . . I mean, I
didn't give birth, so I don't have any . . . and around the
house, it's . . ." S/he realized hir words were tumbling
over each other in hir excitement. "All I have is
Scotch."

"That would not be wise," Slon said. "Do not concern yourself. I have brought an artificial nourishment
beverage with me in substantial supply. It is, after all, a
lengthy trip from Vulcan, and obviously Xyon did not
go hungry all this way. I have brought the formula for it
on a chip so that you can program it into your replica-
tor. I will feed him for the moment from a bottle; you
may wish to attend to your own presentation."

Burgoyne didn't quite get it, but then s/he looked down
and seemed to notice for the first time hir lack of attire.

"One of us is dressed inappropriately," commented
Slon. "If this is to be put to a vote, I would prefer that
you acquire clothing rather than that I divest myself of
mine. Although it is your home, and I shall abide by
your rules."

"Just give me a minute," said Burgoyne, and s/he
hurried into the adjoining room. S/he came back out
moments later with a simple shift tossed over hirself
and sat on the floor, staring up in wonderment as Slon
bottle-fed Xyon. Xyon was clearly having no trouble
with the formula; indeed, he seemed quite content with

it. "What," s/he finally managed to ask, "are you doing here? I don't . . . I don't understand."

"I am here with your son."

"Yes, I can see that. And Selar—?"

"Is not."

"I can see that also." S/he took a deep breath to steady the pounding of hir heart. "Look, Slon . . . you're an intelligent man. You must know all the questions that are tumbling around in my head right now, so let's not pretend they're not there. Tell me what's going on."

"Selar," Slon said calmly, "is still on Vulcan. Xyon is here, as am I. I will be returning to Vulcan. Whether Xyon returns with me . . . is up to you."

"To me?" S/he was having trouble wrapping hirself around what s/he was hearing. S/he wanted to believe s/he was interpreting it correctly, but almost didn't dare. "Why . . . up to me? Selar . . . wait. Selar knows you're here, doesn't she?" s/he asked with sudden suspicion.

"Of course. You could not possibly think I kidnapped my own nephew."

"I don't know what to think anymore."

"Perhaps this might help you in your thought process," said Slon, and he handed a computer chip to Burgoyne. S/he held it up, and knew it immediately for a mail card. Hir eyebrows puckered questioningly, but Slon was as readable as a rock. So s/he went over to hir computer screen and popped the chip into the slot.

Immediately an image of Selar appeared on the screen. She looked no different than she ever did. Her manner was calm, detached. She might just as easily have been commenting on the unchanging weather of Nevada.

"Hello, Burgoyne," she said. Burgoyne wasn't sure, but there seemed to be just a hint of strain in her voice. Her outward manner, however, remained unchanged.

"By this point you are, most likely, trying to determine whether I am aware that Xyon is there with you, and that Slon has him."

"She's good, I'll give her that," admitted Burgoyne.

"The answer to both of those questions is: Yes. I am quite aware. It was, in fact, my suggestion. Actually, I suppose 'suggestion' is too mild a word, considering the circumstances." She paused a moment, as if steeling herself, and then continued, "I have given great thought to the matter, and have decided that—if you are still interested—Xyon will benefit more from being in your care than in mine."

Burgoyne couldn't believe it. S/he turned and looked at Slon questioningly. Slon simply nodded and then pointed at the screen, indicating that Burgoyne should pay attention to the rest of what was being said.

"You will notice," she said, with remarkable clinical detachment, "that Xyon is continuing to develop at an accelerated rate. My studies and tests indicate that that acceleration will slow as he grows older . . . which is fortunate, since at this speed he would be an old man by age five. Nevertheless, this aspect and . . . others have forced me to conclude that Vulcan may not be the right environment for him. I think he may not fit in here very well. I have done a good deal of self-evaluation as well, and have concluded that—if he does indeed encounter the problems I feel he will—that I lack the emotional and maternal capabilities required to see him through his trials. It is an unfortunate admission to make, but I have always prided myself on knowing my capabilities. I think you will be better suited to meet his emotional needs than someone for whom emotions are an . . . inconvenience at best. As for me, I will be remaining on Vulcan. I think it the best place for me for the time being. I will very likely return to Starfleet active duty at some future date. But, naturally, I will not want to risk interfering with your childrearing, should you choose to return to shipboard duty as well. So, I will make certain to request that I not be assigned to the same vessel as you. I know that, being an emotional individual, you might consider that request some sort of personal slight, should you hear of it. So I believed it best to inform you of it now. That way you will be able to take it in the spirit in which it is intended.

"Naturally, you will not raise Xyon as a Vulcan. I ask, though, that you respect aspects of our culture enough to teach him some of our history and philosophies. Considering the amount of time you spent in our library, I suspect you have already familiarized yourself with much of it, and will be able to use it in a more constructive endeavor than trying to defeat me in combat." She hesitated then, as if trying to decide whether she could continue. Finally she said, "It is my belief that you could have won our battle. I believe you chose not to. The fact that you made that choice . . . makes it easier for me to make this one. Teach him my name, Burgoyne, and make certain that he knows who his mother is . . . and who he is. Peace . . . and long life." She held her hand in the Vulcan salute.

"Live long and prosper," s/he replied, returning the gesture. Selar, naturally, could not hear hir, since the message was prerecorded. Yet she nodded ever so slightly, as if reacting to Burgoyne's response, before the picture faded out.

There was silence for a time, broken only by Xyon's occasional gulping as he drank down his nourishment. Then, slowly, Burgoyne turned to Slon. "Is this for real?" s/he asked.

"You still doubt it?"

"I . . . suppose I don't, no. It's just hard to believe, I mean . . ." S/he shook hir head. "What brought this on?"

"She did not go into specifics with me. She simply told me what she had decided, and asked me to bring Xyon here."

"Why didn't she tell me ahead of time?"

"Because she said she wanted you to react with your gut instincts when Xyon was already here. She said she has little use for instincts herself, but that you seem to function best when you depend upon them. For what it is worth, I think that is an accurate enough assessment."

"So . . . what do I do now?" Burgoyne was staring numbly at Xyon, not quite sure what to think.

"You do as she suggests: you follow your instincts. Do you want him?"

"Of course I want him!"

Slon nodded approvingly. "You see? You answered that with immediacy and conviction. That alone should provide you with the answer you seek."

"I . . . suppose you're right. May I . . . ?" S/he gestured with hir arms, and Slon understood. He rose and, without missing a beat, eased the still-drinking Xyon over into Burgoyne's arms. Burgoyne slowly rocked the child as, apparently oblivious to the change in "ownership," he continued at his bottle. He was holding it in his own hands, rather than requiring someone to hold it for him. "Incredible. He feels like he weighs nothing."

"I know. You would almost think his bones are hollow. But he is very strong, very resilient."

"You sound almost proud," observed Burgoyne.

"I am his uncle, after all. That would certainly be my prerogative."

"You're right. Slon . . . did you have something to do with this? With getting her to change her mind?"

"No. It was entirely her doing, her initiative." Slon stood there and watched hir for a few moments more. "Curious."

"What?"

"I am not exactly expert in the realm of emotions, as you might surmise. But I cannot help but think that your reaction is a bit . . . muted."

"It's just that . . . well . . ." Burgoyne looked down at Xyon as if s/he couldn't quite believe that he was really there. "When this all started . . . when I got this house, made plans . . . it was never with the thought that I was going to be Xyon's sole parent. Even if I had won the judgment, I was then going to do everything I could to get Selar to be there right alongside me, raising Xyon the best we could. I never wanted to be the one parent in his life."

"My understanding is that Hermats are not raised by a father and mother."

"That is correct. To be blunt, part of the reason I'm now something of an outcast in some quarters is precisely because I wanted to provide that sort of life for my son. I was looked upon by many of my own people as a freak, a misfit."

"Ironic, considering that Selar was worried that that would be the way that Xyon would be perceived."

"Maybe we deserve each other at that." Burgoyne noticed that Xyon was drifting off to sleep. Gently s/he removed the bottle from his mouth. Xyon's lips fluttered slightly, but otherwise he continued to sleep soundly.

"Are you saying you are sorry that you will be raising Xyon?"

"No. I'm saying I'm sorry that we—Selar and I, together—won't be." S/he eased hirself onto the couch. Xyon stirred a little, but Burgoyne rocked back and forth, and Xyon drifted back to sleep.

"After everything that happened, you still love her."

Burgoyne nodded. "Stupid, isn't it?"

"No. But it is illogical."

"And I'm worried." Burgoyne looked up at him. "I'm worred what Selar is going to do now. I'm worried that she's going to beat herself up over this. Second-guess herself, make herself feel as if she's inadequate."

"I would not worry about that happening."

"You wouldn't?" Burgoyne felt a bit relieved. This was, after all, Selar's brother. If anyone knew how she was likely to react in any given situation, it was he.

"No," he said confidently. "I believe it is already happening."

"What?" That was certainly not the answer Burgoyne had been expecting.

But Slon nodded slightly. "I am seeing it already. In her bearing and posture, in the things she says. She is having difficulty coping with her decision, even though she is confident of its correctness. And moreover—"

"Moreover what?" Burgoyne was beginning to feel frustrated. It was as if s/he had to fight for every scrap of information.

"I do not wish to instill within you false hope . . . but it is my belief that she feels deep affection for you. So much so that she does not know what to do with it or how to handle it. That makes matters very problematic for her. I am not saying she loves you. I do not think she would know what to do with the feeling if she had it. I am simply saying she is very confused."

"Well, that makes two of us." Burgoyne now looked

a bit uncertainly at Xyon. "Maybe I'm . . . maybe I'm not doing the right thing by taking Xyon. Maybe—"

"You should force him back upon a mother who is in turmoil?" Slon shook his head. "I do not see the logic in that plan."

"Then what am I supposed to do?"

"Be as good a parent as you possibly can. It is Xyon who needs you now. Allow me to attend to Selar."

"Attend to Selar?" Burgoyne regarded Slon with open curiosity. "What have you got up your sleeve? I mean, what have you got planned?" s/he amended quickly when s/he saw Slon looking blankly at his sleeve and the arm that occupied it.

"Planned?" Slon said blandly. "I did not say I had anything planned. However . . . I do have some . . . interesting connections. As does T'Pau."

"Connections? T'Pau? What does she have to do with any of this? What connections? What are you up to?"

"Up to?"

"Stop that! Stop repeating what I say while adding this whole inscrutable Vulcan attitude that you revel in. If you're planning something, just come out with it and tell me!"

"There is really nothing to discuss at this point," Slon told hir firmly. "I will simply say this: There are always . . . possibilities."

THE AMBASSADOR

IF BURGOYNE'S DAYS HAD BEEN one much the same as the other, so, too, had it been for Selar. Patients came. Patients went. They got cured or got sicker, they lived or they died. Doctor Selar made her best efforts in all cases, but her clinical detachment seemed to have become even more detached. It wasn't that she didn't care about what happened to them. It was that they had ceased to be living, breathing individuals in her eyes. They were instead simply . . . objects. Problems to be solved. A series of ailments to be diagnosed, ministrations to be tended to, cures to be prescribed. They were an endless parade of problems. Nothing more than that.

She did not think this especially odd, or sad, or anything. It simply . . . was.

Every so often she would go into the room that had served as Xyon's nursery. She would stand there for a time, thinking about the life that he was now leading on

Earth. She wondered if he remembered her at all. He probably would . . . at least for a brief time. Would he forget her after weeks? Months? Certainly a year or so from now, only the face and voice of Burgoyne would have any meaning to him.

Burgoyne . . .

She found herself thinking about hir more and more these days. She found that she would watch other Vulcans engaging in something as simple as walking, and she would be comparing those movements to the way that Burgoyne carried hirself. There was a grace, an elegance to Burgoyne's movements that she really hadn't appreciated until after Burgoyne was out of her life. It was . . .

Sad?

Whenever her thoughts would wander in that direction, she did everything she could to shake it off. Burgoyne was gone, that's all, just gone out of her life, and no amount of regrets was going to benefit anyone. Besides, she did not have regrets. She was Dr. Selar of Vulcan. All her training, everything that she was, everything that she knew, taught her that decisions were arrived at in a solid, logical manner. Once the decision was made, no amount of second-guessing or reconsideration was worthwhile. She had done what was best for Xyon. For Burgoyne. For herself.

She sat in her office and laughed.

At first the sound was so odd that it didn't immediately register on her what it was. She had never heard her own laughter before. When it leaped out at her in that manner, it prompted her to put her hand to her mouth, as if she had just, against her will, called T'Pau by a profane epithet. She had no idea what had prompted her to act in such a manner.

She had been thinking about Burgoyne. That much

she knew. Something s/he had said, or something s/he had done. Selar couldn't remember clearly now what it might have been. S/he had said or done it many months ago, and at the time, Selar had just shaken her head and let it pass without comment. But now, unbidden, it had come back to her . . . what was it . . . ?

"When I die . . ." Burgoyne had said. What was it . . . ?

They had been lying in bed together, and Burgoyne had suddenly propped hir head up on one hand and looked at Selar with what appeared to be utter sincerity.

"When I die," s/he had said abruptly, with no preamble whatsoever, "I want to go like my grandfather did: peacefully, in his sleep. Not screaming, like his passengers."

And she, Selar, had looked at hir blankly and said, "Was your grandfather a shuttle pilot of some sort?"

Burgoyne had stared at her for a long moment, and then a grin had split hir face. S/he rolled onto hir back and proceeded to laugh, to Selar's utter confusion. She did not press Burgoyne on the matter because it seemed rather pointless. An out-of-context recollection of hir grandfather was a most illogical way to start off a conversation.

For no reason, the comment had suddenly come back to Selar after having given it no thought for months . . . and the thinking behind the joke suddenly made sense. That's what it was. A joke. The grandfather had fallen asleep at the controls of his vessel and died while slumbering, leaving the rest of the craft's passengers to die horribly.

It was, of course, not especially funny or logical. The death of innocent passengers, for starters, was a tragedy, not a cause for amusement. Then there was the practical aspect of it. If the pilot of any vehicle or vessel suddenly became incapacitated, shipboard computers—a basic part of any vessel manufactured for centuries now—would kick in and be able to continue guiding the vessel to safety. From a humor point of view, it made no sense at all. Which was what made it humorous: it was absurd.

But the most absurd thing of all, and the thing that had seized momentary hold of Selar's control, was that she had not comprehended that instantly. She herself, by her actions and reactions, was the true butt of the joke. As well she should be, for failing to comprehend such a simple and trivial display of jocularity. She felt as if she was seeing herself from outside herself, and she might well have been the most absurd figure ever to result from thousands of years of Vulcan evolution and discipline. Certainly that was worth a bit of a giggle.

But just as quickly as she came to that realization, she brushed it off, having no desire to deal with it. Anyone who had thought they heard her laugh from within her office would have stopped and listened for some further sign of uncharacteristic merriment. They would have been disappointed, for she was in control of herself once more. And she felt that the sooner she had managed to distance herself from that inexcusable noise she had uttered, the better off she would be.

She heard a noise from the examining room next door. Someone had entered. That was rather unusual, because she was not expecting her first patient for another twenty-seven minutes. Perhaps the arrival was early. She had no need to recheck her agenda for the day; she had glanced at it once when she had first arrived and committed it to memory, as she did every day. Today's first patient was a new one, one Seklar by name, who had been having aches in his joints for close to a year now. If there was any aggravating aspect to being a doctor for Vulcans, it was the damned Vulcan stoicism. Here was a man who had not known an absence of pain for months, and yet he had refused to see a doctor. He had borne up under the pressure of incessant muscle aches because—since he was so disciplined—he refused to acknowledge that he might, in fact, be in need of medical attention.

She rose from her chair and stepped into the next room. A tall, slightly stoop-shouldered, gray-haired Vulcan was standing there with his back to her. He was wearing a grayish robelike garment, and much of his hair was turning a pale white. This was definitely someone who had quite a few years on him . . . which was odd, considering that Seklar's bio file (which, naturally, she had also studied with blithe ease) didn't seem to indicate that he was so old. Perhaps the premature aging might be a secret to some other aspect of his condition. Even as the possibilities ran through her mind, she said crisply, "Kindly lay down on the diagnostic table and undo the front of your robe."

"That," said the Vulcan, "will not be necessary."

The response took Selar aback slightly. "I believe that it will," she said. "Since I am the doctor, I am somewhat familiar with this procedure."

"And were I the patient, I would defer to your wisdom in the matter. But I am not, and therefore am under no such constraint."

Until that moment, she had been busy checking her diagnostic instrumentation as she spoke. But his response brought her up short, and she turned and really looked at the man. "If you are not a patient, why are you in my examining room?"

"I was looking for you." His voice was a bit gravelly, but there was something in his tone that commanded her attention. When he looked at her, she felt as if she was being watched by a pair of eyes that had seen just about everything that the galaxy had to offer by way of challenge, triumph and tragedy. There was a world-weariness in those eyes, and yet just enough of a sparkle that seemed to indicate he was always more than willing to see just what else might come his way. "You are Selar. One should never jump to conclusions on these matters."

"Yes, I am. And who are you?"

"My name is Spock."

It was as if a hammer-blow had struck her in the ribs. She knew the name instantly, of course. Who wouldn't? Indeed, she felt a degree of chagrin that she had not recognized him at once. "Ambassador Spock," she said. "It is an honor." She brought her hand up in the Vulcan salute.

He returned the gesture with a slight nod of his head.

"May I offer you something? A beverage of some kind . . ."

"That will not be necessary. I felt we should talk."

"Talk?" It took all the discipline she had to contain her astonishment. "I do not understand, sir. I am naturally gratified that you would see fit to speak with me . . . but the reasons for doing so elude me."

"I have heard from several different sources that you might benefit from a dialogue."

"Sources . . . ?" Then it began to occur to her. "Slon," she said slowly.

"He was one," Spock agreed readily. "We have met on one or two occasions, during diplomatic functions. He is a rather . . . interesting individual."

"Not precisely the word I would have used," said

Selar. "May I ask what other individuals felt that I was in need of discourse with you?"

"T'Pau."

She was genuinely taken aback by that. "T'Pau? That is . . . intriguing. May I ask—"

"I notice, Doctor, that you tend to ask permission before posing a question. That tendency could be rather time-consuming, if continued. It would very likely be of benefit to both of us if you simply posed your queries in a straightforward manner."

"I am simply trying to show proper respect, sir," she said stiffly.

Spock made a slight noise that sounded like *"Henh."* "One would think that such things become more important when one gets older. I certainly thought as much. But I have come to realize that I care less and less about such niceties. Perhaps it is because, as one finds oneself with less time, one comes to appreciate the economy involved in not wasting that remaining time with endless formalities."

"Point taken, sir," she said, although she did not really know if she agreed. "My office might be more comfortable than this examining room, however."

He glanced around. "Perhaps. But there is a certain appropriateness to discussing the matter here. It is, after all, a matter of examination."

"I do not understand."

"An examination of self, Doctor. Your insecurities . . . are not appropriate."

She blinked in confusion. "My insecurities? Ambassador . . . I am not insecure."

"With respect, Doctor, I disagree. From what I have been told by both T'Pau and Slon, you have displayed a singular lack of security in yourself, both as a parent, and as a female."

"Ambassador," she said with thinly veiled annoyance, "with all the respect to which you are due by dint of your many accomplishments, I do not feel that you have the right to stand in judgment of me."

"I do not think the word 'judgment' is appropriate. I would say 'assessment' is more accurate. Determining the value of what you say and what you do."

"But—"

He spoke right over her. "You abandoned your child."

"I did no such thing, Ambassador," Selar said. She had taken several steps back, unconsciously putting a greater distance between herself and Spock. "It was not 'abandonment' to realize where the greatest good for his welfare would be served."

"You made the judgment too hastily."

"Ambassador, again, with all respect—"

"More time-consuming niceties that are of little value, Doctor," Spock remonstrated. "Do not be concerned about respect or lack thereof. Speak your mind. As a doctor, you should know that that is the best medicine."

"The humans claim laughter is."

"That is why they live half as long as we do," Spock deadpanned.

Not quite sure how to take that remark, Selar wisely chose to ignore it. "Very well, then. I witnessed for myself the cruelty that children are capable of inflicting upon another child who is seen as different."

"As have I," Spock said. "Firsthand."

Her mouth opened, then closed. "Oh," she said softly. "Yes, of course. I should have . . . remembered that."

"The capacity for hurting others is the second most

common element in the universe, coming only behind stupidity," Spock said.

"And you believe what I did was stupid."

"No. It was, however, unfortunate, for you sold yourself short."

"It had nothing to do with me, Ambassador. It was only my concern for Xyon's welfare that motivated me."

"No, Doctor. It had everything to do with you."

"With all resp—" She caught herself, and dropped the honorific way of addressing him. "To be blunt," she corrected herself, "while your concern is appreciated, Ambassador . . . you do not know me. You are not in a fit position to make such judgments."

"You believe I speak from ignorance."

"Yes. I do."

"Would you care to enlighten me?"

For a moment she did not have the faintest idea what he was talking about, but then she understood. She hesitated, his piercing gaze seemingly capable of drilling a hole right through her. The truth was that she felt as if he was capable of analyzing every aspect of her soul just by looking at her, but she wasn't about to say that, of course. So, instead, she took a deep breath and said proudly, "I have every confidence in my decisions, Ambassador . . . and nothing to hide. I would ordinarily not sanction such contact with someone whom I know so little, but out of . . . deference to you, I will accommodate whatever you feel is necessary for the efficient exchange of ideas."

"Very well," he said, inclining his head slightly. He brought a hand up to her forehead, and extended his index finger. When he touched the side of her head, it was as if an electric current jolted into her. There was such strength, such force of will within him, that she realized he was holding back. He had to. Otherwise it would be too intrusive, too much. "Our minds," he said in that low, gravelly tone, "are merging."

She had never had an experience quite like it before. She had not been offering any deliberate resistance . . . and yet, the moment their minds were joined, she realized that she had been doing so unconsciously. She had been more than ready to hold back certain aspects of her innermost motives, motives she didn't even realize were there. But the instant her mind merged with Spock's, such aspirations proved to be utterly hopeless. Typically, the Vulcan mind-meld was like the peeling of an onion, one layer being pulled back to reveal another and another, and so on. That was not the case here. It was as if a knife had been brought down, gently but firmly, into the onion, slicing right through it, revealing the core in one quick, smooth motion.

By the same token, his revelation of self was remarkably restrained. He presented to her exactly what he wanted her to see: his own hurt, pain and humiliation, experienced as a youth when other children rained their hostility upon him.

And then, just like that, it was over. She felt his hand behind her back, and she realized belatedly that it was because she had been about to topple over. The only thing that prevented her from doing so was Spock's strong arm. "Are you all right?" he asked.

"I am . . . feeling a bit lightheaded," she admitted. He helped her to a chair, and she eased herself into it. She looked up at him in wonderment. "How long . . . were we merged?"

"Two point seven seconds."

"Is that . . . all?"

"Yes," he said. "That is all that was required."

"Why . . . do you say it like that?"

"Like what?"

"As if . . . I am so shallow. As if I have no depth of character or personality at all."

"If that is the impression I have given you, I apologize," he said stiffly. "It is, as I said, simply a matter of time. As one gets older, one tends to appreciate economy of movement and endeavor. I was able to discern what I needed to discern so quickly not out of any character flaw on your part, but simply because . . . I have been doing this for some time."

"Very well," she said evenly. "And what have you discerned?"

"As I suspected . . . your actions in the case of your son have less to do with him than they have to do with you. You believe that you will be inadequate as a mother in being able to help him and prepare him for the world."

"That, Ambassador, is simply not—"

But she stopped. Because she knew it was pointless to deny any such assertions he might make. He had, after all, been within her mind, however briefly. He knew whereof he spoke, and continued protests would simply be . . . humiliating.

Spock, for his part, seemed to understand her dilemma. He changed his tone to sound a little less accusatory, but the conviction and firmness of voice were still very present. "The problem, Selar, is control. For you, it is very much a matter of either/or. Either you must have total control of a situation . . . or else you do not wish to be involved in it at all. I believe this mindset was ingrained to some degree, but became exacerbated after the death of your mate. You felt—as illogical as it may sound—that by surrendering to passion, by giving up control, you were being punished by the traumatic loss of your mate."

"I see," she said stiffly.

"If you do not wish to continue this discussion—"

"No, no. I find it . . . fascinating."

"You find yourself now in a similar position regarding your child. You wish to be able to control every aspect of his life—to shield him from all hurt, to plan out every aspect of his development, of his future. Yet you have come to realize that such is not possible, while at the same time thinking that that is all you have to offer him. That it is an all-or-nothing proposition. If you cannot control him or the world that he is to live in, then there is nothing at all that you can do for him. You have set yourself a goal that is unattainable, and because you now know it to be unattainable, you would cease the endeavor entirely rather than simply set new goals."

"And what do I have to offer him, realistically?" Selar asked. She was leaning against the diagnostic bed, trying to look comfortable when, in fact, she had never been more ill-at-ease. "All I will ever be to him is a symbol of what he can never be: truly Vulcan. Is that not what your father was to you? Was that not the core of the rift between the two of you? You would look upon him and see the Vulcan that you would never be . . . and he would see in you the human you would always be, no matter how closely you might follow our teachings."

The faintest hint of a smile touched the edges of Spock's mouth. "So . . . you did discern a few things from the mind-meld."

"It could not be helped."

"Indeed not. The rift between my father and I had less to do with my biological heritage than it did my career choice."

"Did it? Or was your career choice predicated on the concept that you could never do what your father did . . . because you could never be what he was?"

The faint smile faded. There was silence for a time, and Selar felt uncomfortably guilty, which annoyed her. Naturally, she allowed neither to show.

"Everyone," Spock said softly, "makes mistakes. To make them from ignorance . . . is unfortunate. To make them with full knowledge is illogical."

"And that is what you think I am doing?"

"Selar . . . one should never ask more of oneself than one is fully capable of giving. Do you feel that you have given everything possible in this instance? That you have done your best?"

She looked down, looked deep into her own heart, which had just been shredded and revealed with such facility during the mind-meld. "Perhaps . . . not," she admitted after a long silence. "But what would you suggest? Go to Burgoyne and inform hir that I have changed my mind again? How much trauma am I supposed to visit upon hir . . . and him?"

"Burgoyne . . . is another subject entirely."

"Burgoyne usually is."

"The truth is," Spock said slowly, "that you love hir."

"No," was her immediate response, but she said it without her customary conviction.

Spock was not the least bit deterred by the denial. "The bond that was formed between the two of you is genuine. If it were not, you would not be so daunted by it. The thing is, most of your attraction is self-referential. That is, you are struck by hir dedication to you, hir passion for you. Hir determination. Hir bravery. Hir strength of character. The problem is that you do not believe that you have anything to offer back. Your concerns are less about hir and more about yourself. You do not think yourself capable of it . . . and, of course, you are afraid of it because of what happened before. 'Loss' is not an abstract term for you. You do not wish to risk further hurt."

"Let us say . . . for sake of argument . . . that you are correct. What possible advice could you offer to address that concern?"

"I could offer what was possibly the best advice on the subject ever given me."

"And that would be?"

Once again, that hint of a smile came to him, as if his thoughts were a hundred miles . . . or perhaps a hundred years away. As if he was genuinely hearing someone else's voice in his head when he spoke.

" 'Risk,' " he said, " 'is our business.' "

"Our 'business'?" Selar didn't understand. "This is not business, Ambassador. This is life."

"The lives we lead are the most important business with which we have to deal," he said. "If I can impart anything to you, let it be that. You must live your life, Selar, and not live in fear of it. If you committed yourself to your patients with as little confidence as you do yourself, you would have the highest mortality rate in the history of medical practice."

There was a sound from the outer room, the patient reception area. Spock drew himself up and said, "It would be best if I left now."

"Ambassador . . . I thank you for your efforts, but I . . ." She hesitated and then realized that it would be best to simply come out and say it. "I have not been the least convinced by anything that you have said."

"Yes. You have been."

She couldn't quite believe that she had heard him

properly. "No . . . I haven't," she said. "And I am not going to reinsert myself into Xyon's life."

"Yes. You will."

"And I am not going back to Burgoyne to try to make a life with hir."

"Yes. You are."

She shook her head in disbelief. "And what," she demanded, "makes you so certain, and me so wrong?"

"Experience," he said. That being all the explanation he felt he needed, he left the examination room—and a thoroughly perplexed Selar—behind.

THE DINNER PARTY

THE SHAKESPEARE TAVERN was even more raucous, if such was possible, than it had been the time that Rafe, Nik, Morgan, and Robin had first assembled there. People were laughing, chatting, and having a great old time. Around the table, the four vacationers were likewise relaxing and soaking in the atmosphere. Drinks were in front of them, appetizers had been ordered, and there really was no reason to assume that the evening was going to be anything other than splendid.

"So you're going to be extending your stay? That's great!" said Nik.

"Well, it was Mother's idea."

"I didn't hear you voicing any strenuous objections, dear. Then again, I'm assuming that you've found something here to engage your interest, right?" She winked lazily in Nik's direction.

"It was a good idea, all right?" Robin admitted, her cheeks coloring slightly. Obviously desiring to change the subject as quickly as possible, she continued, "Nik, Rafe . . . perhaps you gentlemen and Mother and I could spend the day together tomorrow. The whole day. You know, there's other areas of Risa that we haven't even touched. We could get on a shuttle, or—"

"Actually, we've already got plans for tomorrow," Rafe said apologetically. "Nothing we can cancel. A shame, really. We would have liked to do as you suggest, but, well . . ." He shrugged.

"That's very much a shame," Morgan said. "It sounded like it would have been a marvelous idea. But . . . it's not as if you're leaving Risa for good, right?"

"Of course not," Rafe assured her.

But Morgan was watching his eyes very carefully. "You're not leaving?" she said again.

He laughed softly. "Morgan, you did hear me the first time, I assume? No. No, I'm not leaving. Nor is Nik. To be honest, we're perfectly happy to extend our own stay for as long as you're going to be here."

"How nice," she said, her lips thinning. Her eyes were still locked on his. "Tell me, Rafe . . . what do you think of Montgomery Scott?"

"The engineering fellow?" Nik spoke up. "Good heavens, why get into discussing him, of all people?"

"Absent friends," said Morgan.

Robin was looking at her mother strangely. There was something going on, and she wasn't exactly sure what it was. "Mother . . . ?"

"I'll save you time, Rafe. As you know, Scotty seems to be not around. The thing is, Mr. Quincy's office has no track of where either of them might be. I checked. It doesn't seem right that they would simply disappear."

"No, it doesn't," Rafe said earnestly. "I share your concern."

"Do you." Morgan's face was now a mask, unreadable.

"Mother . . . what's going on here?" said Robin slowly, beginning to draw conclusions that she wasn't happy about. "You're not saying—"

"Anything. I'm not saying anything," Morgan replied coolly. "I'm simply asking, that's all. You see . . . when someone's been around for a while—as I have—one tends to take very little on face value. One tends to overthink. Sometimes that can be a hindrance . . . sometimes a help."

The Klingon and human Shakespeare were having their scheduled argument. No one at the table was looking at them. Instead, their attention was fully upon Morgan.

"Where's Scotty, Rafe? Where's Mr. Quincy?" Morgan's tone was very even, and very frosty.

"Morgan, as much as I adore the way you gaze into my eyes, I can't say I appreciate the insinuation," Rafe replied. There was just a hint of warning in his voice.

"I can understand that, Rafe," she said sympathetically. "But here's something you *can* appreciate: The eyes are the mirrors to one's soul. And, interestingly, when someone lies, there's frequently some dilation in the pupils."

"Of a microscopic variety," he countered. "Something that can't be detected with the naked eye."

"Ohhh, you'd be amazed what I can and cannot detect," Morgan said.

"Robin, could you give me some idea why your mother feels the need to insult my father?" There was a hardness to Nik's voice that Robin had never heard before.

"I don't think she's insulting him . . . exactly," she said uncertainly.

"Then what would you call it?"

"I'm not sure. Mother . . . ?"

"Where . . . is he . . . ?" Morgan said. There was no longer any pretense of sociability in her voice.

"You know, Morgan, I'm beginning to wonder if this evening was altogether a good idea," said Rafe. "Especially if that is the attitude you're going to take."

From the other side of the room, there was the unmistakable sound of a sword being drawn, the rasp of metal coming out of its scabbard. They paid it no mind, caught up as they were in the tension that was now at the table. It was probably just going to be another encounter between the Klingon and human Shakespeare, and when you'd seen that once, you'd pretty much seen it all you needed to.

Suddenly, however, their attention was caught by the alarmed voice of one of the waiters, who called, "Sir! Sir! That's the property of the tavern! Put that down before you hurt yoursel—" And if that hadn't been enough to pull their focus away from one another, certainly the sound of a fist impacting with the waiter's face would have done it.

Robin turned, looked, and was thunderstruck as she saw who had entered the tavern. Morgan reacted with open amazement as well. Rafe and Nik, on the other hand, looked very icily at the newcomers.

"Si Cwan!" Robin cried out. "Kalinda!"

For, indeed, it was the two Thallonians, the only surviving members of the once-sprawling empire's royal family. It was Si Cwan who had pulled the sword from the wall, and he was standing perfectly still in the middle of the room, Kalinda at his shoulder. Both of them had fierce expressions on their faces, looking as if they were giving their full concentration to containing their anger.

"Sir! Put it down, right now!" shouted a man that Robin could only take to be on the security staff. He was a couple of feet away, and in the midst of pulling a weapon from the inside of his jacket.

Si Cwan, looking as if he had all the time in the world, lashed out with his foot. He struck the security man just under the chin, snapping his head back and sending him unconscious to the floor.

Customers cried out in panic, starting to get to their feet with the clear intention of bolting from the restaurant. But Si Cwan, in a voice that had been used to issue commands to armies, shouted effortlessly above the din, *"No one move!"* Amazingly, everyone froze where they were. Then Si Cwan extended his arm and pointed the sword straight at Rafe.

Slowly, Rafe stood, facing Si Cwan from across the room. "That was a good move, Cwan. You haven't lost a second off your speed. If anything, you're faster."

"Fast enough to take you," Cwan said harshly.

Rafe smiled patronizingly. "Not quite that fast."

"Cwan . . . what the hell is going on?" said Robin. She and Morgan had now risen from their seats, each taking several steps away from the table. Nik had likewise risen, but had gone to his father's side. "Where did you come from? What's Rafe done—?"

"His name isn't 'Rafe,' " Si Cwan said, never taking

his eyes off his target. "Kalinda and I have been chasing down lead after lead, following a path of destruction that this man has left behind. His name is Olivan. Sientor Olivan. He killed my old teacher, Jereme. And now . . ." He drew a steady breath. "Now I'm going to kill him."

BURGOYNE & XYON

BURGOYNE CAME UP from the bottom of the lake, taking a deep breath of the fresh, warm air and glancing in the direction of the shoreline, where Xyon had been romping around. He had been there only a moment ago . . .

. . . and now he wasn't.

"Xyon!" Burgoyne called. S/he wasn't concerned just yet; s/he was all too aware just how capable hir son was in terms of handling himself, but, nevertheless, his absence was reason for pause. "Xyon!" s/he called again.

Suddenly there was a little splash of water, and Xyon's head popped up a few feet away from Burgoyne's. Xyon grinned gleefully, his eyes wide, as his arms and legs pumped furiously to keep him afloat.

"Well, hello!" laughed Burgoyne, and s/he glided toward him. "Look who's taken to water so . . . swimmingly." S/he took Xyon in hir hands and glided him to the right, then left, and then back again. Xyon giggled, the water splashing around him, and then he slapped it a few times with his palms, delighting in the droplets that splattered around.

The time that had passed since Xyon had come to him had been nothing short of idyllic. It was something to see, the way he was developing. The speed was not unusual for a Hermat, of course, but seeing it in a child with a Vulcan cast was nothing short of amazing. More and more, Burgoyne was beginning to see the wisdom of Selar's decision. At first, s/he had wondered whether Selar wasn't simply washing her hands of the entire situation as soon as the first problem had presented itself to her. But now Burgoyne was perceiving what Selar had seen all too readily: Despite his exterior, Xyon was far more Hermat than had originally been thought. There were the Vulcan ears and eyebrows, certainly, but the Hermat fangs were starting to come in nicely, and his first claws were already developing. If they followed the normal course, they would become brittle, fall off, and the adult version would grow out in short order.

Selar would simply not have had the emotional tools required to raise the child alone. As one of two loving parents, yes, but not alone. For the briefest of moments, regret flickered through Burgoyne's mind, but s/he quickly discarded it. S/he had promised hirself that s/he simply would not dwell on such depressing things. Selar had made it painfully clear that she did not reciprocate Burgoyne's affections for her, and that was that. In fact, with each passing day, Burgoyne found hirself wondering what s/he had ever seen in her anyway. Of course, when one of those things that s/he'd thought to be attractive did present itself to hir, s/he would quickly dismiss it from hir mind. Instead, hir focus was put entirely on Xyon and, yes, everything was developing correctly and expeditiously.

Everything, except one thing. Xyon displayed the characteristic Hermat exuberance, but he was surprisingly mute. Oh, he made burbling sounds, toyed with syllables. But he had not yet uttered a specific word. It wasn't anything to concern oneself about, but it did bother Burgoyne slightly. Continuing to glide hir son back and forth, Burgoyne said, "Say, 'Daaaaaddy. Daaaaaddy.' "

Xyon watched hir mouth movements carefully, entranced. He reached out and touched one of Burgoyne's fangs gently and giggled, and then said, "Aaaaaaaaaa." The basic sound was there, but still, "Aaaaaaa" was not a word.

"Nothing to worry about," Burgoyne said confidently. S/he looked into those gorgeous, round eyes and then couldn't help but add, with just a touch of melancholy, "Still . . . I wish your mama could see you."

Xyon tilted his head slightly, as if trying to comprehend what it was that Burgoyne was talking about. "Aaaaaaa," he said again.

"Yes. Mama." Supporting the paddling Xyon with one hand, s/he brought one of the child's hands up to his pointed little ears. S/he used that hand to caress the tip of the ear and said again, "Mama." Then s/he brought Xyon's hand over to hir own ear. "Daddy." Although, truthfully, with Hermat physiology being what it was, s/he could just as easily describe hirself as "Mama" as well. But something in hir made hir want to reserve that title for Selar . . . even though it was more than likely that Xyon would not see her for years, if ever.

S/he wondered what Selar was going to do next with her life. Would she return to Starfleet? Stay on Vulcan? Choose a third option? For Burgoyne, it was pretty straightforward: S/he had every intention of signing back on with the first vessel that allowed families. S/he certainly wasn't going to leave Xyon behind in the care of someone else. S/he was the child's parent, and that was all there was to it.

Xyon looked as if he was starting to shiver slightly. Although the water was relatively warm, perhaps he was getting a bit of a chill at that. Burgoyne drew him closer to hirself and moved toward the shore with strong, powerful thrusts of hir legs. Once there, s/he wrapped hir son in a towel until the shivering stopped. Xyon cooed once more. "Daddy," Burgoyne encouraged, but still Xyon was mute on the subject, although he did snuggle closer to enjoy the warmth of hir body.

Burgoyne headed toward the house, lost in thought. S/he found hirself wondering what hir social life was going to be like on a new vessel. Before, s/he had been totally left to hir own devices, not having any obligations or worries. S/he could do what s/he wanted, when s/he wanted. What was going to happen now, though? There would be central child-care facilities available during hir shift, certainly. But when s/he was off shift, how could s/he turn around and head out on dates or assignations? Certainly that would be when Xyon craved hir time. S/he couldn't just ignore him while s/he satisfied hir social impulses. The odds were that s/he was going to be staying in a lot more. S/he felt just the least twinge of regret, because the life ahead of hir was going to be very, very different. But then again, why shouldn't it be? S/he had, after all, fought with every fiber of hir being to be with Xyon. Now that s/he was, s/he'd be damned if s/he had the slightest bit of regret over it. No social life? No lovers? Fine. A very small price to pay for what would be a very joyous period of hir life. S/he would spend long and quiet evenings hearing about every aspect of what Xyon's day was like, and telling him in turn what s/he had experienced. Naturally, s/he thought with amusement, Xyon would be speaking by that point. That was a given.

"Maaamaaa . . ."

Burgoyne, hir nude body still cooling in the warm air, came to a dead halt and looked with delight at hir son's face. "Did you say 'Mama'?"

"Maaamaaa . . ." There was absolutely no question about it. He was pulling at his ear, his eyes wide, and he was squirming in hir arms. His nostrils were flaring as if . . .

Burgoyne tilted hir head back, suddenly trying to pull in the air hirself. S/he would have noticed it earlier, except that s/he had been thinking about so many other things. But yes, there it was . . . that scent. A scent that Xyon, even though he'd been parted from her all this time, had detected immediately. He was practically bouncing with excitement, so much so that Burgoyne almost lost hir grip on him. For a moment, Burgoyne considered putting him down and letting him run on his own, but then s/he realized that s/he could get the two of them there far more quickly.

Immediately s/he bolted in the direction of the house. For a heartbeat, s/he thought that there was a chance s/he had been mistaken somehow, but no. No, impossible. The scent was there, clear and strong and pure. It was she; it could be no one else.

S/he dashed into the house, skidding to a halt as s/he saw Selar standing there, her arms down at her sides, her face carefully neutral. Her gaze flickered along the lines of Burgoyne's body, but she withheld comment. Instead, she focused on Xyon, who was twisting like mad to get to her. Burgoyne put him down, and he was across the room like a shot, practically scaling Selar's leg. Selar lifted him, cradled him in her arms. "He is getting big," she observed as Xyon wrapped his arms around her neck. "And he is clearly healthy. That is—"

"Maama," Xyon said proudly, with certainty.

Selar, for all her training and discipline, was unable to keep the surprise off her face. "Yes. That . . . is correct. Mama." She looked at Burgoyne. "Did you teach him that?"

"In a sideways manner, yes, Selar . . . what are you doing here?"

"I am holding our child."

"Yes, I know that, but—" S/he shook hir head, still unable to believe what s/he was seeing. "But, I mean—"

"I know what you mean," she interrupted. "I have . . . been giving a great deal of thought to things. And I believe I have come to a conclusion."

Burgoyne could scarcely voice the words. "And that conclusion . . . would be . . .?"

She let out a slow breath. "I am a physician. It is in my nature to diagnose. I believe that I have been . . . not misdiagnosing, but overdiagnosing my situation. I have not done anything, however, to genuinely treat it. And I believe that this is an instance where the axiom, 'Physician, heal thyself,' is particularly appropriate."

Burgoyne's voice dropped to a whisper as s/he said with amusement, "Look." Selar did. Xyon had dropped off into a peaceful sleep, content in his mother's arms. Selar looked around, and then to Burgoyne with a mute question, and Burgoyne promptly understood and nodded. The nursery was indeed in the same place it had been when Selar was last there, and that was where Selar brought the sleeping child. She lay him gently down in his crib, keeping a hand resting peacefully on his back for some minutes. In that way, she felt the rise and fall of his back, the warmth of him, the beating of his heart.

"Checking to make sure he's still alive?" asked Burgoyne. S/he was speaking from the door to the room in a voice that was barely above a whisper. Selar, naturally, heard it with no problem.

"I had no doubt of that," Selar whispered back as she turned and walked out of the nursery. She stood there, facing Burgoyne, who still had a few bits of the lake dripping on the floor at hir feet.

Burgoyne braced hirself and asked the question s/he had been dreading. "Have you come here . . . to try and take him back?"

"No," Selar said immediately.

"Oh . . . a visit, then. All right, then, uhm . . ." S/he started to step away from Selar. "Why don't I get dressed and we can——"

"Putting on clothing would be a poor use of time."

The remark caught Burgoyne off guard. "It . . . would?"

"Yes. For I will simply have to remove them again."

She extended the first two fingers of her right hand and held them out.

Understanding, but almost afraid to, Burgoyne—in-stead of returning the touch with hir own fingers—took Selar's hand in hir own and gently kissed the knuckles of Selar's extended fingers. Selar let out a low sigh.

"This is . . . highly illogical," she said softly as Bur-goyne kissed the nape of her neck.

"Yes, I know. Isn't it great?"

They were eye to eye, and Selar said softly, "I will never tell you I love you."

"Not true. You will never say with words that you love me. There are . . . other ways."

"Really. And what," said Selar, the edges of her eyes crinkling slightly, "would those other ways be?"

"I'll show you," said Burgoyne.

And s/he did.

SI CWAN

"IT WASN'T HIM," said Kalinda.

Si Cwan's sword never wavered from its place, nor did he take his eyes off the man he had identified as Olivan. "What do you mean? That is him. It's been many years, but I would know him in—"

"I'm telling you, it wasn't him. It was him," and Kalinda pointed with utter confidence at Nik.

"What . . . in hell is going on?" demanded Robin.

"Robin," Morgan said sharply, in a tone that clearly indicated she expected Robin to silence herself.

But Robin wasn't buying that for a moment. "No, Mother. I'm a lieutenant in Starfleet. Si Cwan, whose aide I formerly was, has just come in here, throwing around accusations, and I insist on knowing what's going on?" She had been addressing her mother, but the statement was as much aimed at Si Cwan as it was at her.

"Olivan . . . this man," and he indicated Rafe, who

had not moved from the spot," was a former student of a teacher of mine. A man who taught me the art of self-defense, of camouflage. How to move, to fight . . . in some ways, to think. But they came to a falling-out, many years ago. Some weeks ago, Olivan returned . . . and killed him."

"How do you know it was him—I mean, this, 'Oli-van.' "

"Kalinda saw it. In a dream."

"And you trust the imaginings of some young girl?" Nik said scornfully. "Based on that, you'd accuse—"

"Nik." His father spoke, and there was something different in his voice. "Nik . . . let it go. This is unworthy. Is it not unworthy, Si Cwan? We were students of Jereme, after all. Denying who and what we are, and shying away from a battle . . . these are inappropriate things, wouldn't you say?"

"Very much," agreed Si Cwan. He had not relaxed a muscle.

"But it wasn't him!" said Kalinda, pointing at Rafe. "He's not Olivan! The other one is!"

"He's much too young."

"But he's the one who killed Jereme!"

"It does not matter who did," Rafe said evenly. He hooked his thumbs into his belt, pressing them against the belt buckle. "We are both responsible. Singling out one or the other is not relevant. If you have a grievance with one . . . you have it with both."

Robin had never, ever seen Si Cwan like this. The fury was palpable, and when he spoke, it was like a voice from the grave. "Then I will kill you both," said Si Cwan. "One or two . . . it matters not to me. For you killed my teacher, and you will die."

"Oh, my God," whispered Robin.

Si Cwan took a step toward him, and suddenly froze in place as he saw the grim smile spread across Rafe's face. Kalinda was advancing next to him, but he put up a hand. She looked at him in confusion. "What's wrong?"

"He's done something. I don't know what, but he's done something."

"My, my. You have learned a good deal, Si Cwan, even with the limited training that Jereme gave you," said Rafe. He was starting to circle the table, his gaze locked with Si Cwan's. "You see, Si Cwan . . . the true art of war is to plan for it, even if you do not know that you're going to be in one. There is no such thing as too many backup plans. Tell me . . . does the name Gerrid Thul mean anything to you?"

It was Robin who spoke up. "A madman. Someone who created a computer virus that came close to wiping out the Federation. His allies introduced a virus into the *Excalibur* that nearly destroyed it—"

"Did . . . destroy . . . it."

There was dead silence.

"No," whispered Robin. "It was . . . it was two separate incidents."

Rafe shook his head. "No. You thought it was. But it wasn't. The virus that led to the destruction of the *Excalibur* was a delayed farewell present from the incident your Federation has termed the 'double helix situation.' And I . . . helped create it. I helped conceive it, and my resources, my scientists, aided in its development. I'm rather clever when it comes to creating such things. And I like to spread the joy. That's why I have introduced a virus into the central computer of the El Dorado, which I've just triggered," he tapped the belt buckle, "with this. Within two minutes, this entire resort will become one gargantuan death trap. I am the only one who can stop it. If you kill me, Si Cwan—if you *manage* to do so, which I very much doubt—then you will be dooming everyone you see in this room to a very violent death. Your choice, Si Cwan. For the sake of everyone here . . . I hope you choose correctly."

TO BE CONCLUDED . . .

Look for STAR TREK fiction from Pocket Books

Star Trek®: The Original Series

Enterprise: The First Adventure • Vonda N. McIntyre
Final Frontier • Diane Carey
Strangers from the Sky • Margaret Wander Bonanno
Spock's World • Diane Duane
The Lost Years • J.M. Dillard
Probe • Margaret Wander Bonanno
Prime Directive • Judith and Garfield Reeves-Stevens
Best Destiny • Diane Carey
Shadows on the Sun • Michael Jan Friedman
Sarek • A.C. Crispin
Federation • Judith and Garfield Reeves-Stevens
Vulcan's Forge • Josepha Sherman & Susan Shwartz
Mission to Horatius • Mack Reynolds
Vulcan's Heart • Josepha Sherman & Susan Shwartz

Novelizations

Star Trek: The Motion Picture • Gene Roddenberry
Star Trek II: The Wrath of Khan • Vonda N. McIntyre
Star Trek III: The Search for Spock • Vonda N. McIntyre
Star Trek IV: The Voyage Home • Vonda N. McIntyre
Star Trek V: The Final Frontier • J.M. Dillard
Star Trek VI: The Undiscovered Country • J.M. Dillard
Star Trek Generations • J.M. Dillard
Starfleet Academy • Diane Carey

Star Trek books by William Shatner with Judith and Garfield
Reeves-Stevens
The Ashes of Eden
The Return
Avenger
Star Trek: Odyssey (contains *The Ashes of Eden, The Return,* and
Avenger)
Spectre
Dark Victory
Preserver

#1 • *Star Trek: The Motion Picture* • Gene Roddenberry
#2 • *The Entropy Effect* • Vonda N. McIntyre
#3 • *The Klingon Gambit* • Robert E. Vardeman
#4 • *The Covenant of the Crown* • Howard Weinstein
#5 • *The Prometheus Design* • Sondra Marshak & Myrna Culbreath

Star Trek: The Next Generation®

Star Trek: Voyager®

Star Trek®: The Captain's Table

#1 • *War Dragons* • L. A. Graf
#2 • *Dujonian's Hoard* • Michael Jan Friedman
#3 • *The Mist* • Dean Wesley Smith & Kristine Kathryn Rusch
#4 • *Fire Ship* • Diane Carey
#5 • *Once Burned* • Peter David
#6 • *Where Sea Meets Sky* • Jerry Oltion
The Captain's Table Omnibus • various

Star Trek®: The Dominion War

#1 • *Behind Enemy Lines* • John Vornholt
#2 • *Call to Arms...* • Diane Carey
#3 • *Tunnel Through the Stars* • John Vornholt
#4 • *...Sacrifice of Angels* • Diane Carey

Star Trek®: The Badlands

#1 • Susan Wright
#2 • Susan Wright

Star Trek® Books available in Trade Paperback

Omnibus Editions
Invasion! Omnibus • various
Day of Honor Omnibus • various
The Captain's Table Omnibus • various
Star Trek: Odyssey • William Shatner with Judith and Garfield Reeves-Stevens

Other Books
Legends of the Ferengi • Ira Steven Behr & Robert Hewitt Wolfe
Strange New Worlds, vols. I and II • Dean Wesley Smith, ed.
Adventures in Time and Space • Mary Taylor
Captain Proton! • Dean Wesley Smith
The Lives of Dax • Marco Palmieri, ed.
The Klingon Hamlet • Wil'yam Shex'pir
New Worlds, New Civilizations • Michael Jan Friedman
Enterprise Logs • Carol Greenburg, ed.

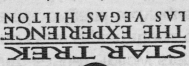

STAR TREK
THE EXPERIENCE
LAS VEGAS HILTON

Be a part of the most exciting deep space adventure in the galaxy as you beam aboard the U.S.S. Enterprise. Explore the evolution of Star Trek® from television to movies in the "History of the Future Museum," the planet's largest collection of authentic Star Trek memorabilia. Then, visit distant galaxies on the "Voyage Through Space." This 22-minute action packed adventure will capture your senses with the latest in motion simulator technology. After your mission, shop in the Deep Space Nine Promenade and enjoy 24th Century cuisine in Quark's Bar & Restaurant.

Save up to $30

Present this coupon at the STAR TREK: The Experience ticket office at the Las Vegas Hilton and save $6 off each attraction admission (limit 5).

Not valid in conjunction with any other offer or promotional discount. Management reserves all rights. No cash value.

For more information, call 1-888-GOBOLDLY
or visit www.startrekexp.com.

Private Parties Available.

CODE:1007a EXPIRES 12/31/00

BUILD YOUR OWN STARSHIPS
AT WARP SPEED!

With easy-to-follow steps
and clear explanations of
classic origami techniques,
<u>Paper Universe</u> will give
you the ability to hold part
of the final frontier in your
own hands. From a simple
piece of paper, create the
<u>Starship Enterprise</u>™,
a Klingon™ bird-of-prey,
a Borg cube, and more!

STAR TREK®
PAPER UNIVERSE

AVAILABLE IN SEPTEMBER
FROM POCKET BOOKS

PAPR